W9-AYN-203

PRAISE FOR *UNDERMAJORDOMO MINOR*

A *New York Times Book Review* Editor's Choice

"Patrick deWitt's new novel, *Undermajordomo Minor*, which is, let's just say this straight out, quick and funny and thoughtful and moving and super. . . . A terrific piece of genre writing, and that's that. . . . [Balances] its narrative whimsy and rhetorical flourish with bona fide heart. For every comic digression, there's a breath of quiet stillness; for every bout of old-fashioned frippery, there's a time for authentic and moving introspection, so the entire project of *Undermajordomo Minor* feels less like a postmodern exploration—a take, if you will—and more like the genuine article, a tale that engages us and haunts us just like the best tales of yore. . . . *Undermajordomo Minor* not only salutes the literature of a bygone era but fully inhabits it, and the result is a novel that offers the same delights as the fairy tales and adventures stories it takes on, while reminding us that in the long game of literature, what lasts is what thrills. My take on Patrick deWitt is that he is a thrilling writer likely to last past our own soon-to-be-bygone time."   —*New York Times Book Review*

"[In *Undermajordomo Minor*,] geography and era are purposely abstracted. Where we are, when we are, or why we're there are all afterthoughts. What matters is Mr. deWitt's imagination, which is a forceful train that ignores the usual tracks."   —*New York Times*

"DeWitt scrapes this stately veneer against the silly and the serious alike, then turns his lens on the friction—or comedy—that comes of it. That friction works wonderfully in the dialogue, where conversations swing from banter to bickering and back again, all while embellished to the point they often overmatch the trivialities they're concerned with. At times, discussions between Lucy and his superior, Majordomo Olderglough, read more like Abbott and Costello skits than anything out of their era.... Out of all the thieving and warring and heartbreak and, yes, the occasional half-eaten rat—he's crafted something worthwhile: humor, and hope."　　　—NPR

"Compulsively readable sentences, oscillating between the prosaic and the lyrical, the modern and the arcane. Told by an omniscient narrator, *Undermajordomo Minor* breezes along in staccato chapters, most no more than a few pages long, a mix of dark comedy and twee world-building ... populated by deWitt's signature menagerie of strange and unsavory folk. . . . Madcap dialogue unfolds like a fencing match, acts of cruelty are dovetailed by tenderness, and backstories of murder, revenge and lost love are nested within Lucy's quest, giving the world texture while amplifying the story's themes of love and longing."　　　—*San Francisco Chronicle*

"Throughout the novel, [deWitt] seeks to play against our expectations, to take the moral lessons inherent in his chosen form and rewire them, give them additional dimension and heft. . . . The result is a novel that carves out its own amusements, much as its protagonist does."　　　—*Los Angeles Times*

"In the tradition of such virtuosos as Vladimir Nabokov and Steven Millhauser, DeWitt seduces the reader with verbal swashbuckling and pyrotechnics while also offering up a charming vision of a Never-Never Land for adults. It's an entertaining read, complete with its own implication that distraction from the mundane travails of life is sometimes exactly what one needs. . . . *Undermajordomo Minor* is a fanciful bit of literary fun, in the spirit of Millhauser's novel *Martin Dressler* (or his elegant story "Eisenheim the Illusionist"). . . . It's not a topical novel—such as, say, Dave Eggers' *The Circle*—but rather its charm lies in how it plays with traditions and the romance of literature itself. Like a whodunit board game, a sense of mystery suffuses the novel and provides the fuel of suspense."　　　—*Dallas Morning News*

"This novel is compulsively readable. DeWitt's facility with point of view and narrative style is astounding. . . . *Undermajordomo Minor* has been engineered by a master craftsman. The pacing is superb and, as I read, I kept thinking how grateful I am to writers who can make me laugh."   —*Boston Globe*

"Poor Lucy. The leading man of Patrick DeWitt's book isn't much to write home about—or look at, or listen to. Lucien Minor is a liar who's no good at lying, an underling to a castle servant and, what's more, a suitor to a taken woman. Still, he makes for a fitting guide—charmingly befuddled and besieged by circumstance—in this twist on the common folk tale. DeWitt takes on familiar tropes just to turn them on their heads, and the results are by turns funny, fascinating and often plain weird—a bit like Lucy himself."

—NPR, Best Books of 2015

"*Undermajordomo Minor*—the title dares you to say it out loud—is set in a Kafkaesque, Alpine but otherwise geographically vague part of central Europe. . . . Our hero is the callow and unprepossessing but still strangely appealing Lucien Minor, known as Lucy, who quits his small town, where he is resolutely unpopular, to take the position of undermajordomo at the vast, rambling, crumbling Castle von Aux. There, amid a pageant of human pettiness and oddity, he gradually discovers within himself a resourcefulness and a curious charm that transform him into an oddly irresistible hero."   —*Time* magazine, 10 Best Fiction Books of 2015

"Relentlessly wry and often outrageously funny. . . . In *Undermajordomo Minor*, deWitt has somehow created a fable in which the comic narrative voice is impossibly accomplished, and nearly every word is funny. . . . A gut-busting and satisfying tale."

—*Paste* magazine

"In his previous novel, *The Sisters Brothers*, deWitt discovered brutal humanity and coal-black humor behind the façade of a recognizable genre, and now he's done it again. *Undermajordomo Minor* bursts with exchanges begging to be read aloud in the village square."   —*Esquire* magazine

"'I don't subscribe to amusements, Lucy. Laughter is the basest sound a body can make, in my opinion,' says the valet. . . . As I read the book, I more than once made the sound the valet finds so base and unpleasant." —*Wall Street Journal*

"This kinda-sorta fairytale has humor and quirky, undeniable charm. . . . The story is surprisingly straightforward and unadorned, though the prose oozes with that odd DeWitt charm that makes it compelling. Told from Lucy's point of view, the tale has a clueless innocence that is both comical and sweet. Dialogue is clipped and formal, but the effect is often laugh-out-loud funny."
—*Washington Independent Review of Books*

"*Undermajordomo Minor* wears a fairy-tale cloak, but at its wondrous and fantastical heart lies an unexpectedly moving story about love, home, and the difficulty of finding one's place in the world. Elegant, beautifully strange, and utterly superb."
—Emily St. John Mandel, author of *Station Eleven*

"In his delightful and dark new novel, Booker nominee deWitt brings his amusingly off-kilter vision to a European folk tale. . . . DeWitt (*The Sisters Brothers*) uses familiar tropes to lull the reader into a false sense of grounding, delivering with abundant good humor a fully realized, consistently surprising, and thoroughly amusing tale of longing, love, madness, and mirth."
—*Publishers Weekly* (starred review)

"Following up on the huge success of *The Sisters Brothers* (2011), de-Witt has another askew masterpiece on his hands, this time turning his unique narrative voice onto the familiar tropes of the fairy tale. Lucien (Lucy) Minor leaves his home, by train, to accept the position of the assistant to the majordomo of Castle Von Aux—aka "under-majordomo." A darkly humorous adventure ensues. . . . The highly nuanced characters are king in this tale. More than a compilation of quirks, each new character adds depth to the story, opportunity for growth in Lucy, and just plain fun for readers. . . . DeWitt has delivered another intriguing, compelling, and thought-provoking winner that will appeal to anyone who wants to be captivated by a smart, entertaining read." —*Booklist* (starred review)

"Patrick deWitt novels don't sneak up on you; they're the kind you love instantly. His latest *Undermajordomo Minor* (a follow-up to his Booker-shortlisted *The Sisters Brothers*), is no exception. From the moment you tumble into its strange world, there is no other world. In that sense, and in its slightly mannered language, it's like a fairy tale, although one with plenty of room inside for thoroughly modern, adult complications."   —*BookPage*

"[A] well thought through modern take on folkloric storytelling. . . . The tale shifts, subtly, from Tolkien to Stoker with a dash of Conan Doyle, but with plenty of humorous touches. . . . DeWitt's yarn is playful and pleasing. . . . Smart entertainment that blends light-hearted moments with more thoughtful reckonings of the human condition."   —*Kirkus Reviews*

"After giving the western genre a makeover in his previous novel, *The Sisters Brothers*, Patrick deWitt conjures up a dark fairy tale worthy of Wilhelm and Jacob Grimm in *Undermajordomo Minor*, a deliciously off-kilter coming-of-age story. . . . DeWitt packs his scenes with sprightly banter and quirky circular arguments. His fairy tale world combines elements of the medieval with more modern aspects such as travel by train, creating a partially historic, partially timeless feel. Although readers will find plenty here to chill their spines and possibly turn a few stomachs, a detached levity dances through every moment. . . . Alongside the humor lies a wry wisdom about the hidden strengths of the perpetual outsider. Take special note of this delightful, wickedly sharp gem."
                                        —Shelf Awareness

"DeWitt is the master of episodic structure. In his hands, the pseudo-simplistic fable form becomes a game of dense social and psychological complexity. His distilled story telling provides exactly enough information to fuel the reader's imagination. With a few brushstrokes he makes vivid, challenging people breathe. Each incident is visually powerful and often surprising. When a particular section ends, we aren't bored or overstuffed. We want more. But deWitt has given us all we need to fill in the gaps for ourselves. He trusts us to do that, to be active participants in his creation. The result is odd but delicious."
                          —Katherine Dunn, *The Oregonian* (Portland)

"[*Undermajordomo Minor*] is characterized by the off-kilter humor and the surprising emotional purchase that made *The Sisters Brothers* so great. . . . A fun, galloping read that's appealingly silly at times and fully engrossing at others. . . . It's a kids' story for grownups, and I mean that as the highest possible compliment."

—*The Portland Mercury*

"*Undermajordomo Minor* is as difficult a story to describe as it is pleasurable to read. . . . [DeWitt] plays around with his canvas, toying with its mythic elements and adding a few modern ones."

—*The Stranger* (Seattle)

"Most of what makes the book a strange read has to do with the way it slowly—and then quite quickly—makes a philosophical case that's wildly different from what we're used to seeing in genre fiction. I won't spoil that revelation; just know that it's definitely worth the initial uncertainty." —Flavorwire

"An electrifying adventure, both tender and profane. Nervy, hilarious, and utterly unpredictable, Patrick deWitt has served up another dazzler."

—Maria Semple, author of *Where'd You Go, Bernadette?*

"*Undermajordomo Minor* is a wonderfully wry and wise novel, and reading it is like coming across some twisted classic—Cervantes by way of Louis C.K. I marvel at all that Patrick deWitt is able to do on the page." —Jess Walter, author of *Beautiful Ruins*

"*Undermajordomo Minor* is brutal, brilliant, sly, absurd, and poignant. It's both gripping tale and hilarious subversion. Once again Patrick deWitt proves his wild, original talent, generous wit, and exquisite control." —Sam Lipsyte, author of *The Ask*

"Patrick deWitt has an untrammelled and utterly original imagination. I cannot think of anyone else who could pull off so beautifully this controlled explosion of drollery, mischief, sly fun, and tenderness." —Neel Mukherjee, author of *The Lives of Others*

UNDERMAJORDOMO MINOR

ALSO BY PATRICK deWITT

Ablutions

The Sisters Brothers

UNDERMAJORDOMO MINOR

Patrick deWitt

ecco
An Imprint of HarperCollins*Publishers*

For Gustavo

———

This book is a work of fiction. The characters, incidents, and dialogue are drawn from the author's imagination and are not to be construed as real. Any resemblance to actual events or persons, living or dead, is entirely coincidental.

UNDERMAJORDOMO MINOR. Copyright © 2015 by Patrick deWitt. "The Looking-Ahead Artist" © 2016 by Patrick deWitt. All rights reserved. Printed in the United States of America. No part of this book may be used or reproduced in any manner whatsoever without written permission except in the case of brief quotations embodied in critical articles and reviews. For information address HarperCollins Publishers, 195 Broadway, New York, NY 10007.

HarperCollins books may be purchased for educational, business, or sales promotional use. For information please e-mail the Special Markets Department at SPsales@harpercollins.com.

A hardcover edition of this book was published in 2015 by Ecco, an imprint of HarperCollins Publishers.

FIRST ECCO PAPERBACK EDITION PUBLISHED 2016.

Designed by Suet Yee Chong

Library of Congress Cataloging-in-Publication Data has been applied for.

ISBN 978-0-06-257270-7

16 17 18 19 20   OV/RRD   10 9 8 7 6 5 4 3 2 1

"It is a very painful thing, having to part company with what
torments you. And how mute the world is!"
—ROBERT WALSER

I

LUCY THE LIAR

Lucien Minor's mother had not wept, had not come close to weeping at their parting. All that day he'd felt a catch in his throat and his every movement was achieved in chary degrees, as though swift activity would cause a breach of emotion. They had eaten breakfast and lunch together but neither had spoken a word, and now it was time for him to go but he couldn't step away from his bed, upon which he lay fully dressed, in coat and boots, sheepskin cap pulled low to his brow. Lucy was seventeen years old, and this had been his room since birth; all that he could see and put his hand to was permeated with the bewildering memories of childhood. When he heard his mother positing unknowable questions to herself from the scullery downstairs he was nearly overcome with sorrow. A valise stood alertly on the floor beside him.

Hefting himself from the mattress, he rose, stomping his feet three times: *stomp stomp stomp!* Gripping the valise by its swiveled leather handle, he walked downstairs and out the door, calling to his mother from the base of the steps before their homely cottage. She appeared in the doorway, lumpily squinting and clapping flour dust from her knuckles and palms.

"Is it time?" she asked. When he nodded she said, "Well, come here, then."

He climbed the five groaning stairs to meet her. She kissed his cheek before peering out over the meadow, scrutinizing the bank of storm clouds roiling up behind the mountain range which walled in their village. When she looked back at him, her expression was blank. "Good luck, Lucy. I hope you do right by this Baron. Will you let me know how it turns out for you?"

"I will."

"All right. Goodbye."

She re-entered the cottage, her eyes fixed to the ground as she closed the door—a blue door. Lucy could recall the day his father had painted it, ten years earlier. He'd been sitting in the shade of the anemic plum tree marking the inscrutable industries of an ant-hill when his father had called to him, pointing with the paint brush, its bristles formed to a horn: "A blue door for a blue boy." Thinking of this, and then hearing his mother singing an airy tune from within the cottage, Lucy experienced a dipping melancholy. He dissected the purposelessness of this feeling, for it was true he had never been particularly close with his parents; or rather, they had never cared for him in the way he had wished them to, and so they'd never had an opportunity to achieve any stable partnership. He was mourning the fact that there was nothing much to mourn at all, he decided.

He elected to linger, a favored pastime. Sitting upon his up-ended valise, legs intertwined fashionably, he removed his new pipe from his coat pocket, handling it with care, much in the way one holds a chick. He had purchased the pipe only the day prior; having never used one before, he took a particular interest as he filled it with the chocolate-and-chestnut-smelling tobacco. He lit a match and puffed, puffed. His head was enshrouded in fragrant smoke, and he felt very dramatic, and wished someone was watching him to witness and perhaps comment on this. Lucy was spindly and pale, bordering on sickly, and yet there was something pretty about him, too—his mouth was full, his black lashes long, his eyes large and blue. Privately he considered himself comely in an obscure but undeniable way.

He adopted the carriage of one sitting in fathomless reflection, though there was in fact no motion in his mind whatsoever. Holding the pipe head in the basin of his palm, he rotated the mouthpiece outward so that it rested between his middle and ring fingers. Now he pointed with it, here and there, for this was what the pipe-smoking men in the tavern did when giving directions or recalling a location-specific incident. A large part of the pipe's appeal to Lucy was the way it became an extension of the body of the user, a functional appendage of his person. Lucy was looking forward to pointing with his pipe in a social setting; all he needed was an audience for whom to point, as well as something to point at. He took another draw, but being a fledgling he became dizzy and tingly; tapping the pipe against the heel of his palm, the furry clump clomped to the ground like a charred field mouse, and he watched the blurred tendrils of smoke bleeding out through the shredded tobacco.

Staring up at the cottage, Lucy cataloged his life there. It had been lonely, largely, though not particularly unhappy. Six months earlier he had fallen ill with pneumonia and nearly died in his bedroom. He thought of the kindly face of the village priest, Father Raymond, reading him his last rites. Lucy's father, a man without God, came home from working the fields to find the priest in his home; he led the man out by the arm, this accomplished in a business-like fashion, the way one shepherds a cat from the room. Father Raymond was startled to find himself treated in such a way; he watched Lucy's father's hand on his bicep, scarcely believing it.

"But your son is dying," Father Raymond said (Lucy heard this clearly).

"And what is that to do with you? I trust you can see yourself out, now. Be a good chap and shut the door when you go." Lucy listened to the priest's hesitant, shuffling steps. After the latch caught his father called out: "Who let *him* in?"

"I didn't see the harm," his mother called back.

"But who summoned him?"

"I don't know who, dear. He just came around."

"He sniffed out the carrion, like a vulture," said Lucy's father, and he laughed.

In the night, alone in his room, Lucy became acquainted with the sensations of death. Much in the way one shudders in and out of sleep, he could feel his spirit slipping between the two worlds, and this was terrifying but also lovely in some tickling way. The clock tower struck two when a man Lucy had never met entered the room. He was wearing a shapeless sack of what looked to be burlap, his beard trimmed and neat, brown-to-black in coloring; his long-ish hair was parted at the temple as though it had just been set with a brush and water; his feet were bare and he sported caked, ancient dirt running to the shinbone. He padded past Lucy's bed to sit in the rocking chair in the corner. Lucy tracked him through gummy, slitted eyes. He was not afraid of the stranger particularly, but then he wasn't put at ease by his presence, either.

After a time the man said, "Hello, Lucien."

"Hello, sir," Lucy croaked.

"How are you?"

"Dying."

The man raised a finger. "That's not for you to say." Now he fell silent and rocked awhile. He looked happy to be rocking, as though he'd never done it before and found it fulfilling. But then, as one troubled by a thought or recollection, his rocking ceased, his face became somber, and he asked, "What do you want from your life, Lucy?"

"Not to die."

"Beyond that. If you were to live, what would you hope might come to pass?"

Lucy's thoughts were slothful, and the man's query was a restless puzzle to him. And yet an answer arrived and spilled from his mouth, as though he had no control over the sentiment: "Something to happen," he said.

The man in burlap found this interesting. "You are not satisfied?"

"I'm bored." Lucy began to cry a little after he said this, for it seemed to him a pathetic statement indeed, and he was ashamed of himself, his paltry life. But he was too weak to cry for long, and when his tears dried up he stared at the candlelight and shadows stuttering and lapping against the pale white seam where the wall met the ceiling. His soul was coming loosed when the man crossed over, knelt at the bedside, put his mouth to Lucy's ear, and inhaled. And as he did this Lucy felt all the heat and discomfort leaving his body. The man exited holding his breath and walked down the hall to Lucy's parents' room. A moment later, Lucy's father suffered a coughing fit.

By dawn the color had returned to Lucy's face, whereas his father's was paler, his eyes rimmed red where the lids sprouted lash. At dusk his father was bedridden, while Lucy took heedful steps around his room. When the sun rose the next morning, Lucy felt perfectly well other than a tenderness in his joints and muscles, and his father was dead in bed, his mouth a gory sneer, hands stiffened to claws. The undertakers came to remove the corpse and one of them slipped going down the steps, knocking Lucy's father's head against the edge of the tread. The violence of the blow was such that it punched a triangulated divot in the skull at the forehead, and yet the wound did not bleed, an oddity which the undertakers discussed and commented on in Lucy's presence. Lucy followed the trio out the door and watched as his frozen father was loaded into an unclean cart. The cart departed and the corpse rocked to and fro, as if under its own impulse. A spinning wind swooped under Lucy's nightshirt and the frost from the earth breathed coolly up his ankles. Dancing back and forth on the balls of his feet he waited for a feeling of remorse or reverence which did not arrive, not on that day or any other day, either.

In the months that followed, Lucy's mother's attitude toward him soured further. Eventually she admitted that, though she knew Lucy was not explicitly at fault, she felt him part-way responsible for his father's death, as he had unwittingly transferred his illness to an otherwise healthy man, and so had struck him down before his time. Lucy wanted to speak to his mother of the visitor in the burlap sack, but he had a sense that this was something he mustn't discuss, at least not with her. The episode proved a nagging burden, however, and at night he found himself starting in his bed every time the house settled. When he could no longer bear this feeling, he sought out Father Raymond.

Lucy had no strong opinion of the Church. "I don't know Adam from Adam," he was fond of saying, one of many self-authored quips he felt deserved a superior audience to the lard-armed women who loitered about the fountain in the square. But there was something in Father Raymond he had responded to— a sincerity, an unpolluted empathy. Father Raymond was a moral and humane man. He followed the word of God to the letter and at night, alone in his chambers, felt the Holy Spirit coursing through his body like bird flocks. He was relieved to see Lucy in good health. In fact he was relieved to see anyone. The village was largely non-religious, and he passed full days without so much as a knock on the door. He ushered his visitor into the sitting room, setting out a tray of ancient cookies which crumbled to sand before Lucy could deliver them to his mouth. A pot of pale tea offered no palatable diversion and at last he gave up on the idea of refreshment altogether to tell the story of the stranger's visit. At the conclusion of the tale Lucy asked who the man was, and Father Raymond made an overtaxed expression.

"How would I know?"

"I was wondering if it wasn't God," said Lucy.

Father Raymond looked doubtful. "God doesn't travel through the night volleying disease."

"Death, then."

"Perhaps." Father Raymond scratched his nose. "Or perhaps he was a marauder. Is anything missing from the house, that you noticed?"

"Only my father."

"Hmm," said the priest. He picked up a cookie, which perished. He brushed the crumbs from his hands.

"The man will come again, I think," said Lucy.

"He told you this?"

"No. But I feel it."

"Well, there you are. Next time you see the fellow, be sure and ask his name."

In this manner, Father Raymond did little to put Lucy's mind at ease regarding the stranger in the burlap sack; and yet he proved to be of assistance in another, unexpected way. When Lucy admitted to having no plans for his future the priest took the trouble to write letters of introduction to every castle within a hundred kilometers, the idea being that Lucy might excel as some manner of servant. These letters went unanswered save for one, penned by a man named Myron Olderglough, the majordomo of one Baron Von Aux's estate in the remote wilderness of the eastern mountain range. Mr. Olderglough had been won over by Father Raymond's romantic description of Lucy as an "unmoored soul in search of nestled safe harbor." (It was rumored Father Raymond spent his friendless nights reading adventure novels, which colored his dreams and waking life as well. Whether this was true or not is unknown; that the priest was partial to poetic turns of phrase is inarguable.) An offer of employment and terms of payment rounded out the missive. The position (Mr. Olderglough assigned it the name of undermajordomo, which Lucy and Father Raymond decided was not a word at all) was lowly and the pay mirrored this but Lucy, having nothing better to do, and nowhere in the world to be, and feeling vulnerable at the thought of the man in burlap's return, embraced his fate and wrote back to Mr. Olderglough, formally accepting the offer, a decision which led to many things, including but not limited to true love, bitterest heartbreak, bright-white terror of the spirit, and an acute homicidal impulse.

Lucy regarded the village of Bury, resting—or collected, he thought, like leavings, debris—in the crease of the valley. It was such a scenic locality, and yet when he looked over the clustered hamlet he felt a sense of loss, a vague loathsomeness. Had he ever been anything other than an outsider here? No, is the answer. In a place famous for its propensity to beget brutish giants, Lucy by comparison was so much the inferior specimen. He couldn't dance, couldn't hold his drink, had no ambitions as a farmer or land-owner, had had no close friendships growing up, and none of the local women found him worthy of comment, much less affection, save for Marina, and this had been the all too brief exception. He'd always known an apartness from his fellow citizens, a suspicion that he was not at all where he should be. When he took the position with Baron Von Aux he made the rounds to share the news and was greeted with benign matter-of-factness, rote well-wishing. His life in the village had been uneventful to the degree that his departure didn't warrant the humble energy required to birth an opinion.

Now Lucy's window was opened and his mother appeared, un-spooling his bedside rug with a muscular snap of her wrists. The concentrated explosion of dust was backlit by the sun; it hung on the air awhile, and he stepped closer to witness its dreamy descent to earth. As the detritus—his own—coated his hair and shoulders, his mother noticed him and asked, "You're still here? Won't you be late for your train?"

"There's time yet, Mother."

She gave a quizzical look and stepped out of sight, leaving the rug to hang like a calf's tongue from the sill. Lucy considered the vacant window for a moment, then took up his valise and wrenched himself away, following the path through the trees and down the valley, toward the station.

He met a man walking in the opposite direction, a shabby satchel in one hand, makeshift walking staff in the other. The man had a field worker's complexion but wore his Sunday suit; when he saw Lucy he ceased walking, staring at Lucy's valise as though it posed some problem for him.

"Did you take the room at the Minor house?" he asked.

Lucy didn't understand at first. "Take it? No, I'm just leaving there."

The man relaxed. "So the room's still available, then?"

Lucy's head banked to the side, the way a dog's does when it hears a faraway whistle. "Who told you there was a room there?"

"The woman herself. She was putting up a notice at the tavern last night, and I happened to be stepping past."

Lucy looked in the direction of the cottage, though he could no longer see it through the trees. When he had asked his mother where she was going the night before, she'd said she wanted to take the air.

"She seemed an honorable woman," said the man.

"She is not dishonorable," Lucy answered, still looking uphill.

"And you're only leaving there today, you say?"

"Just now, yes."

In a covert voice, the man said, "I hope you didn't find the accommodation lacking in some way."

Lucy faced the field worker. "No."

"Sometimes you don't uncover the lack until it's too late. That's how it was with the last house. It was slave's rations by the end of my stay there."

"You'll be happy at the Minors'."

"She seemed an honorable woman," the man repeated. "I pray she doesn't mind my being early, but I've found it best to get a jump on these things." He gestured at the incline. "It's just this way, is it?"

"The path will take you there," said Lucy.

"Well, thank you, boy. And good luck to you." He bowed and walked on. He was disappearing around a bend when Lucy called to him:

"Will you tell her you met me, sir? The woman of the house?"

"If that's what you want." The man paused. "But who shall I say I met?"

"Tell her you met Lucy. And tell her about our conversation."

The field worker seemed to think it an odd request, but he tipped his hat. "Consider it done."

As the man disappeared into the trees, Lucy was visited by an evil thought; and at the same moment the thought became whole, a rush of wind swarmed him, a column of air focused on his chest and face. It was true that at times a gust of wind was like a soundless voice commenting on some private notion or realization. Whether the wind agreed or disagreed with him, who could say. Certainly not Lucy; and neither was he much concerned about it. He continued down the hill. His mind was like a drum, a fist, a sail overflowing, pregnant with push and momentum.

At any rate, he was no longer bored.

Lucy thought he might pay a farewell visit to Marina, and headed to her house to see if she was in. There was no sign of Tor's gargantuan boots on her porch and he knocked, propping himself in the doorway as one merely happening past. But when she answered, she looked so naturally beautiful that his eyes must have betrayed his true feelings, a cleaved combination of adoration and acrimony. For her part, Marina evidently had no care for his being there. Pointing to his valise, she asked,

"Are you going somewhere?"

So, she wasn't even aware of his leaving. "Yes," he said. "I've been summoned to the Castle Von Aux. Likely you've heard of it?"

"I haven't."

"Are you certain? It's in the east, the high mountains—a very picturesque location, they say."

"I've never heard of it, Lucy." She gazed disinterestedly over his shoulder, hopeful for some diversion or another. "What will you be doing in this very famous and picturesque castle?"

"I'm to be undermajordomo."

"What's that?"

"It's akin to the majordomo, more or less."

"It sounds to be less."

"I will be working in concert with him."

"Beneath him, that's what it sounds like." She untied and retied her apron, fitting it snugly around her dainty waist. "What's the wage?"

"It's a healthy wage."

"But what is the figure?"

"Assuredly healthy. And they sent me a first-class ticket, as well. A nice touch, I thought. They mean to keep me happy, that much is clear." In actuality, they had sent a paltry advance which had not quite covered a third-class ticket; he had had to take a loan from his mother for the remainder.

Marina asked him, "How did you get this position?"

"I was assisted by the good Father Raymond."

Smirking, she said, "That old rag doll. He's all powdery, like a biscuit." She laughed at this—laughed loudly, and for a long time. Lucy didn't understand how her laughter could be so blithe and enchanting when she herself was so covetous and ungenerous. Furthermore he couldn't comprehend why he felt such an overwhelming desire for someone who, it was plain enough to see, was patently rotten from the inside out.

He said, "You can laugh at the man if you want, but he alone took it upon himself to help me. This is more than I can say for anyone else in these parts."

Marina couldn't be bothered to take offense. She peered back into the house and seemed to be thinking of taking her leave, but Lucy wasn't ready for farewells just yet. Feinting, he removed his pipe and pointed its stem at the storm clouds, now tabled across the valley. "Rain's coming," he said. She did not look skyward but stared at the pipe.

"Since when do you smoke a pipe?" she asked.

"Somewhat recently."

"How recently?"

"Very recently."

A drugged mien came over her, and in a silky voice she said, "Tor smokes cigarettes. He rolls them in one hand, like this." She see-sawed her fingers against her thumb, her face affecting Tor's self-satisfaction and confidence. "Did you hear he's working out the terms to Schultz's farm?"

Lucy had not, and his mind flooded with insults and epithets, for Shultz's property was the finest in Bury. And yet he held his tongue, wanting his farewell with Marina to be peaceable, not out of any magnanimity, but so that after Tor ruined her—he felt confident Tor would ruin her—and she was once more alone, she would think of Lucy's graciousness and feel the long-lingering sting of bitter regret. In a sober tone, he told her, "Good for Tor, then. That is, good for the both of you. I hope you'll be very happy together."

Marina was moved by the words, and she crossed over to hold Lucy. "Thank you, Lucy," she said. "Thank you." Her hair brushed his face and he could feel her breath against his neck. This unanticipated contact was like a bell struck in the pit of his stomach, and he was reminded of the time of their love affair, which took place during the previous spring.

At the start it had consisted of much forest-walking, hand-holding, and eye-gazing. After a period of a month Marina realized Lucy was not going to make love to her without encouragement, and she encouraged him, and Lucy was scandalized, but not for very long at all. They fell into a routine of daily fornication in the lush, sloping fields below the village. Lucy was greatly relieved to be courting, at long last, and he knew he had the makings of a faithful wife in Marina. As they lay naked in the grass, the clouds moving bovinely over the mountaintops, he pondered their future. How many children would they have? They would have two children, one boy and one girl. They would live modestly, and Lucy would become a schoolteacher or cobbler or poet—some post which did not involve strenuous activity. Each evening he would return to their humble home and his family would swarm him, easing him into his chair by the fireplace. Would he like a cup of tea? Why yes he would, and thank you so very much. What of a scone? Well, why not? These daydreams caused in Lucy a physical reaction, a pleasing tension which ran from his shoulders to the undersides of his feet, toes curling in the sunshine.

His visions of this contented life were bolstered by the field relations themselves, which he had thought were going markedly well. But when, one afternoon, he said as much to Marina, her face darkened. He asked her what was the matter and she told him, "It's just that . . . you don't have to handle me so gently, Lucy." Soon afterward she sent him away, and Lucy spent heartsick months studying the curious words with such fervor that they all but lost their meaning—and he never did deduce just what it was she wanted. What he was keenly aware of now was that Tor's hands were matted in curly brown hair gone blond from sun exposure, and that when he gripped a glass of ale it looked as though he were holding a thimble. Lucy hated Tor, and presently decided to tell a sizable lie about him. Marina was saying her goodbyes when he said, "But before I go I have something I need to tell you about this Tor."

"Oh? Is that so?"

"Unfortunately it is. Most unfortunately, actually."

She crossed her arms. "What is it?"

He thought for a moment. When the lie came to him he clasped his hands solemnly, "I happen to know for a fact that he is engaged to another woman in Horning."

She laughed. "Who told you this? It isn't true!"

"Oh, but I'm afraid that it is. Here is my reason for visiting. I'm quitting Bury forever but couldn't bear the thought of you being made a fool of."

"Who is a fool?"

"You may do with this information what you will."

She said, "I think you're jealous of Tor, Lucy."

"That is a fact, Marina. I am jealous of Tor. But more than that I am in contempt of him. For if you were mine I would never be seen gallivanting around Horning with another woman on my arm, and introducing her to all I passed as my bride-to-be. She is, I understand, several years younger than you."

When Lucy set his mind to it, he was a most accomplished liar, that rare stripe who could convincingly relay information running contrary to reality with the utmost sincerity. He could see that Marina was beginning to take him seriously, and he pushed on, telling her, "The dowry is said to be no trifling sum, either. In a way, you can't really blame Tor."

"Enough, Lucy," she said. "Tell me it's a lie, now. Will you say that it is?"

"I wish that I could. But that's not possible, because what I'm saying is factual, and I once made a pact with you. Do you recall it?"

Her eyes fluttered and cast about; she was only half listening to Lucy. "A pact," she said softly.

"You asked me to always be true to you, and I swore that I would be. Oh, but you must remember, Marina. For you made the same pact yourself."

Her eyes were hollow and doleful and she believed him completely, now. "Lucy."

"Goodbye!" he said, and he turned to take his leave of her.

Walking away on the springy legs of a foal, he thought, *How remarkable a thing a lie is.* He wondered if it wasn't man's finest achievement, and after some consideration, decided that it was. He experienced a sterling enthusiasm for his future, and his would have been a triumphant getaway were it not for the fact that the assistant train engineer, two hundred kilometers away in Ravensburg, had insisted upon eating a second helping of cheese for his dessert on the night prior.

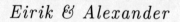

Eirik & Alexander

The assistant train engineer, named Eirik, was entertaining disappointment in the tavern after hearing news that his junior colleague Alexander would be made full engineer, an insult considering Eirik's seniority and years of loyal service to the company. He had had nine plum brandies when Alexander entered the tavern, nodding his small greetings all around but making no announcement of his advancement, which somehow was worse than if he had, for it was plain just to look at him that he was distending with pride. He took a seat beside Eirik and laid a palm on his back. Eirik felt a measure of pity in that hand, and he rolled his shoulder to remove its weight. Alexander volunteered to buy Eirik a drink but he declined. "Thank you all the same, but I'm not quite destitute yet."

"I wish you wouldn't take it that way," said Alexander.

"Wishing is a pastime for disappointment, nothing more," Eirik replied. "Take it from one who knows."

Now Alexander became serious, and he spoke with an edge to his voice Eirik had never heard before: "Look, now. We've got to work together. Tomorrow morning and each morning after. You and I have always got along well enough; I do hope there won't be any problems between us now."

Eirik found himself regarding the ringed baby flesh of the man's neck, imagining what it would feel like to grip it in his hands. And in that same unsettling way one realizes he's left the door to his home ajar, Eirik knew that he could kill Alexander. Not that he would, but that it was possible.

"There won't be any problems coming from me," Eirik said, and he excused himself, bowing exaggeratedly before weaving from the tavern and into the road. He went home for his supper but found no solace there, his foul mood compounded by his wife's miserly cheese portion. His wife was always miserly with her cheese portions but the amount he received that night was even more scant than usual. He sat at the table alone, staring at his empty plate and considering his private theory, which was that his wife secretly ate the cheese herself while he was at work.

"More cheese," he called.

Her voice, from the larder, was unemotional: "There is none left."

"How in the world did we eat through an entire wheel in less than half a month?"

"What can I tell you? You eat it, and then it's gone."

"But I don't eat it, that's just the problem." He moved to the kitchen and found her stacking plates, her back to him. "You eat it!" he said.

She stiffened, then turned to look at her husband, loathing everything about him: his weak chin, his sour odor, his lopsided mustache, his stoop. The thing was, she really did secretly eat the cheese. No sooner would Eirik leave for work than she would go for the hidden wheel and tug away a goodly sized piece, savoring this in a corner nook otherwise unused save for this lone and lonely activity. But she was unsatisfied in most every aspect of her life, and the cheese was one of the very few pleasures she had. And now it appeared that this, too, would be stolen from her. *All right, then*, she thought. *Take it all, even my smallest happiness.* Reaching her arm deep into the cupboard, she removed the hoarded cheese and laid it on the counter before making for the privacy of the attic, where she wept in the full-throated style, feeling just as sorry for herself as a person could ever hope to feel.

Eirik stood awhile, swaying and listening to his wife's jerky, breathy sobbings. He knew he should move to comfort her but found the desire to do so entirely absent, being far too excited about this unexpected surplus of Gouda. *I'll pay her a visit after a snack, perhaps,* he thought, and brought the cheese to the dining room table, consuming the entire half wheel in addition to a bottle of elderberry wine, afterward passing out in his chair and suffering through a cycle of horrific dreams and visions: Alexander furiously copulating with his wife while eating his, Eirik's, cheese; his wife lying on the table nude while Alexander carved elegant swaths into her broad white calf with a paring knife, for she herself was fashioned from cheese; that his penis was cheese which broke off while he urinated; that his penis was cheese his wife nibbled on while he slept—all through the night like this, and so in the morning, in addition to the state of his head from the wine and plum brandy, his sense of peace was compromised as he set out for work.

He arrived at the station ten minutes late with bloodshot eyes and a halo of fumes swarming his head. Alexander recognized the man's impairment and felt a professional impulse to chastise him.

"So you kept it up last night?" he asked.

"I did what I had to do."

"And now?"

"Now I'll do the same."

An uneasy beginning, then. They spoke little as the hours went by. Eirik's pain and insult were stubbornly insistent but he knew he would get through the day, and that the next day would not be quite so bad. In passing time, he thought of the loveliness of a glass of brandy, the first glass after a shift, the way it drew down his throat and coated his insides with flammable heat, afterward leaving an aroma of smoked plum smoldering in his nostrils and mouth when he exhaled. It was very invigorating, that first plum brandy, and he began to look forward to the tavern with earnest, uncomplicated appreciation. His anger diminishing, he decided he would buy his wife a wheel of cheese on the way home from the tavern, and that he would encourage her to eat as much as she wanted, in plain sight—just so long as he could have his fair share as well. And when this ran out, so what if they had to buy another? Perhaps he wasn't a full engineer, but he earned a good wage and there was room for occasional extravagances so long as they weren't too dear. Eirik hit his stride with his coal spade and the flames shimmied and spit in the firebox. Sweat ran off his nose and chin and into his eyes, and this was agreeable to him. Life was not such a trial after all, he mused. It wasn't easy, but then, how dull an experience it would be if it were so. He began to whistle, and this meant that he was happy.

Alexander sensed the change in his partner's mood, and felt calmer for it. Allowing his mind to drift, he fell to thinking of the difficulties of his youth: his mother dead mere months after his birth; his father, waylaid from sorrow, vanished one autumn morning, never to return, never sending word. From the start Alexander was instilled with the knowledge that whatever shape his life took, it was up to him alone to sculpt it, and so to have risen to the level of engineer, he couldn't help but feel proud of himself. Surely this is understandable, but half an hour shy of Bury, he made the mistake of verbalizing his satisfaction: "My maiden voyage as engineer," he said. "I can't deny it, but it feels good." He turned to Eirik, who said nothing, but looked stonily ahead. Alexander said, "Won't you allow me a moment of boasting, old friend?"

"Boast away," Eirik said. "I won't stop you."

"Why can't you be happy for me?"

"Who's to say I'm not?"

"But how would I know if you were?"

Eirik jammed the spade in the coal tender. "What do you want me to do?" he asked.

Alexander became sheepish. "Typically, when a man has a turn of good luck, his fellows will offer their congratulations."

At this last word, Eirik's black mood returned, a virulent poison which leached through to the deepest parts of his soul. Alexander's neck looked velvety soft to the touch, and Eirik's fingers began to twitch and grip. He resumed his feverish shoveling and as the train barreled along the rails he waited for his hatred to ebb, but it never did, and in fact it only doubled and redoubled, so that he felt lost to it. Resignedly, he waited for the best moment to exorcise this feeling.

The train eased into the station at Bury. Alexander peered out, an attitude of calm defining his person. He turned to Eirik, meaning to offer some minor encouragement or compliment, when he saw his co-worker was watching him with a fanatical look, his eyes dreadful, grotesquely transformed. The look made Alexander wary, and he asked, "What's the matter?"

"You want me to congratulate you?" Eirik asked.

"Don't you feel it's in order?"

"Indeed it is. But you're *certain* you want me to?"

What manner of test was this? Would Eirik strike him with a fist? Well, then, better to have it out. Alexander was a healthy man, if portly, and had seen his share of tavern battles—he was not afraid of the stingy wretch who stood before him. Resting his hand on the brake lever and gripping it in his fist, he struck an upright and confident pose, and said, "I'm certain, Eirik. Let's have it."

The spade stuck out at an angle from the coal tender. Later, speaking to his cellmate, Eirik would muse that it was as if the spade were leaning toward him, offering itself for assistance. He swung it in a quick, tight circle, bringing the edge down on Alexander's hand, severing cleanly the man's foremost three fingers, while the fourth hung as if on a hinge. This swayed up and back and Alexander stood there watching the blood drain from the stumps with the look of a man who had just witnessed a baffling illusion.

"Congratulations," Eirik said. He collected the fingers with the spade and tossed them into the churning firebox.

Lucy knew none of this, and would never know. By the time he arrived at the station Alexander had been led away in a dizzy stumble, and Eirik was being helped down from the train and onto the platform by the constable. It seemed a friendly gesture, and Lucy found nothing amiss about the two men as they walked away, though he was curious about where the assistant engineer might be going five minutes before the scheduled departure, and why the constable was so insistent about holding the spade.

Rain fell in plump drops which made Lucy blink and wince, but he didn't mind getting wet. He felt triumphant about the lie he'd told Marina, and rather than hinder his optimism, the foul weather merely added to the feeling he was embarked on an adventure. He entered the third-class compartment, stowed his valise, and found a sliver of space among the charwomen and laborers and scattered elderly. No one spoke, and Lucy wondered why it was that the impoverished classes were biased toward public silences.

The train was delayed for reasons already discussed, and Lucy passed forty-five minutes in the airless cabin while the conductor and stationmaster searched for someone to fill in as engineer. He was lost to his own plotless thoughts when there came a knock on the window from outside the train. He turned and saw Marina hovering in the air above the platform; her fist remained aloft next to her face and she wore the pleased expression of the cat after a kill. The effect of her countenance, along with her floating in the window like that, was unsettling to Lucy, and he felt a premonition of danger which brought about a head-to-toe rash of gooseflesh.

Now he noticed a pair of brutish, hairy hands were holding Marina aloft at the waist; presently these hands returned her to the platform, and she and Tor stepped back, that they might both see inside and be seen by those inside the compartment. They stood arm in arm, smiling at Lucy, perfectly at ease with each other. If they had had an argument relating to Lucy's lie then it was past. The conductor happened by and Tor called the man over, speaking imploringly to him and pointing at Lucy directly. The conductor watched Lucy while Tor spoke; when Tor had finished, the conductor made for the train, and Lucy's compartment.

"May I see your ticket, please?" he said.

"My ticket?" said Lucy.

"Please."

"Why do you want to see my ticket?"

The conductor held out his hand. Miserably, Lucy passed it over. The man studied the stub and shook his head. "Whatever is that gentleman talking about?" Looking out the window, he addressed Tor and Marina, rapt in their waiting. "It's third class!" He waved the stub back and forth. "A third-class ticket!" Tor held a hand to his ear, pretending not to be able to hear. Marina slapped him on the arm, as though he were being too cruel; and yet, she didn't truly want him to stop—she was enjoying the sport they made of Lucy. The conductor waded through the compartment to the window and slid it open. "The young man has a third-class ticket," he said.

Tor, perplexed: "The stick-like fellow? The red-faced chap just there? The famished one? You're certain he's not in first class?"

"Would you like to see the ticket for yourself?"

Tor performed a slight bow. "I would never deign to tell you your own business, sir," he said, and he rested his mitts on his hips and pursed his mouth, an approximation of confounded frustration.

"Oh, but I was certain he was to be in first class. The young man possesses a noble bearing, wouldn't you say?"

The conductor, along with the others in the compartment, regarded Lucy dubiously. "Well," said the conductor, "the lad is where he is meant to be. And I don't know what else to tell you about it."

"Yes," Tor agreed. "What else is there to say, after all?"

"Good day," said the conductor, closing the window.

"Good day to *you*, sir," Tor answered, his volume halved by the pane of glass. He offered a parting wave to Lucy, and to the compartment in general; Lucy did not respond, but others around him did. Now Tor and Marina turned and walked into the village, arm in arm, and by the looks of them they were deeply in love. Everyone watched them go; once they were out of sight the collective attention returned to Lucy. His face was no longer red, but pale, his gaze darkened, impermeable.

"Friends of yours?" asked the man beside Lucy.

"No."

"They're a handsome couple."

Lucy closed his eyes, not to sleep, but to be alone in the well-appointed room he housed deep within his mind.

The train headed east, crossing the great green valley and ascending into the mountains, winding ever higher as they followed the broad, back-and-forth swoops of the track. As the stars assembled it looked to Lucy that the train was hurrying the night along by plunging into the stomach of the sky. He slept sitting up, propped by a body on either side of him.

In the night there occurred an untoward happening. Lucy awoke or partially awoke to find two men, one tall and one small, creeping into the compartment. Their movements were stealthy beyond the call of good manners, and this, combined with the fact of their faces being obscured behind the upturned collars of their coats, brought about a wary interest in Lucy, and he watched them with half-shut eyes.

The compartment was quiet, the dozing occupants' faces cast in silvery moonlight, and the men moved to stand before a bony older woman clutching a tartan satchel to her chest. Her mouth hung slackly and a rill of spittle drew down the side of her face; the larger of the men regarded her with a cocked head, then set to work removing her fingers from her bag. This was accomplished in delicate stages, one finger at a time, and Lucy was expectant that at any moment the woman would come to and let fly a bloodcurdling shriek. But the man was so adept, as though he were precisely aware to what extent he might molest the woman's person without interfering with her slumber, that she gave no indication of disturbance.

Soon her grip was unfurled, and so the man could gain access to her bag, from which he removed unknown objects, passing these to the smaller man, who tucked the booty away in his long coat. After gleaning all he could or cared to, the larger man returned the bag to the woman's grip and stepped to the side, that he might focus on the body to the woman's left. It was in this workaday manner that the duo robbed each person on the bench opposite Lucy; and now they were doubling back to do the same to him and his benchmates.

As the men drew closer, a fearsome unease came over Lucy, for he had not a clue what he should do. He might put up a fight, but there were two men against his one, and it was a safe assumption that these bandits were all the more familiar with the ways of violence than he. Mightn't he leave the compartment? Simply stand and go, without a glance back over his shoulder? But no, the men would notice his exit, and perhaps it was that they wouldn't want him to leave. What option remained, then? In the end he could think of no alternative other than feigning sleep and letting the men make away with his meager possessions. A shameful conclusion, it was true, but still preferable to the other chilling possibilities, and so there Lucy sat, awaiting the inevitable.

The men were just setting upon him when a train traveling on the westbound track hurtled past, rocking the compartment, drenching it in flashing light, and disturbing most everyone's rest. The thieves quit the compartment like shadows thrown across the wall; and though many passengers were momentarily awakened by the passing train, none had seen the pair go, and so none realized they had been robbed. Lucy looked about for a body to speak with, but all had resumed sleeping. He buttoned his coat to the throat and looked out the window at the world of night. The moon held its position admirably and unwaveringly, pegged as it was to its corner of the sky.

Lucy awoke in thin winter sunlight, lying on his side, now. The train had stopped any number of times and the compartment was empty except for a shabbily dressed man sitting on the bench across from him. The man was staring at Lucy expectantly, as though waiting for him to awaken, that they might make discourse. But Lucy didn't want to speak to anyone just yet, and so resumed his window-gazing.

They were above the snow line, well beyond the first pass and into the deeper ranges where the drifts formed impossible meringue shapes and were painted blue and green in their shadows. The first- and second-class compartments were heated with engine runoff, but not so the third; the wind rattled the windows, and Lucy could make out his breath before him.

Lucy studied the man in the reflection of the pane. He seemed to be neither young nor old, or rather, young and old—his eyes were adolescent, full of verve and mischief, yet the flesh beneath the sockets drooped to water-filled crescents; his hair was thick, swept back in a high-crested roll, but its ink-black coloring was run through with white strands, these creeping upward from the sideburns to the crown. The man could have been eighty years old or he could have been forty. He removed a handkerchief from his breast pocket and blew his nose; as he returned the handkerchief to his coat, the visual of fingers slipping past a lapel reminded Lucy of the thieves from the night prior, a recollection which must have upset his composure, for the man asked, "Are you quite all right, boy?"

"I am, sir," said Lucy, "but tell me, please, did you pass the night on this train?"

"I did."

"You'll want to check your purse, then, for there were two thieves preying upon the passengers while we slumbered."

A look of dread came over the man. "Oh, dear," he said. "Is it really so?" He patted the pockets of his coat and trousers; finding his possessions accounted for, he told Lucy, "No, all is where it should be."

"You're a lucky one. Luckier than the others, anyway. You should have seen the way these devils roamed about the compartment. It was as though the notion of consequence never entered their minds."

"Is that right?" the man said. "They do sound devilish, anyway. And what about you, boy? How did you fare?"

Lucy waved the thought away. "Nothing to worry about there. It was that I chased them off when they came too near."

The man leaned forward. "Did you really?"

"I did."

"Chased them right off, eh?"

"Indeed."

"That was very daring of you."

"I've no patience for shirkers and thieves, is what."

"That much is clear." The man stood and bowed. "I salute you."

Lucy thanked the stranger; he was pleased to be making such an impression. Again he looked out the window. They were passing through a dense forest, now. A deer stood in the distance, away from the track, considering the train with a sidelong glance. When Lucy returned his attention to the compartment he found the man was studying him much in the same way.

"Yes, sir?" said Lucy.

"Well," said the man, "it's just that I find myself wondering, at what point did you do this chasing away?"

"At what point, sir?"

"Yes. That is to say, did you actually see these thieves robbing anyone?"

"I did indeed. Half a dozen people at least."

"And why did you not intervene before they got to you, I wonder? As one who proclaims to have no tolerance for thieves, for shirkers—for devils, as you yourself call them—I would think you'd have leapt into action at the first sign of wrongdoing. And yet you did nothing, until they came your way." The man blinked. "Or perhaps it is that I've got the story wrong."

"Well," said Lucy, "yes, hmm," and he sat awhile, thinking about what he might say in his defense. In the end, all he could come up with was to state that he'd been slow to act due to his being heavy-minded from slumber.

"Ah," said the man, nodding. "Still sleepy, were you?"

"I was."

"A foot in each world?"

"Correct."

"That explains it, surely."

Lucy felt he had deflected the interrogation handily, and yet he also wondered if he couldn't identify a suppressed smile upon the man's lips. Was this frayed individual making fun of him?

"May I ask you where you're headed?" the man said.

"The Castle Von Aux. Do you know it?"

"I do indeed. You wouldn't perhaps be Mr. Olderglough's new man, would you?"

"I am. How did you guess it?"

"Poke in the dark."

"Do you live at the castle?"

"I most certainly do not."

Lucy thought he detected in these words some trace of pique, and so he asked, "Why do you say it like that?"

The man held up a finger. "For one, I am not welcome there." He held up another finger. "For two, I have no inclination to visit such a place." He held up a third finger, opened his mouth to speak, shut his mouth, and balled his hand to a fist. He sighed. "Do you know," he said, "I was saddened about Mr. Broom."

"Who's Mr. Broom?"

"Your predecessor."

It hadn't occurred to Lucy that there'd been a predecessor. The man deduced this and asked, "Have you heard nothing about him?"

"No."

"I find that strange. There's a story there, after all. Poor Mr. Broom."

Lucy sat watching the man, who apparently did not plan to elaborate.

"Won't you tell me?" Lucy asked.

"It's not for me to tell. Ask Olderglough. Though he'll likely not tell you either, that rascal. Ah, well. We've all got our lessons to learn, haven't we?"

"I suppose that we do," said Lucy, finding the sentiment, and indeed the man himself vaguely threatening. Hoping to mask this feeling, Lucy casually removed his pipe from his pocket, to study and admire it. The man took an interest as well, and asked if he might have a look for himself. Lucy handed the pipe across, and the man held it this way and that. He nodded his appreciation. "This is a very fine pipe."

"Thank you," said Lucy.

"Very fine indeed."

"Thank you, yes. May I have it back, please?"

The man returned the pipe, but there was an unhappiness in his eyes, as though to part with it pained him. When Lucy tucked the pipe away in his breast pocket, the man stared at Lucy's chest.

The mountains had eclipsed the sun and the compartment dropped to a cold coloring; the conductor passed in the corridor, stating it would soon be time to disembark. The man stood as the train eased into the station.

"What's your name, boy?" he asked.

"Lucy."

"Lucy? I like that. I'm Memel." He pointed out the window. "And there's your new home."

The Castle Von Aux stood a half mile beyond the station; Lucy could make out a broad, crenellated outer curtain wall and two conical towers. It was built at the sloping base of a mountain range, standing gray-black against the snow—a striking setting, but there was something chilling about it also. Lucy thought it was somehow too sheer, too beautiful.

Memel was buttoning up his coat. Once accomplished, he did a curious thing, which was to tilt his head back and speak into the empty space before him: "Mewe," he said. "We've arrived. Will you come out, yes or no? I'm sorry that we argued." Bending at the waist, he peered under the bench and made a beckoning gesture. "Come on, already. What are you going to do? Stay here forever?"

A boy rolled like piping from beneath Lucy's bench and stared up at him. Lucy took in the boy's features, which were a source of fascination; for whereas Memel was an old man who seemed far younger than his years, here was a boy of perhaps ten with the mark of bitter time impressed upon his face: a hollowness at the cheek, a bloodless pallor, wrinkles bunching at the corners of his eyes. When he extended his hand, Lucy shook it, but the boy, Mewe, said, "I meant for you to help me up." Lucy did help him up, and now the three of them made for the exit. The wind was swirling snow outside, and Memel and Mewe flipped up the collars of their coats before disembarking. Only now did it occur to Lucy just who these people were.

They stepped into the shin-high snow blanketing the platform. The station was a fallow cabin with its door half off the hinges and the windows knocked out. Animal tracks darted in and out of the homely structure but there were no human footsteps to be seen. Neither Memel nor Mewe had any baggage; they pushed on in the direction of the castle, punch-punching through the frosted snow, while Lucy stood awhile by the train tracks, preferring to be apart from these two. But when they noticed his falling behind they ceased walking and called for him to hurry along, that they might travel together. Lucy could think of no alternative other than to fall in line, and so he did this, saying to himself, *I am alone with two bloodthirsty thieves. We are walking into an anonymous field of pale snow.* Hoping to keep their criminal minds occupied with chatter, Lucy spoke, asking Memel if Mewe was his son, or grandson. Memel said no, they were merely friends.

"Not today we're not," said Mewe.

"No, that's true. Today we're not friends. But normally, yes."

"Why aren't you friends today?" Lucy asked Mewe.

Mewe shook his head. "Memel likes to talk; he'll tell you."

"You'll only interrupt me," Memel said.

"No, I won't."

"It's an unremarkable thing," Memel admitted to Lucy.

"If idiocy is unremarkable," added Mewe.

"Of course idiocy is unremarkable. That's its chief attribute."

"I've found your idiocy to be quite remarkable at times."

Memel rolled his eyes. "Mewe takes refuge in insult," he told Lucy.

"Quite remarkable indeed," Mewe said. But Memel remained silent; he wouldn't participate in the lowly discourse. Mewe kicked at the snow. Wearily, he said, "We just like to fight, is what it is."

Memel pondered the statement, apparently a virgin notion for him. "It's true. We do." He was displeased by the admission; it appeared to make him remorseful.

Lucy had been watching the pair for a time, but as their conversation fell into a lull, now he looked up at the castle, and when he did this he startled, for it was much closer than he'd sensed it to be, as if the property had uprooted itself and met them halfway. Lucy considered its facade with a dour expression, and he thought about how buildings often took on the qualities of a living being for him. His own home, for example, was the architectural embodiment of his mother; the tavern was a tilted, leering drunkard; the church was the modest yet noble double of the good Father Raymond. But what was the castle representative of? It was too early to name it. He only knew that it spoke of something colossal and ominous and quite beyond his experience.

They approached a shanty village, built up in a cluster apart from the base of the castle, a hundred or more haphazard domiciles linked side by each in the shape of a teardrop. A series of larger, open-air structures formed a cross through the center—marketplace stalls, Memel explained. Lucy watched as the villagers went about their business: shawl-covered women ducking in and out of doorways, children wrapped to their breasts or trailing behind; men standing in groups of threes and fours, speaking animatedly, gesturing, laughing. Memel pointed out his shanty to Lucy, and with pride, though it was indistinguishable from the others: a warping shack fashioned from tin scrap and mismatched timber. A chimney pushed through the roof, tall and tilted, issuing wispy woodsmoke.

"And does Mewe live with you also?" said Lucy.

"No, I live alone," said Mewe. "Just this side of Memel's, do you see?"

Lucy nodded. He asked Memel, "How long have you lived here?"

"I was born here. Mewe, too. We all were."

"And how long has the village stood beside the castle?"

"Just as long as the castle has been here, so has the village."

"But where do you all come from originally?"

"I don't know, actually." He turned to Mewe. "Do you know?"

"Nowhere, I should think."

A second silence, and Lucy's attention drifted away, to the face of the mountain looming beyond the castle. At first he was simply reviewing the scenery, but then he realized there was some manner of human industry taking place in the snow: bodies moving about, and puffs of smoke floating along on the air. "Those are people up there," he commented.

"Ah, yes," said Memel.

"What are they doing?"

"Wasting their time."

"Wasting their time doing what?"

"Playing a silly game."

"And what is the point of the game?"

"To kill but not be killed oneself."

"Killed?" said Lucy.

"Yes. Did Olderglough not tell you about that either?"

"There was no mention of killing."

Memel chuckled. "Rascal! Well, not to worry. You aren't in any danger."

"No?"

"Very little danger. A small danger. Keep on your toes, and you'll be fine, I would think. The others are much worse off."

"What others?"

"The killed, the killing. The rebels and their tyrannical opposition." He pointed to one side of the mountain, then the other. "They are often out and about."

"These two parties are at odds, is that what you're saying?"

"They are at war."

"Why are they warring?"

"Ah," said Memel. "Long story."

"And what is the story?"

"It is most complicated and long."

"Mightn't you tell it to me in shorthand?"

"It would never do but to tell it in total."

All this was troubling to Lucy. "Perhaps you will tell it to me later," he ventured.

"Perhaps I will," Memel said. "Though likely not. For in addition to being a long story, it's also quite dull."

They had arrived at the edge of the village. Memel and Mewe said their goodbyes, the former taking up Lucy in a lurching embrace which went on far longer than was seemingly necessary. Lucy was embarrassed by the show of affection but made no objection, thinking it likely a local custom, something he decided to endure as an example of his tolerance.

Lucy trudged uphill to stand before the massive riveted doors of the castle, knocking bare-knuckled in the cold. But it was like knocking on the trunk of a tree; it produced a sound so slight that he himself could hardly hear it. He spied a middling-sized bell hung away and to the side of the entrance, and pulled on the dangling rope to ring it; only the rope came away from its pulley, slipping through the air and disappearing with a whisper into the snowbank beside Lucy's feet. He looked all around, then, for what he couldn't say, it simply felt an apt time to take in his surroundings. And what did he see? He saw trees and snow and too much space. He upended and sat upon his valise. Reaching for his pipe, he found it missing. He thought of Memel embracing him, and he scowled. "I don't quite know what to do just now," he admitted.

An inventive notion came to him, which was to throw stones at the bell. Rooting about in the snow, he was pleased with himself for thinking of the scheme, or for receiving it; success proved elusive, however, for the stones were hard to come by, the bell was placed very high, and Lucy's aim was abominable. Now he was panting, and a clammy sweat coated his back. Abandoning the project, he pressed his belly against the castle and peered up. From this angle the facade looked concave, and its height invoked a queasiness, so that he felt his legs might give way, and he would topple backward down the hill, the thought of which made him laugh. He listened to his own laughter with what might be described as an inquisitive detachment. Much in the same way he had never been able to reconcile the connection between his reflection and his mind, Lucy could not recognize his voice as relating to his person.

He resumed his valise-sitting. Sunlight drew down the front of the castle, bisecting his face levelly, a lovely yellow warmth from the nose-bridge to the apex of his cap, while below there clung a beard of bitter, blue-white chill. He closed his eyes, considering the activity of his own padded heartbeat, the transit of his blood. For a moment Lucy was happy, though he didn't know why.

When he opened his eyes, a peripheral movement originating from the forest to the east of the castle caught his attention. He turned to witness a sheet of dry snow drop from a tall branch and to the ground, this landing with a soft-clapping *shump*. Through the aftercloud he saw a man's famished face emerge from behind the broad trunk of an oak tree. This face held Lucy's gaze, and Lucy, alarmed, sat upright. A second face, similarly famished, appeared from behind another tree, and Lucy stood. Now a third face came into view, now a fourth, and all at once a group of twelve or more men materialized from the shadowy wood. They were each of them holding a bayonet, and they walked in a huddle toward Lucy, who retreated some steps so that his back pressed flat against the cold wall of the castle.

The men affected a militarily homogeneous air, the lot of them wearing top to bottom gray-green wool, with bands of red encircling their arms at the biceps and black sashes cinched about their waists. As they drew nearer, however, Lucy could see that the cut and style of each man's outfit was dissimilar to his fellows': one wore long trousers, another knickers with tall boots; one sported a shearling collar, while his neighbor trailed a scarf. Even their rifles were dissimilar, the lengths of the bayonets varying drastically. It was as though they had each of them made their own garments in the privacy of their homes, with but the vaguest aesthetic prescription to guide them. Only their unshaven, haunted faces were alike.

Lucy was afraid of these men, naturally, for they carried themselves so grimly, and it seemed they intended to set upon him and for all he knew bring him to harm. But when at last they reached him they merely stood there, breathing in and out, and watching him as though he were some part of the scenery. They were looking at him but thinking of their own lives, and not of his.

A man stepped from the rear of the pack, and from the moment Lucy saw him it was clear he was one apart from the others. While the rest possessed the swollen-eyed expression of malnourished desperation, this man's skull wore the hunger well, and his gaze described intelligence and the most natural manner of confidence. He was, in fact, exceptionally handsome, so that Lucy could not look away from him. The man was perfectly serious as he stepped closer, and when he spoke, his deep voice denoted no hostility, only a measure of import, as though time were a pressing consideration for him.

"What's your name, boy?"

"Lucy."

"Lucy?"

"That's my name, sir, yes."

"What's all this with the stones, Lucy?"

"I was trying to strike the bell."

"And why?"

"I'm eager to gain entrance to the castle."

"And why?"

"That I might begin my appointment there. Also because I'm cold."

"I don't believe I've seen you before." He pointed down the valley. "Do you come from the village?"

"No, I come from Bury."

"What's Bury?"

"A location, sir. I come from there."

The exceptionally handsome man puzzled a moment, as one completing an equation in his mind. "So you are Lucy from Bury, is that what you're telling me?"

"I am."

"And you mustn't tarry, as you're in a hurry?"

"Yes."

"Because you're chilly?"

"I suppose that's all correct, sir, yes."

The soldiers were stifling laughter, as was the exceptionally handsome man, and Lucy stood by, considering the enigmatic nature of charisma. If he could change a single thing about himself, it would be to possess that atypical luster certain people were blessed with. The exceptionally handsome man was rich with it, and in witnessing and identifying this, Lucy experienced both covetousness and admiration. He watched the man whisper into one of his soldiers' ears; the soldier nodded and saluted before hurrying away into the woods. Now the exceptionally handsome man spoke again to Lucy, only all of the playfulness from the moment before had gone:

"Do you have any food?"

"No."

"A biscuit, perhaps? Or a piece of cheese?"

"Nothing whatsoever, sir, no."

"Any money?"

"I have a very small amount of money."

"May we have it?"

"It's all I've got, sir."

The exceptionally handsome man stepped closer, gripping his bayonet, and there entered into his voice an emotionless, droning tone. "May we or may we not have the money, Lucy from Bury?"

Lucy handed over his small purse of coins, and the exceptionally handsome man emptied it into his palm.

"This is all you have?"

"Yes."

"This is all you have in the world?"

"Yes."

The exceptionally handsome man returned the coins to the purse, sulkily stuffing this into his coat pocket. He appeared to take Lucy's insolvency personally, and a cumbersome quiet came between them. Lucy was casting about in his mind for some bit of chit-chat when the soldier who had gone on scout returned, whispering in the exceptionally handsome man's ear. The exceptionally handsome man received the news, then addressed the others, who stood at attention, ready to receive his instruction. "All right, we're heading back to base camp in a single push. The bastards are up to something or I miss my guess, so let's stay on our guard. Are we up for it, yes or no?" The soldiers called back in a single voice that shocked Lucy with its volume and alacrity: "Aye!" And then, just as quickly as they'd come, they departed, with their leader bringing up the rear.

Rounding the corner of the castle, he ceased walking, as though plagued by an unknown anxiety. Turning, he leveled his rifle at Lucy; his expression was stony, and Lucy once more found himself concerned for his own safety. But there was no danger; the rifle was raised higher, and higher still, and now the exceptionally handsome man took aim and fired his weapon. The bullet ricocheted off the hip of the bell and the peal pulsed in the air, this mingling with the echo of the rifle's discharge. As Lucy was standing under the bell itself it was as though the noise created something physical surrounding him, a chamber of vibration and sound. Looking upward, he watched the bell's slow, circular sway. When he looked back down, the exceptionally handsome man was gone.

After some minutes, the door was unbolted from the inside. It budged a laborious half inch, then another. Lucy couldn't see who was responsible for these efforts, but there came from the black crack a wispy, whispering voice:

"Who's there?"

"Lucien Minor, sir."

"Who?"

"Lucy, sir. I'm reporting to my post under a Mr. Olderglough. Is that you?"

"Mmmm," said the voice, as if unsure.

"I'm happy to make your acquaintance. Thank you again for the position. I'm eager to begin my appointment, and I should think you won't regret taking me—"

Lucy heard the distant pop of a rifle discharging. It was a miniature and cotton-wrapped sound, and he wondered at the chasm separating the quaintness of this noise and the actuality of a hurtling bullet. There came another report, and a pause; now there followed a rushing crescendo of pops, like a handful of tacks strewn over hardwood. Lucy's feet were numb, and his stomach felt airy and scooped out.

"May I come in, sir?"

The voice uttered a reply but Lucy couldn't make it out.

"What was that?" he asked.

The voice rose to a shriek: "Push the fucking door!"

Lucy's recovery from the directive was admirable and timely. He pushed with all his strength; the heavy door hesitated, then swept slowly, evenly open.

II
—

MR. OLDERGLOUGH

Mr. Olderglough stood in the underlit entryway, an elegantly skeletal man of sixty or more outfitted in a suit of black velvet. His white hair was uncombed or unsuccessfully combed; a lock spiraled past his brow and over his eyes, to roguish effect. His right arm hung in a sling, his fingers folded talon-like, nails blackened, knuckles blemished with scabs and blue-yellow bruising. Bowing a bow so slight it hardly amounted to a bow at all, he said, "I apologize, young man, for my vulgarity of a moment ago. I woke up in a foul mood this morning, and the world's been against me ever since."

"I'm sorry to hear that, sir."

"I had a terrific nightmare, is what." Mr. Olderglough leaned in. "Eels," he said.

"Eels, sir?"

"That was what the dream was about." But he offered no further information regarding the eels, no description of what malice they had represented. Lucy made no inquiries about it, the reason being that he didn't wish to know any more. As his eyes became accustomed to the darkness, now he saw that Mr. Olderglough's attire, which had appeared so regal at the start, was actually quite scruffy—buttons mismatched, and stains illustrating his lapels. Lucy thought he looked like an aesthete chasing a run of foul luck. Pointing at the sling, he asked,

"Have you had an accident, sir?"

Mr. Olderglough stared at his hand with what Lucy took for regret. "No, not an accident," he answered, and now he laid his left hand atop his injured right and began to stroke it consolingly, which summoned in Lucy a revulsion he couldn't put words to. Mr. Olderglough emerged from his reverie and asked if Lucy would like a tour of the estate; before Lucy could answer, the man tottered away down the darkening corridor. Lucy followed after, not because he wanted to particularly, but because he could think of no other option, and because he didn't like the idea of standing alone in the dim, dank place. Other than the stillness of the air it was not noticeably warmer inside the castle, and he did not unbutton his coat.

Mr. Olderglough was not an enthusiastic guide.

"This is a room," he said, pointing as they passed. "Not much use for it these days. Better not to go in at all, is my thought. And here, here too is a room, just a room, serving no purpose whatsoever."

In fact, most every space in the castle was not in use, and the property in general had fallen into disrepair: the furniture was covered with canvas, the heavy velvet curtains drawn, and clumps of dust had built up in the corners and doorways. None of the fireplaces they passed were in use, and Lucy asked,

"Do you never light a fire, sir?"

"I wouldn't say never. I'll admit that it's rare. Room."

"I wonder," said Lucy, "on what occasion do you light one?" For the deeper they traveled into the castle, the more the temperature fell, with the light growing dimmer all the while.

"I avoid them, myself," Mr. Olderglough answered. "It seems I get nothing done with a fire going other than have a fire going. The notion of reading by the hearth is pure farce, so far as I'm concerned. Every half a page I have to set my book aside to nurture the flames—not at all my idea of a relaxing evening." He gave Lucy a reproachful look. "You're not cold, are you?"

"I am not warm, sir."

"Well, if you're after a fire, you may be my guest. But you'll have to forage your own wood, as the little we have stocked goes to the scullery stove."

"That's fine, sir, thank you."

"Yes, boy. And now, if you'll follow me, please." They entered a cavernous ballroom. Ringing the high walls were any number of ornately framed oil paintings, portraits of similarly regal-looking individuals, the Barons and Baronesses of yore, Lucy supposed, and correctly. Mr. Olderglough stepped to the center-point of the space; when he spoke, his voice was staggered by an echo on the air. "Yet another room," he said, "and a very large and empty room it is, wouldn't you say?"

"It is large and empty, sir."

"This dingy chamber once was filled with music and dancing and laughter and gaiety. And look at it now. Quiet as the grave."

Indeed, the ballroom gave Lucy an uneasy feeling, as though it had been host to some godless occurrence or other. "And where have all the people gone to, sir?"

"After the Baroness left us, then we fell into our Decline."

"Do you mean to say she died?"

"I don't mean that, no. Only that she departed, and hasn't returned, and likely will not return. But her leaving was like a death, if you'll allow me my small melodrama."

"Please."

"Thank you."

"You're welcome."

"Yes. Well, we're coming on a full year now that she's been away, and not a day goes past without my lamenting her absence."

"You were very close to her, sir?"

"As close as one in my position can be. She extended me every kindness—kindnesses many of her stature would have forgone." Mr. Olderglough moved to stand before a painting of a swan-like beauty in a light blue silk and lace gown: the Baroness Von Aux.

"A light in a dark place," Mr. Olderglough said.

"She looks to be afraid of something."

"Yes. Oh, but she was very brave, as well."

Lucy asked, "And where is the Baron currently, sir?"

"The Baron goes where the Baron wishes. And often as not he wishes to go nowhere at all."

"I should like to thank him for the appointment, if I might."

"The Baron has no knowledge of your appointment. In fact he hasn't the remotest interest in the mechanics of the castle. Six days out of seven he won't even leave his room. Seven days out of seven."

"And what does he do in there, sir?"

"I suspect it involves a degree of brooding. But this is not your problem to ponder; it'll be months before you lay eyes on the man, if you lay eyes on him."

"I will wait to thank him, then," said Lucy.

Mr. Olderglough shook his head, with emphasis. "You don't understand what I'm telling you, boy. Don't speak to the Baron if you see him. As a matter of fact, don't see him at all, if you can avoid it. That is to say, don't let him see you."

Lucy asked, "Am I not meant to be here, sir?"

"No one is *meant* to be here." Mr. Olderglough was gripped by a shiver. Once it passed he turned to Lucy and asked, "Are you ever seized up like that, boy?"

"We all catch a chill, sir. I should think a fire would allay it."

"No, it's quite something else, I fear." He pointed to the exit. "Moving on, then," he said, quitting the ballroom in what could be described as a hurry.

They resumed their trek down the hallway, their heels clicking in time, then not.

"What of your trip, Lucy?"

"What of it, sir?"

"Will you tell me about it?"

"There isn't much to tell, I'm afraid. I met a pair of villagers on the train."

"Oh? And what did you make of them?"

"I found them somewhat strange, sir. I believe one of them stole my pipe."

"You've met Memel, it sounds like." There was an amusement in Mr. Olderglough's tone, but also something like derision. Lucy asked,

"Don't you approve of him?"

"My approval or disapproval is irrelevant. The villagers are like children, and children can be dangerous entities in that they have no God. Do you understand what I mean when I say this?"

"Not quite, sir."

"If there are no consequences for a person's actions, what might his motivation be to do right by his fellow man?"

Lucy wasn't sure if he was expected to answer the question or not. At any rate, he didn't know what the answer might be, and Mr. Olderglough didn't press for a response. A quiet moment passed, much in the way a cloud passes, and Lucy found himself wanting to defend Memel, which was odd, considering he didn't know the man, and that he had been victimized by him. Pondering this curiosity, he pushed on after Mr. Olderglough, the pair of them descending a flight of stairs, and then another, where the air became thicker, almost swampy. It was scarcely credible to Lucy that this gloomy locale was now his home; presently he fell to wondering what his time would be like there, and so he inquired after his duties.

"Easier asked than answered," said Mr. Olderglough. "For our days here are varied, and so our needs are also varied. On the whole, I think you'll find the workload to be light in that you will surely have ample free time. But then there comes the question of what one *does* with his free time. I have occasionally felt that this was the most difficult part of the job; indeed, the most difficult part of being alive, wouldn't you say, boy?"

"Perhaps you're right, sir."

"Surely I am. Oftentimes I'm confronted with an afternoon or evening off, with not a stitch of work to do, and do you know, I meet this fact with something akin to panic." Mr. Olderglough sighed. "At any event: in the simplest terms, your foremost function is to anticipate my needs and see to them. Your predecessor was most gifted in this."

"Mr. Broom?"

A cold look crept across Mr. Olderglough's face. "How did you know his name?"

"Memel told me."

"And what else did he tell you, I'd like to know?"

"Nothing else."

"Nothing at all?"

"Not so very much. Will you tell me what happened with Mr. Broom, sir?"

"Later, perhaps."

"May I ask where he is now?"

"Later, boy."

Lucy heard another volley of rifle fire occurring up the mountain.

As casually as he might, he asked, "And who are these men with bayonets, sir?"

Mr. Olderglough peered curiously toward the ceiling, as though clarification would meet him there. "Men with bayonets," he said.

"They ran into the forest? To shoot at or be shot at by a second party?"

"Oh, them." Mr. Olderglough flapped his wounded wing dismissively. "Harmless. Nothing but a lot of noise. Ignore them, that's what I do."

Lucy found this unsatisfactory, naturally. "May I ask who it is they're fighting?"

"Other men." Mr. Olderglough shrugged. "Men, like them."

"And what are they fighting about, do you know?"

"Well, now, what does anyone fight about, boy?"

Lucy was baffled. And while he sensed his questions and comments were annoying Mr. Olderglough, he couldn't help but add, "I do wish I'd known about this beforehand."

"Oh? And why is that?"

"Sir, there is a war taking place outside the castle."

Mr. Olderglough rolled his eyes. "It's not a *war*," he said.

"Bullets are flying through the air."

"That doesn't make it a *war*. A war is a much bigger production. This is a trifle by comparison." He thought awhile. "I hope you don't think anyone will shoot at you."

"I pray they don't."

"Of course they won't. Why would they? A nice young fellow such as yourself." Mr. Olderglough reached over and pinched Lucy's cheek, hard. The man's fingers felt as though they were made of wood. *What a long hallway this is,* Lucy thought.

Having reached the far end of the castle, Mr. Olderglough led Lucy back in the direction they'd come, though by a separate series of labyrinthine passages, these no less unpleasant than the others. They were going to visit the scullery, Mr. Olderglough explained. He talked as he walked.

"You will awaken at five-thirty in the morning, to bring me my tea by six. This will be waiting for you on a tray in the scullery, having been prepared by Agnes, whom you will soon meet, and whom you will surely come to admire, as she is admirable in any number of ways and you are, it would seem to me, a lad with a good head on your shoulders, the sort in possession of the ability to separate wheat from chaff."

"I hope that I am, sir, and thank you."

"You're welcome. I will take my tea abed, and so you should be prepared to witness me in my sleeping attire. It is nothing too terribly flashy, mind you, only I thought it prudent to warn you ahead of time."

"That's fine, sir."

"Good. Now. I will ask you to ferry me the tea tray as it stands. That is, do not pour the tea from the pot, and neither should you add the cream or sugar to the teacup, as these are small actions I prefer to perform in my own way, and according to my personal tastes, known to no one save for myself."

"I understand."

"Negligible accomplishments adding up to something significant over a period of time, and cumulatively, do you know just what I mean here, boy?"

"I believe I don't, sir."

"I shall not sit idly by and settle for anything other than a perfect cup of tea."

"No."

"Compromise is a plague of sorts, would you agree, yes or no?"

"I don't know that I've thought of it before, sir."

"A man accepts an inferior cup of tea, telling himself it is only a small thing. But what comes next? Do you see?"

"I suppose, sir."

"Very good. Now. After my breakfast, you will return to find your own breakfast awaiting you in the scullery. Do not forget to compliment Agnes's fare, even if the fare does not warrant it."

"I understand."

"The fare will not warrant it."

"I understand."

"You will not starve here, boy, but neither will you grow fat."

"No."

"After eating, Agnes will likely send you into the village to fetch us our stores for the day. Have you much experience in the marketplace?"

"No, sir."

"Can you identify a fresh vegetable versus a non-fresh vegetable?"

"I surely can."

"What we're after is a vegetable in its prime."

"Yes."

"Too young will not do. And too old—worse yet."

"I will seek out the freshest vegetables."

"That's the attitude. Now, might I ask what you know of haggling?"

"I know of its existence."

"But have you yourself haggled?"

"No, sir."

"They will name a high price, but you must not pay this price," Mr. Olderglough explained.

"No."

"You must pay a lower price."

"This is haggling."

"Just so. And now. What of meat."

"Meat, sir."

"Have you bought it?"

"I've never, no."

"You will want to keep a sharp eye on the wily butcher."

"Is he wily, sir?"

"Is he wily! He will sell you gristle with a smile on his face, then sing a carefree tune all the way home."

"I'll watch him closely, sir."

"If you bring gristle to Agnes, it will be unpleasant for you."

"I will not do it."

"All is right with the world, then." Mr. Olderglough smiled at Lucy. "This is going quite well, isn't it? You and I?"

"I hope so, sir."

"It certainly seems it, if you ask me."

"Very good, sir."

"Indeed. And now, here we are. Let's see if our grande dame is scampering about."

They had arrived at the scullery, an incongruous space in that it was orderly, clean, and well lit, with many candles ablaze, a row of low windows lining the east-facing wall, and a cheering if modest fire crinkling in a small hearth in the corner. This last, in addition to the heat from the stove, made for a warmer room than any other Lucy had met at the castle, and he stood awhile, basking in it. Agnes was nowhere to be seen. Mr. Olderglough was standing with eyes closed, swaying slightly and grinning, as one enamored of a fond memory.

"Are you all right, sir?" asked Lucy.

Mr. Olderglough opened his eyes. "There once were twenty souls in our employ here, boy. Can you imagine it? Coachmen, waiting maids, porters, a cook, a nurse. All gone now, alas."

"I thought you'd said Agnes was the cook, sir?"

"Originally she was the chambermaid. When the cook left us, then did Agnes step forward, claiming a deft hand."

"But it seems you take issue with her cooking, is that correct?"

"Not so far as she knows. But in my private mind, yes, I am unenthusiastic."

"And why do you not speak with her about it, may I ask?"

"Because I dislike unpleasantness. Also there is the fact of my being somewhat afraid of her. And then, too, I'm not much interested in eating." He looked at Lucy. "Are you?"

"I like to eat," Lucy said.

"Is that right?" Mr. Olderglough shook his head, as if to accommodate an eccentricity. "Personally, it never held much sway for me."

Lucy said, "May I ask what became of the others?"

"Well, they've gone away, haven't they?"

"But why have they, sir?"

"I suppose they thought it the wisest course of action, is all." Mr. Olderglough looked wistfully about the room. "Twenty souls," he said, "and here, what's become of us? Well, we've got you in our company now, boy, and this heartens me, I can tell you that much."

Lucy was not so heartened. He followed Mr. Olderglough to the larder; the shelves were all but bare. There came from the corner the scratching of rodents, and now began a thumping, squabbling battle, a lengthy affair concluding with the agonized squeal of the defeated: high and sharp at its commencement, distantly windy at its resolution. Mr. Olderglough wore a satisfied expression, as though the outcome were favorable to him. Drawing back his cascading forelock, he said, "I find the constant upkeep of the body woefully fatiguing, don't you?"

M r. Olderglough led Lucy up a tight spiral stairwell, impressive in its dizzying, seemingly endless redundancy, in addition to its airlessness and general gloominess. They passed a landing outfitted with a stubby-legged bench of hardwood which Mr. Olderglough addressed with a tap of the toe of his boot. At the top of this stairwell was Lucy's room, a cramped space with a slanted ceiling and a small window located in the center of the lone exterior wall. The furnishings consisted of a two-drawer dresser, a rocking chair, a modest bed, and a potbellied stove pushed into the corner. Lucy laid his valise on the bed and opened it. Mr. Olderglough, standing at his back, said, "I suppose you must be tired after your journey."

"I suppose I must be," Lucy replied. He was considering his possessions. Here was every single thing he owned, and it didn't seem like much to him, because it wasn't.

Mr. Olderglough said, "Then you may rest, or not rest, as per your desire. At any rate, the afternoon is yours. Tomorrow you will begin your appointment proper, does that agree with you? Well, then, good day to you, boy."

"Thank you, sir. Good day to you as well."

Mr. Olderglough left the room and closed the door, and Lucy sat down upon the bed. Mr. Olderglough opened the door and re-entered the room, and Lucy stood.

"I forgot about the letters."

"Letters, sir?"

"The letters, yes. The Baron maintains a robust correspondence with the Baroness, living currently, apparently, or so he believes I should say, in the far eastern province. Every morning you will find a sealed envelope on the side table in the entryway. This will be taken by yourself to the station, where you will meet the nine o'clock train. The train will not stop. The letter will be passed off to the train engineer himself, and achieved thus." He lifted his good arm high above his head.

"He will snatch it up from my hand, do you mean?" Lucy asked.

"Just so, yes. It is an unorthodox method, I know, but we are on our own, here, and we must make do." Mr. Olderglough scratched his chin. "You're looking at me as though you have a question."

"Yes," said Lucy. "I'm wondering how it came to be that the mail was collected in this way."

"Ah, I bribed the engineer," said Mr. Olderglough. "Actually, I continue to bribe the engineer. Possibly that sounds untoward, but it's only a pittance, and if the truth should be known, I get a thrill from it. Touch of criminality, thickens the blood—you didn't hear it from me, boy. Now you're looking at me with another question."

Lucy nodded. "The engineer, sir. Will he have letters for me as well?"

"No, he won't. The Baron's is a one-sided correspondence."

Lucy pondered the definition of the word. "I was unaware there was such a thing," he admitted.

Mr. Olderglough's face puckered, as one stung by a discourtesy. "Is this a comical observation?" he asked.

"It was not meant to be, sir, no."

"I certainly hope not. Because I don't subscribe to amusements, Lucy. Laughter is the basest sound a body can make, in my opinion. Do you often laugh, can I ask?"

"Rarely."

"How rarely?"

"Very rarely, sir. Extremely rarely, in fact."

"Good," Mr. Olderglough said. "Good. Now. These letters are of the most pre-eminent importance to the Baron, and must be handled with the greatest respect and discretion. No peeking, is what I'm saying here."

"I would never, sir."

"You will want to."

"Be that as it may."

"And, if there ever comes a day where the engineer *does* have a letter for you, this should be treated with utmost seriousness. I suspect this will never happen. Actually I can say with confidence that it won't. Still and all, you have been instructed, have you not?"

"I have been instructed, sir."

Mr. Olderglough stole a glance at the contents of Lucy's valise. "Where is your day suit, boy?"

"I haven't one, sir."

"What—do you mean?"

"I mean that I am not in possession of a day suit, sir."

"Well, what do you have in the way of evening attire, then?"

"This is my attire in its entirety," said Lucy, pointing to his worn out suit of clothes.

Mr. Olderglough regarded the ensemble with unambiguous indignity. "Did it not occur to you," he said, staring glumly at Lucy's sheepskin cap, "that you would be expected to dress in a manner befitting your appointment?"

Lucy considered the question. "I will admit to being aware of a style of dress common among those working in places such as this," he conceded. "But I suppose I assumed that my employer might furnish me with said attire, were it required of me to wear it."

"I see. And who was it that gave you this idea, I'd like to know?"

"No one, sir. It came to me independently."

"It's a bold notion."

"I was not after boldness."

"You achieved it."

"I'm sorry if I've offended you."

"You have annoyed me mildly. It is abating as we speak." Mr. Olderglough looked out the window, and back. "Has anyone ever told you you possess a likability?"

"Not that I can recall, sir, no."

"You possess a likability."

"I'm happy to hear as much."

"Yes. Well. Perhaps something can be done about the situation at a later date, but until that point in time, we will get by with what's available to us."

"Just as you say, sir."

Mr. Olderglough moved again to exit the room, but in turning the doorknob he found himself transfixed by its apparatus, so that Lucy asked him, "Is there something the matter with the door, sir?"

Mr. Olderglough didn't reply for a moment; when he spoke, his voice was dimmed nearly to a whisper. "Would you describe yourself as a fitful sleeper?"

"I suppose I would, sir, yes."

"Good. May I also ask, do you typically retire early in the evening, or later on?"

"I would say that it varies. Is it safe to assume that you have a preference?"

"It is indeed. In fact, I will request, with a friendly firmness, that you come to your room no later than ten o'clock, and that you should lock yourself in each night."

Lucy wasn't sure he'd heard correctly. "Did you say you want me to lock myself in, sir?"

"Yes."

"Is that really necessary?"

"Yes."

"And why is it necessary, sir?"

"Hmm," Mr. Olderglough said. "You should lock yourself in because I've asked it, and because I'm your superior, and so it will avail you to heed me, just as it will please me to be heeded." After speaking he stood by, happy with his skillful avoidance of the question put to him. He tocked his heels together and left, and Lucy began unpacking his valise. In the drawer of his dresser he found a heavy brass telescope; carved on the side was the name BROOM. He assumed his predecessor used this to chronicle the goings-on of the shanty village, which sat far beneath the tower window, and now he himself did just the same.

When he peered into the device, the village leapt into view, colorful and fast-moving. He caught a glimpse of young Mewe exiting his shanty, stepping with speed and purpose but suddenly stopping, an expression of doubt on his face. Now he doubled back and returned to his home, and he did not exit again. Memel was standing outside his shanty just next door, arguing with a slight girl whose features Lucy couldn't make out, as she was facing away from him. When she stalked off, Memel called after her, to no avail. He was smiling as he watched her leave; their argument, at least for him, was not a vicious or serious one. Alone now, he removed a pipe from his pocket and began filling this with tobacco. Lucy had forgotten Memel had stolen it. He decided to retrieve it, and after tucking his valise beneath the bed he descended the corkscrewed stone stairwell.

III

—

KLARA THE BEGUILER

It had just gone six o'clock as Lucy ambled down the hill before the castle. The winter sun had dipped below the mountain, and the village wore the properties of night prematurely. The cold stung at his ears and he pulled his hat down to cover them. As he walked past the shuttered stalls in the marketplace, a half-dozen children assembled behind him, stepping in a clutching cluster to observe him and wonder at his arrival. They were giddy to be stalking the newcomer, and while there was an element of danger to this adventure, they themselves knew, in the way children know such things, that Lucy was not a bad man. Still, when he spun about to greet them, they scattered in individual directions, each one shrieking ecstatically. Lucy blushed at the attention but also felt happy, even proud in a way, as though he had been formally announced.

Passing Mewe's shanty, he noticed the window was ajar, and he paused to peer inside. Mewe sat at an uneven table, playing cards fanned out in his hands. His face bore the penitent look of one who has just been caught cheating, because he had just been. Across from Mewe was a young woman, and she was very pretty indeed, if the truth would be known. In point of fact she was more than pretty: she was exquisite.

She was his age, Lucy supposed, or slightly younger. She wore her abundant brown hair stacked atop her head, exposing a delicate jawline angling into a long, tapered neck. The silhouette of her face was backlit by candles, and he could see no flaws about her, not an angle out of place, as though she were a marble figurine crafted by the sure hand of a master wishing only to share an ideal of the purest beauty. Her comeliness was counteracted by the state of her coat, a shapeless, sack-like thing with cuffs gone thin to the point of fraying. But she herself was so very lovely to behold that Lucy wouldn't have looked away for the world; he couldn't have. Her black eyes flashed in the stuttering flamelight as she chided her playmate.

"Why do you do it, Mewe?"

"I don't know why. It's like an itch that must be scratched."

"But it isn't any fun for me when you cheat."

"No?"

"How could it be?"

"I should think it might be exciting for you."

"And why would you think that?"

"It follows some manner of logic."

"Would you like me to do the same to you?"

"I suppose I wouldn't, actually."

She snatched up the cards from his hand, shuffling these into the deck. "Even if you win, you lose, don't you understand?"

"I don't know about *that*," Mewe said.

She ceased shuffling. "Will you or won't you stop it?"

Mewe put on a brave face. "I will try."

A days-old puppy, black in color, clambered onto the table and arched against an earthen jar sitting between Mewe and his enchanting guest. When the jar toppled, Mewe righted it automatically and dragged the puppy from the table to his lap. The girl dealt the cards and they resumed play, and Lucy had the feeling he was watching a painting come to life; there was something enduring about the scenario, something timeless and vividly evocative, and this appealed to him in a sweetly sad way. The spell was broken when Mewe spied him at the window and said, "Oh, hello, there." The girl turned to look, and when her and Lucy's eyes met he was filled with a shameful panic, and he spun away, huddling at Memel's door, his heart knocking against his throat.

"Who was that?" he heard the girl ask.

"Lucy's his name. We met him on the train. He's at the castle, now. Gone after Mr. Broom."

She paused. "Is he nice?"

"He seems it. But who can say? Perhaps he's a scoundrel in hiding."

The girl softly laughed, then was silent. Lucy heard the scrape of her chair, and now she appeared at the window. She stood mere feet from Lucy but owing to the darkness had no idea of his proximity. She was pondering some distant thought, a lonely one, according to her expression; when she shut the window and drew the curtain, Lucy stood awhile in the snow, feeling foolish and trembly.

He turned and knocked on Memel's door. Memel answered with a puppy in his hand, this likewise black, but with white boots.

"Did you take my pipe?" Lucy asked.

"Yes," said Memel.

"Can I have it back, please?"

Memel left and returned with the pipe.

"Thank you," said Lucy.

"You're welcome." Memel nodded to the castle. "How are you settling in?"

"Fine."

"What have you had for your supper?"

"Nothing."

"Are you hungry?"

"I don't know if I am."

"Shall we find out?"

Memel ushered him into the shanty.

The front room of Memel's home brought to mind an animal's burrow. The floor was dirt, and the air smelled of roots and spices. The walls were made from tin scrap of varying degrees of corrosion, and they shuddered in the wind. But it was not an unpleasant space: a copper cauldron hung in the fireplace, its fat, rounded bottom licked by flames, and oil lamps throwing off a honey-colored light lined the rafters in neatly pegged rows. Lucy sat beneath these at a low-standing table. There was a litter of puppies roaming about, yipping and knocking things over and pouncing on one another; the exhausted mother lay on the floor beside the table, stomach bagged, dead to the world. "Poor Mama," said Memel. "She's had just about enough." He nudged her with his foot and she retired to one of two small back rooms, with the puppies following after. Memel removed the cauldron from the fire and set it in the center of the table to cool. Tilting back his head, he shouted, "Mewe!"

Mewe's muffled voice came through the wall, from his own shanty. "What?"

"Is Klara with you?"

"Yes."

"Is she still angry at me?"

Lucy could hear the girl named Klara murmuring, but couldn't decipher her words.

"She says she's not," Mewe called.

"And do you believe her?"

"Yes, I think I do."

"And you? Are you still angry?"

"Not at all."

"Will you please come and eat with us, then?"

A pause; more murmuring. "Who is 'us'?" Mewe asked.

"Lucy has come to visit. The lad from the train?"

"Yes, he was spying on us a moment ago."

Memel looked at Lucy with a questioning glance. Lucy shook his head. "I was only passing by," he whispered.

"He claims not to have been spying, Mewe."

"Oh? And what would he call it, then?"

"Passing by, is how he describes it."

Yet more murmuring. Mewe said, "Ask him for us, please, if he believes one must be in motion to be passing?"

Lucy admitted that yes, he supposed one did have to be, and Memel restated this.

"Well, then," Mewe continued, "how does he explain the fact of his being stationary at my window?"

Memel raised his eyebrows. "Were you stationary, Lucy?"

"Perhaps I lingered for a moment."

"Now he is calling it a momentary lingering," Memel said.

"I see," said Mewe. Murmuring. "We would like to know, then, just what is the difference between the two?"

Lucy thought he could hear some restrained laughter coming from Klara. To Memel he said, "Spying suggests a hope to come by private information. My intentions were much simpler."

Memel digested, then repeated the words, which precipitated further hushed discussion between Mewe and Klara. At last the former said, "Would Lucy describe himself, then, as idly curious?"

Lucy was now certain he could hear both Klara and Mewe stifling their amusement.

"Well?" Memel asked, who was smiling.

"I think that would be fair," said Lucy.

"It would be fair, he says," Memel said.

For a time, Lucy could not hear any further chatter from next door. Finally it was Klara who spoke. "Give us a moment to finish our game, Father," she said.

S tew's too hot yet, anyway," Memel said, peering into the cauldron. He stepped away from the table and invited Lucy into his room, a drab cube with no window or furnishings save for a straw mattress on the ground and a wood crate doubling as a bedside table. The puppies lay in a heap in the corner, feeding off their mother, who regarded Memel and Lucy with a look beyond concern. Memel leaned down and stroked her with a gentle hand, his face drawn with worry. "They're going to kill her." Cocking his head, he asked, "Would you like a puppy, Lucy?"

"Oh, no, thank you."

"You're certain?"

"Yes."

"Well," he said, "this simply won't do." He picked up the puppy with white boots and left the room. An uneasy feeling visited Lucy; he followed Memel and found him standing at a water barrel beside the front door, his arm submerged to the elbow. "If the mother dies, then they all will," he said, regarding the black water with a look of grave determination. Long moments passed, and when he slipped his arm from the water, there was nothing in his hand. He returned to his room and re-emerged with another puppy, making once more for the barrel. Why this was being carried out in Lucy's presence, and just prior to eating, Lucy could not fathom. Whatever the reason, he felt impelled to intervene. When he spoke, he was not motivated by any one thought or combination of words, but in response to a kind of pain, much in the way one involuntarily cries out after being injured:

"Stop it," he said. "If it's come to this, then I'll take him."

Memel came nearer and deposited the puppy in Lucy's palm. "Her," he said, and moved to the table to ladle out the stew.

The puppy was the runtess of the pack. Sleekly black, her head tottered creakily, as though she were feebly aged. She peered up at Lucy and opened her mouth but no sound came out; lowering her head, she closed her eyes and Lucy tucked her into the breast pocket of his coat. Her snout pushed proud of this, her tiny jaws ajar. Lucy rubbed the fuzz above her nose and she licked his fingertip, which prompted a flutter in his stomach. There is an instance of import when one experiences the conception of love, he realized. It was as though you had been waiting for it all along; as if you'd known it was approaching, and so when it arrives you reach out to greet it with an innate familiarity. Behind him, Memel said, "All right, Lucy, the stew is cooled."

When Lucy turned to face the table he gave a start, for Klara and Mewe had snuck in and were sitting upright, hands laid flat before them, a portrait of obedience but for the hint of mirth clinging to their lips. Lucy suspected their sneaking in was a prank played on him, some bit of mischief for his benefit or at his expense. It was harmless enough, as pranks went; but why did his face burn so as he sat down? Klara, spoon in fist, covered her face and silently shuddered; Mewe produced a series of discreet snorts. Memel, sitting, took note of their good humor but had no inkling of its origin. He leaned forward on his elbows and asked hopefully,

"Is there a joke?"

"No," said Mewe and Klara together.

"There's not a joke?"

"No."

Memel tried to let it go, but could not: "Oh, tell us the joke, already." He was genuinely curious; he himself wanted to laugh with the others—he wore a smile on his face, in anticipation of the introduction of something amusing. But when they offered no explanation, he grimaced, and told Lucy, "This is rude behavior."

Lucy stared at his stew, waiting for the painful moment to pass. Quietly, he told Memel, "It's something private between them, I suppose." Klara sat up alertly when he said this, as if she'd been stuck with a pin, and now she scrutinized Lucy for such a length of time that he thought nothing else would do but to face her.

When their eyes met, and held, he felt once again the instance of import, only more powerfully than before. There was in him an actual reverberation, and his blood hurried every which way. He could not intuit what Klara was experiencing, if anything, but there was something in his expression which alarmed her, and she suddenly looked away. When she did this, his heart caught, and he wished to reach out to her, to take up her hand in his own. Now it was her turn to blush, he noticed.

Lucy settled into his supper. The stew was deliciously spicy, so that sweat beaded at his temples under his cap, and his tongue was singed with a pulsing heat. Memel poured him a glass of water but Lucy, recalling what lay at the bottom of the barrel, opted for wine. He only rarely drank alcohol, and it birthed in him a feeling of jauntiness, and he decided he might have some small celebration with himself. By the time he had finished his stew he was working on his third glass, and a confidence or sense of ease settled over him. Mewe and Klara carried on with their private whisperings and gigglings, but Lucy wasn't embarrassed by this; in fact he thought it just that they were devoting these attentions to him. Was he not a funny one, after all? This pale and underfed young stranger with a puppy in his pocket? He made no protest, he took no offense, but began to prepare his pipe, for now he finally had his audience, and they would witness his smoking and wonder at the complexity of his thoughts. Alas, when the sharp smoke jabbed at his naked throat he emitted a single cough which blasted the pipe's contents fully over his head. Memel, Mewe, and Klara found this a glad event; the three of them laughed frankly, loudly, and for a lengthy period of time. Lucy knew, even while the tobacco was hurtling through the air, that he could never recover from this social blunder; he solemnly returned his pipe to his coat pocket, drained his wine, and poured himself another.

The room was in motion, slowly wheeling, bringing to mind the dizziness he'd experienced when climbing the stairwell to his quarters in the castle—a moderately unsettling yet not entirely displeasing sensation. He removed the puppy from his pocket and laid her on the table, tickling and teasing her. She reared and bit his hand, but she was so slight that this caused no pain, and he laughed at the futility of it. Klara's features were blurred in the woozy candlelight; she was watching Lucy with seeming indifference. And yet she didn't look away, either.

The wine was going down like water, and Lucy had arrived at the point of drunkenness where he couldn't hold a thought. His lips became lazy and his words were slurred; this amused the others, who put any number of questions to him, that they might expose and celebrate his state.

An ugliness took shape in Lucy's mind. It was obvious to him that these people would never welcome him into their society, and that they wanted him around only to make sport of him. When he saw the white-booted puppy peering out from behind the water barrel, he knew he had been tricked by Memel, and this was the final insult. He stood and lurched toward the door, with the others calling after him, their voices choked with cackling, gasping laughter. Memel crossed over, clinging to Lucy's coat and imploring him to stay; Lucy pulled away, stepping clear of the shanty and into an oceanic windstorm which instantly plucked his cap from his head and gobbled it up. Realizing the puppy still was clutched in his hand, Lucy turned, thinking to return it to Memel, but Klara was standing in the doorway with a repentant look on her face and Lucy felt he couldn't meet her again. He tucked the puppy away in his pocket and resumed his uneven snow-marching toward the looming, blacker-than-night castle.

His mood was profoundly resentful as he caromed off the walls of the spiral staircase, bumbling in the dark, hands outstretched like a blind beggar. He had had it in his mind that once he left Bury he would become a second man, and this man would command, if not respect, then at least civility. But here it was much the same, it seemed: he was derided and made to look the fool; the villagers had identified him on the spot as one who could not be considered a serious person. In remembering his departure from the shanty, it occurred to him that Memel had stolen his pipe again. Checking his pocket, he found this to be so, and he paused at the top of the stairs to issue a hissing sound.

He fell into bed, not bothering to undress. The puppy crawled from his pocket and began nosing about under the blankets; Lucy watched the lump creeping toward this and that cavern and crevice. He drifted into uneasy slumber, his dreams descriptive of impossible frustrations, a vanishing doorway here, a never-ending staircase there. This marked the completion of his first day at the castle.

IV

—

THE CASTLE VON AUX

In the morning there stood at the foot of Lucy's bed a small round human woman wearing an exceedingly white smock and a look of displeasure. She had short gray hair and her face was also gray. Actually her hair and face were similar in color to the point of being confusing, even jarring to Lucy. Her hands, resting atop her stomach, were so deeply red as to appear scalded. This was Agnes, the cook.

"Were you not told to lock the door?" she said.

"Hello. Yes. Good morning, ma'am. I was." Lucy's head was throbbing, and his throat was so dry that it was difficult to speak. His boots were peering out from beneath the blankets and Agnes, pointing, asked,

"Is this the custom, where you come from?"

"I fell asleep," Lucy explained, sitting up.

"That's to be expected, when one is in bed. But why did you not take the boots off before sleep came, is my question." Agnes drew back the blanket; the sheets were stained with earth and snow. When the puppy clambered out, Agnes gasped. "Goodness! I thought it was a rat."

"It's not a rat, ma'am."

"That's clear *now*." She reached down and scratched the puppy's chin. "Does Mr. Olderglough know you keep an animal?"

"No."

"And how long were you planning on hiding it from him?"

"It's nothing I've been hiding, ma'am. That is, it's only just come to pass."

"It's something he will want to hear about."

"I will be sure to tell him."

"Very good. And when will you be rising, I wonder? Mr. Olderglough has had to fetch his own breakfast, and yours is getting colder all the while."

"I'm sorry about that, ma'am; it won't happen again. I'm getting up now."

Agnes nodded, and crossed the room to go. Pausing at the door, she said, "You will remember to lock up?"

"Yes, ma'am."

"It's not something to be forgotten." She looked over her shoulder at Lucy. "Or possibly you don't understand how important this is."

Lucy swung his boots from the bed, and to the floor. "I suppose I do." He scooped the puppy up and deposited her in his pocket. "Actually, I don't," he said. "Why exactly must I lock my door, please?"

"We all must lock our doors."

"But what is the reason?"

She measured her words. "It's not for nothing, and that's all you need to know."

Agnes took her leave, and Lucy sat awhile, pondering. "I should like to know quite a lot more than that," he said at last. Later, he would wish to know less.

He moved to the window, telescope in hand.

M r. Olderglough was sitting in the servants' dining quarters, a cramped and cheerless room annexed to the scullery. His hand was free from its sling, apparently on the mend, and he was poring over a large leather ledger, to the side of which sat his breakfast, consisting of a bowl of porridge, a thin slice of dry bread, and a cup of tea. An identical setting had been laid out for Lucy; he sat, sampled the porridge, and was not in any way impressed by its flavor, texture, or temperature. His tea was likewise cold, in addition to being bitter, but it washed away the taste of wood shavings the porridge imparted, and so he drank it down in a gulp.

"Good morning, sir," he said, gasping.

Mr. Olderglough nodded but did not respond verbally, distracted now by the sawing of his bread, three cuts lengthwise and three on the height, making for nine squares in total. Once this was accomplished, he stuck out his tongue and laid a square on the fleshy pink appendage. Withdrawing his tongue, he chewed, proffering a look which dared Lucy to comment. Lucy did not comment. He said,

"I find myself wondering, sir, if I might keep an animal."

Mr. Olderglough swallowed. He was moderately alarmed. "An animal?" he said.

"A dog, sir, yes. A puppy."

"Where in the world did you get a puppy?"

"From Memel, sir. His dog gave birth to a litter."

"I see. Sloughed the burden off on you, then, did he?"

"I wouldn't say sloughed."

"Every man for himself?"

"Not exactly, sir. In point of fact I'm happy to have the puppy. If you'll allow me to keep it, that is."

A look of confusion had affixed itself to Mr. Olderglough. "When did all this *happen*, may I ask?"

"Only recently, sir."

"Clearly." Staring into space, now, Mr. Olderglough said, "Do you ever get the feeling the world is passing you by?"

"I don't know about that, sir."

"An occasional rapidity of time? Things occurring in an instant?"

"I'm not sure, sir."

"A speediness of events? And then, once the speedy event has happened, it cannot unhappen?"

"I suppose that's true, sir."

"Yes. Well, at any rate, if you desire a companion, then who am I to stand in the way of your happiness?"

"So I may keep the puppy, sir?"

"And why not? It's none of my affair what you get up to of a Sunday. I'm a proponent of individual freedom."

"Yes, sir."

"One should search out his heart's desire, wouldn't you agree with me?"

"Oh, yes, sir."

"We've only got one go-round, eh, Lucy?"

"One go, sir."

"Once around the park?"

"That's right."

"Let's make it count, why don't we?"

"Let's do that, sir."

Mr. Olderglough pointed. "Why aren't you eating your porridge?"

"Because of the taste of it, sir."

Mr. Olderglough looked about the room, then leaned in and whispered, "Dump it in the fireplace, why don't you. And mine as well. Agnes stomps and clomps if the plates aren't licked clean."

Lucy did as he was told, then returned to his chair.

"Is it a he or a she?" Mr. Olderglough asked.

"A she, sir. I hope that's all right."

"I have no preference. I'm just making conversation at this point. Would you like another cup of tea?"

"No, thank you."

"I believe I'll go again." Mr. Olderglough poured himself a second cup and took a dainty sip. He said, "Did you know that I myself keep a bird?" This last was spoken as though he'd forgotten it to be so, and only just remembered, and was surprised by the fact of it.

"I didn't know, sir, no," said Lucy.

"A mynah bird," said Mr. Olderglough, "named Peter. I had thought he might brighten my room with his chirping song. Alas, not a peep."

"I'd thought the mynah was the chatty one."

"That's what I'd been led to believe as well. Consider my displeasure, then."

"Yes."

"Study on it."

"I surely will. I wonder if there's something the matter with him."

"Or else the showman's desire is absent. Anyway, Peter is mute as a stone." Mr. Olderglough sighed. "I could do with a bit of music, to tell you the truth, Lucy. I could do with a bit of cheer." He propped his head against the back of the chair. "I've always liked the name: Peter. That's what I'd have named my son, if I'd had one. Well, it wasn't for the lack of trying. If I had a penny for every barn dance I attended in my youth."

"Yes, sir."

"Some of us are fated to roam the earth alone, it would seem."

"Sadly true, sir."

Mr. Olderglough pushed his plate away. "Would you like to meet him? Peter?"

Lucy did not particularly care to, but it seemed to be expected of him, and so he said that he would. Mr. Olderglough clapped and stood and began expediently buttoning his coat.

P eter was a deeply antisocial bird. A passerine of middling size with drab brown plumage and a sharp orange-yellow beak, he squatted sullenly on his perch, looking not at but through his visitors. Actually, Lucy thought his expression, if a bird can have an expression, denoted legitimate hatred.

"This is Peter," Mr. Olderglough said.

"Hello, Peter."

"Say hello, Peter."

Peter did not say hello, but burrowed his face in his breast and pulled up a leg, standing motionless, and it seemed he would be thus forever.

"Closed up shop," said Mr. Olderglough. "You see how it is, then?"

"Yes, sir, I think I do. And you say he's never made any sound whatsoever?"

"None."

"Something which will make him sing, sir."

"Nothing will."

Mr. Olderglough moved to rest upon a faded fainting couch in the corner of his parlor. Muttering to himself, the man was lost for a time to his reveries, and Lucy took advantage of this to survey his superior's quarters: at once tasteful and dire, formerly grand, utterly dated, and coated uniformly in dust. It was a room in which time hung more heavily than was the norm, and Lucy had the feeling he was the first to pay a social call in a long while.

A wall clock chimed, and Mr. Olderglough said, "You'll be wanting to meet the train, now, Lucy. In the entryway you'll find the Baron's letter on the side table, as well as a list of what's needed from the village."

"And with what shall I pay for the goods?"

Mr. Olderglough stood, patting his pockets but turning up nothing. "Do me a favor, boy, and pay for them yourself. I'll get it back to you soon enough."

"I'm afraid I can't do that, sir."

A twinge of panic struck Mr. Olderglough. "Haven't you any money handy at all?"

"None." Lucy paused. "Perhaps, sir, if you were to give me an advance on my wage?"

"Hmm," said Mr. Olderglough. "No, I don't believe I'll do that."

"I was wondering when I might be paid," Lucy admitted.

"You will be paid on payday, naturally. For now, you will wait in the entryway, please."

As Lucy traveled from Mr. Olderglough's room to the castle's entrance, he was struck by the fact of his enjoying the position, enjoying being told what to do, the marvelous simplicity of it. He had always sensed in his mother and father a desire for him to do something, to do anything, but they were remiss in sharing particular instructions and so, being unambitious himself, he accomplished nothing, and only continued to disappoint them. But now, all at once, he was useful, was being used, and this filled him with a sense of dignity. Arriving at the entryway, he stood by the side table awaiting Mr. Olderglough and basking in this feeling. Alas, as the minutes passed by, Lucy's buoyant attitude turned to restlessness, which then evolved to candid boredom. He scanned the shopping list but this offered nothing in the way of entertainment, and so he found himself wishing to steal a glance at the mysterious Baron's letter. He knew he must not do this, that it was in direct opposition to what Mr. Olderglough had told him, but the desire grew and grew further, and soon he gave in to it. Edging a fingernail under the wax seal, he opened the envelope and unfolded the paper.

My Darling,

What news have you? Will you tell me you no longer love me? Whether or not I would prefer this to the damning silence, I won't say. The truth is that I am no longer steering this devastated ship. I took my hand off the wheel long ago, and have no concerns or thoughts for a destination. May we be dashed over merciful rocks!

Why do the happy times dim in my memory, while the evil ones grow ever more vivid? And furthermore: why do I bother asking you anything anymore? A marvel: how can the days be so full of someone wholly absent? The scope of your void humbles me. It is vast to the point that part of me hopes you have died. This at least would explain your nonappearance, and so would afford me some slight comfort. Also it would make it simpler for me to die. And yet I love you still and more, with every day that floats past.

I am yours alone,

Baron Von Aux

Lucy read this in a rush, and then again, more slowly. It seemed there was a dim rumble or vibration emanating from the words, and it caused him to bend his ear nearer the page so as to drink it in. He recognized something of himself in the letter; but also he found himself feeling envious of the Baron's heartsickness, which was surely superior to any he had experienced. This jealousy struck him as childish, and yet he wasn't in any way ashamed of it. He returned the letter to the envelope and had just set it back on the side table when Mr. Olderglough arrived. "You'll have to make this stretch, boy," he said, pressing some coins into Lucy's hand. Calculating their worth, Lucy thought it impossible, and said as much to

Mr. Olderglough, who in turn espoused the merits of a credit-based society. It was at this point that Agnes came around the corner. Her red fists stabbed and jabbed at the air as she walked, punctuating her evident rage.

"Which of you dumped his porridge in the fireplace!"

"It was Lucy," said Mr. Olderglough, quickly quitting the room. Agnes did not notice his leaving; she moved toward Lucy as if on oiled wheels.

Lucy received his reprimand with what he hoped was something approaching grace. He wiped away the traces of spittle adorning his face and stepped outside, lamenting having lost his cap, as the cold set upon him at once, clinging to his neck, ears, and scalp. He turned up his collar and pushed on; he could hear the train but could not yet see it. Walking toward the tracks, he peered sideward at the village. There was a trickle of smoke seeping from Memel and Klara's chimney, and Lucy wondered if it was she who had made the fire. He decided she had; and he thought of her crouched before the stove, the flame drawing across the wood. He imagined the smoke spinning in cresting coils before the draft from the flue pulled it taut, encouraging it upward, and to the open spaces. Lucy felt an aching in his chest. He wanted to know just what Klara's days looked like.

Arriving at the station, he found Memel and Mewe on the platform, standing toe to toe, engaged in another argument. Memel held a dead hare in his hand, which Mewe lunged for once, twice, three times. Memel yanked it just out of reach; Mewe was fuming. "Hand it over," he said.

"I will not," Memel answered.

"But you know that it was in my snare."

"If it was in your snare you'd be holding the hare, for I would never claim an animal that was not my own."

"But that's precisely what you are doing!" Mewe lunged again, and again Memel held the hare at arm's length. "The most disturbing part of all this," Mewe said, "is that you're actually starting to believe your own lies."

"God Himself only knows what the most disturbing part of it is."

Mewe wagged a finger. "You always bring God into arguments you know you're losing, for the liar is lonely, and welcomes all manner of company. Now, I'll ask you one last time: will you hand over the hare or won't you?"

"You know that I won't."

"Very well." Mewe brought his boot heel down on Memel's toe. The old man bellowed, and the hare was flung into the air, with Mewe dashing after. At the same moment he caught the somersaulting thing, Memel tackled him, and now the pair wrestled about in the snow, pulling at the hare and gritting their teeth and damning each other in the most base and common manner. Lucy found this spectacle more than a little intriguing and was curious to see who would emerge hare in hand; but now the train was approaching the station, and so he was forced to turn away.

Stepping to the edge of the platform, he held the letter high in the air. As the train bore down upon him he studied the darkened cockpit for a sign of the engineer; seeing no movement there he grew fearful something had gone amiss, when at the last moment there emerged a meaty hand, fingers splayed, poised to pounce. Lucy held his breath, and as the train hurtled past he was engulfed in a frigid wind, this of such force that he couldn't tell if the letter had remained in his grip or not. Peering up, he saw that it hadn't; he spun about to witness the blue envelope flapping in the engineer's fist. Now the fist was withdrawn. The letter had been posted.

Lucy felt a sense of dizzy satisfaction, an amusement at the strangeness of the event. Being lost to the novelty of this occurrence, he stepped too near the train, so that he felt his body shudder, as though he would be jerked from the platform and into the grinding metal wheels and shrill mechanisms. All at once he understood the train's unknowable weight and power, and he stepped cautiously backward as it passed. He didn't like to think of anyone's death, least of all his own.

When he turned he saw that Memel and Mewe had ceased their fighting and were standing before him, panting and snow-coated, each of them clinging to opposite ends of the hare. They were smiling. Behind them, at the apex of the looming mountain, Lucy could make out the pops and puffs of the area war, the soldiers scrabbling about, insects swarming cream.

To Memel, he said, "You have taken my pipe again."

"Yes, that's true," said Memel. "Did you want it back?"

Lucy said that he did, and so the pipe was returned to him. He found the mouthpiece was scored with teeth marks, and that the basin smelled of Memel's rank, inferior tobacco. In a stern tone, he said, "I want you to stop taking it from me, do you understand?"

Memel raised his eyebrows, his head bobbing side to side, as though the notion were a fascination to him.

"Will you stop it or won't you?" Lucy asked.

"Oh, all right."

Lucy struck out for the village. That he had no use for company was clear, but Memel and Mewe were blind to this, and they hurried after, that they might walk alongside him. "We're happy to see you, do you know?" said Memel. "You left in such a rush last night, we weren't sure what to think."

"Just that it was time for me to go, I suppose."

"Clearly it was that. But will you come by this evening, I wonder? I've bagged a fine hare this morning, and Klara will prepare us a stew."

"Actually," said Mewe, "it was I who bagged the hare."

"A hare was bagged, is all he needs to know."

"I should think he would want to know the truth."

"Yes, and how will he hit upon it with you spouting untruths?"

Lucy interrupted them. "I don't think I will visit you tonight," he said.

Memel and Mewe were taken aback by this. "And why not?" asked the former.

Recalling their leering, mocking faces in the candlelit shanty, Lucy told them, "I would rather not come, is all."

Now the pair shared a solemn look, and Memel said, "Do you know something, Mewe? I don't believe Lucy likes us."

"I think you may be right," said Mewe.

Memel meditated on it. "But *why* doesn't he?"

"I don't know why."

"Well," said Memel. "It doesn't feel very good, does it? Being disliked?"

"No, it certainly doesn't."

Memel meditated further. "Do you think that perhaps he likes us a little bit, though?"

"Perhaps. But not enough to dine with us, it would seem."

"It's a pale flame, is that what you're saying?"

"He likes us, but barely," Mewe said, nodding.

"A pale flame indeed. Well, what can we do about it, eh?"

"Yes."

"If he thinks we'll beg after his friendship, he might think again."

"Yes."

"And, who's to say? Perhaps he'll acquire a taste for our company in time."

"That's quite possible."

"I suppose there's nothing but to wait and see, then."

"That's all, yes."

"Wait and see and hope for the best."

"That's all."

Chatting in this breezy manner, Memel and Mewe stepped away from Lucy. Memel was twirling the hare in a carefree fashion; he tossed it to Mewe, who caught it, and tossed it back. Lucy had fallen back to watch them go but now resumed walking, following them at a distance. He had his shopping to do.

Regarding the vegetables, Lucy fared moderately but not particularly well. The grocer, a grimly lipless woman in her later middle years, sold only potatoes, squash, carrots, and onions, and those available were not all that fresh. Upon inspecting the goods, Lucy requested superior merchandise, and was confident superior merchandise existed on the premises, but the grocer was disinclined to do a stranger favors, and made no attempt to mask this. Thinking in the long term, Lucy accepted the partial defeat with a brave face, wishing the woman a happy day as he stepped away from her stall. But he knew he must not falter in respect to the meat, for if this came to pass, then his maiden outing would surely be considered a failure.

As he entered the neighboring stall he took on the posture of a man who could not conceivably be taken advantage of. He was confronted by a blood-streaked brute of a fundamentally dissatisfied man: the wily butcher, who might have said a hundred things in response to Lucy's greeting, but who chose to say nothing, he merely stared, with a look in his eye that somehow imparted both malice and indifference. When Lucy pointed out the fact of his being newly installed at the castle, the wily butcher said, "No more credit."

"Oh, I've got money, sir," said Lucy, passing over the coin he'd received as change from the grocer. The wily butcher held the coin in his palm, studying it for a time. "What do you want," he asked, and Lucy began to read aloud the list Mr. Olderglough had made out for him. Halfway through this, the wily butcher said, "Stop."

"But I'm not done with the list yet, sir."

"That's all you're going to get for the coin."

"Mightn't you extend our credit just the once more?"

"I might not."

"May I ask how much is owed you?"

The wily butcher named a figure which was much higher than Lucy would have thought. It was so much more than he'd have guessed that he could think of no words to say in reply, and he wished he'd never requested the information in the first place. The very naming of this numeral set the wily butcher off; his breathing quickened, and his face became increasingly red. "I'd be within my rights to take this coin and give you nothing, what with the amount due me. Is that what you want?"

"No, sir."

"Then you'll get what the coin allows, and go away happy." Now he took out his long knife and began sharpening it, his back to Lucy, who stood considering what he might have done differently to have won the unpleasant man's approval. But he could think of nothing, for he had done nothing wrong; the animus belonged to someone else. And yet, it occurred to him, if he came away with faulty goods, who would receive the blame? He alone. His reputation thus imperiled, he called out, "No gristle, now." When he said it, the wily butcher became statue-still.

"What did you say to me?" he asked.

There was in his voice a just-contained fury, and on hearing this, then did Lucy become aware of the magnitude of his error. When the wily butcher turned to face him, the man's expression was so grotesque that Lucy became fearful of physical violence.

"I meant no offense, sir," Lucy told him.

"But what did you *say*," asked the wily butcher, long knife gripped in his fist.

Lucy was considering retreat when a voice sounded behind

him: "You heard perfectly well what he said." He turned to find Klara standing there, a look of mischief on her face. "Now give him what he asked for already, you mean old bull."

"Oh, hello, Klara," said the wily butcher, his eyes dropping shyly to the ground. With her arrival, all the nastiness had left the man, and now he resumed the sharpening of his knife. Klara stepped closer to Lucy. "Hello," she said.

"Oh, hello."

"Father says you won't visit us again. Is it true?"

"I suppose it is," he said.

She peered searchingly into Lucy's left, then right eye, as one trying to locate something in a dark room. "But why won't you?"

"Well, I'm very busy, is all."

"What is it you're so busy with, can I ask?"

"There are many tasks befallen me."

"And will you name some of these tasks?"

"I suffer through any number of time-consuming endeavors."

She said, "I noticed you watching us from your window." Lucy hadn't thought anyone could see him spying, and he blushed terribly to learn that it was so. Surely Klara noticed his embarrassment, but she had no reaction to it, which exhibited a kindness, he thought. Was there anything crueler than a body commenting on another body's shame?

"What do you see, when you look at us?" she asked.

Bowing his head, he said, "Just, people."

"No one special?"

"I didn't say that."

In a tight voice, she said, "But Father claims that you don't like us."

"No," he told her. "That's not what it is."

"Well, what is it, then?"

"Just that I don't enjoy being made to feel foolish."

"And who is it that makes you feel foolish?"

"You do, for one. And Mewe, and your father."

"But we were only teasing you." She was picking at her sleeve, and Lucy noticed again how mangy the coat was, how worn and homely and unbefitting such a person as Klara. She'd got hold of a thread, and as she pulled on it the sleeve became ever more sorry-looking, and Lucy grew rankled by her intentional worsening of the garment. "Stop it," he said, and she did. The thread had come loose and was sticking to her fingers; she snapped her wrist and the thread slipped away on the air, and they both watched this.

She turned back to face him. "Don't you know why we tease you? Why I do?"

"It's likely you find me funny in some way," Lucy ventured.

Her face softened. "No, Lucy. That's not what it is at all."

"What is it, then?"

She thought a moment, then shifted her weight. She was opening her mouth to speak when the wily butcher laid Lucy's goods on the counter with a thud. "Here," he said. "And tell that Baron he might settle his debts one of these days." Lucy took up his bundles, nodded to Klara, and exited without another word. As he cleared the village, his mind was teeming with notions and possibilities. It occurred to him that, much in the way one experiences a brightening when walking beneath a cherry tree in bloom, so too did Klara generate and throw light.

That night Lucy couldn't sleep. He sat in his rocking chair before the stove, feeding twigs into its black mouth and staring out the window at the village, half-hidden in a shroud of unmoving fog. It was past midnight when, intermingled with the crackling of the fire, he became aware of an extraneous noise, a muffled bustle taking place behind him, and he turned to look, assuming it was the puppy settling in her sleep. But no, she was dozing leadenly atop his pillow, and Lucy thought he must have imagined the sound. He had resumed his window-watching when it occurred a second time, only more distinctly, and now Lucy's attentions were drawn to the door.

The knob was turning. This was being performed slowly, as though whoever was doing it did not wish to draw attention to the fact that he was. When the knob reached the limit of its rotation, the door swelled in its jamb; but being bolted, it couldn't be opened, and the knob turned backward, just as cautiously as before, to its point of origin. Lucy stared, rooted by fright. When the knob began again to turn, he called out,

"Who's there?"

The reply registered scarcely above a murmur. The voice was a man's, and his tone was illustrative of one possessed by deep confusion and hurt:

"Why are you in my room?"

A simple enough question, and yet these six words summoned

a tingling dread in Lucy. He stood away from the rocker, creeping sideways, and to the bed. Locating the heavy telescope under his pillow, he took this up in his hand, never looking away from the door. "This is not your room," he answered, as evenly as he could. "This is my room."

"No," said the voice, and again: "No." Now the man began pacing in the hallway, pacing and whispering to himself, hissing some unknown threats or remonstrations. Suddenly he struck the door with his fist, so that Lucy jumped back, holding the telescope high in the air like a club. "No," said the voice a third time, then shuffled away down the stairs. Lucy moved to his bed but sat up a long while afterward, regarding the doorknob with an anticipatory anguish, and he thought that if it began turning once more he would cry out from the shock of it. When he awoke in the morning, the telescope was still gripped in his cramping fist, and the puppy was sniffing at the base of the door.

L ucy entered Mr. Olderglough's room, breakfast tray in hand. Mr. Olderglough drew himself up in his bed, patting his lap, casting back his sleeping cap, and looking pleased at the fact of being doted on. After the tray was delivered he began the artful preparations of his tea; Lucy stood by, wondering how he might give voice to his thoughts. At last he decided there was no other way than to simply say it, and so he did: "A man tried to enter my room last night, sir."

Mr. Olderglough was distracted by the cautious measuring-out of his sugar. "What's that, my boy?" he asked. "What is it, now?"

"A man, sir. Tried to enter my room last night."

"A man?"

"Yes, and a strange man he was."

"Is that right?" Mr. Olderglough said wonderingly. Pouring in the cream, he stirred and sampled his tea; finding its taste satisfactory, he nodded in appreciation at life's small but dependable comforts. "And what was so strange about him, I wonder?"

"Well, the fact of him trying to get into my room was strange."

Mr. Olderglough pondered this. "I don't know that I would call that strange, in and of itself. What are rooms for if not entering, after all. Or else exiting. Indeed, think of how many rooms we enter and exit in our span of days, boy. Room to room to room. And we call it a life." He chuckled at the folly of it. But Lucy was in no mood for Mr. Olderglough's wistful opining; in fact he was feeling peevish toward his superior, who was quite obviously acting the innocent when he surely knew just what Lucy was talking about with regard to the visitor of the evening prior.

Lucy said, "I most certainly would describe it as strange, sir. For we must consider that it was not a common-use room, but my own room, and that I was abed, and that it was the middle of the night. If that isn't strange, then I don't know what is. To say nothing of the fact of his attitude."

"Oh, was his attitude strange as well," asked Mr. Olderglough flatly.

"It was. He seemed in a fever, and was speaking to himself—cackling and grumbling and disagreeing."

"As though he were two people, do you mean?"

"Or several people, yes, sir. You are aware of this person?"

"I am, lad. And aren't you glad you locked your door, like I told you? I'm no spring chicken, I won't deny it, but I know of what I speak."

"But who is he?"

"He is very rarely about, these days."

"And what is the matter with him?"

"This and that. Actually, I suspect he's mad."

Lucy took a breath. "That he's mad."

"Yes."

"You're telling me that there's a madman stalking the halls of the castle at night, is that correct?"

"Stalking," said Mr. Olderglough, shaking his head as he spread marmalade over his bread. "There you go with your theatrical wordage again."

"Is he not stalking, sir?"

"He is walking."

"But what does he *want*?" said Lucy, his voice taking on a shade of exasperation.

"Who can tell? Surely it isn't only one thing."

"And why is that?"

"Because no one wants only one thing."

As calmly as he might, Lucy asked, "Can nothing be done about him?"

"What would you suggest, boy?"

"Expel him?"

"Excellent idea. And do let me know how that pans out for you, eh?"

"All I know, sir," said Lucy, "is that I shall never feel safe here, knowing he might pounce on me at any moment."

"No, no. He only comes out late at night. This I can say with certainty. You get to your room at a decent hour, and lock up your door before turning in, and all will be well with you. Now if you don't mind, I—"

"The man thought it his room, sir."

"What?"

"The man thought my room was his own. He seemed quite sure of it."

"Is that so?" said Mr. Olderglough.

"It is so. And would you care to tell me why?"

"Why?" said Mr. Olderglough, blinking politely.

Lucy said, "Whatever happened to Mr. Broom, sir?"

Mr. Olderglough's face formed a scowl, and a low growl came from the back of his throat. "No," he said at last. "I won't speak of it."

"And why not?"

"Because it is unspeakable."

Considering the grandly mysterious awfulness of this statement, Lucy became lost in private thought; this was ongoing for such a length of time that Mr. Olderglough felt it necessary to admit, "I find myself wondering when you'll leave my room, boy."

Lucy retired in a sort of daze, and spent the rest of the morning feeling chased by his anxieties. His duties were performed in half measures, and he found his thoughts turning increasingly to recollections of Bury, the safety and comforts of his home. Mr.

Olderglough, intuiting this mood, and hoping to re-establish a bond of congeniality between them, came to Lucy in his room that afternoon bearing the news that Lucy would travel to the town of Listen the next day, to be fitted for a new suit of clothes. This made little impression on Lucy, who was sulking in earnest, now; but when Mr. Olderglough passed over Lucy's cap, this captured his imagination.

"The little village girl brought it," Mr. Olderglough said.

"Klara?"

"I don't know her name. The small one with the twinkly eyes."

The cap issued a muted crumpling, and Lucy discovered a note folded beneath the sheepskin flap. Klara's penmanship was cautiously deliberate, and the words fell at a slant, as though they would march off the edge of the paper:

> *It's because we like you that we tease you, Lucy. Please will you come and visit us? Your Klara.*

Mr. Olderglough peered over Lucy's shoulder, that he might also read the note. "Are you in the midst of an intrigue?" he asked.

"I don't know yet, sir."

"Will you tell me when you find out?"

"I will."

"Because I'm curious to know."

"I'll tell you, sir."

"Very good," said Mr. Olderglough, and he left the room.

Lucy spent some moments rereading and handling the note and considering its importance, the influence it might wield over his future. The puppy sat at his feet, looking up at him.

"*My* Klara," Lucy said.

The tailor was a sallow man with a monocle, a wisp of a mustache, and blackly shining, harshly parted hair. He read Mr. Olderglough's letter of introduction and instruction with a serene detachment, elbow akimbo, one eye—the non-monocled—gently shut. After folding the letter away, he looked Lucy up and down and said the word: "Fine." Lucy was made to disrobe to the essentials and stand upon a dais surrounded by tall, gleaming mirrors. Regarding his reflection, and being unused to such events and attentions, he felt self-conscious, this made all the more pronounced by the sorry state of his undergarments. His shirt was pitiable; his shorts, grievous. The tailor must have had an opinion regarding these unsavory articles but kept it hidden, throwing himself headlong into his work. Tape in hand, he fairly crawled all over Lucy, calling out measurements to an assistant who remained out of sight and who in fact never made any sound whatsoever.

Afterward, Lucy dressed and rejoined the tailor in the front of the shop, where he was told the suit would be ready in two weeks' time, and that it would be sent by train to the castle. Lucy thanked the man and was on his way out the door when he caught sight of a richly blue three-quarter-length cape hanging from the wall. He pointed.

"And how much is the cape, there?"

"That is a ladies' cape."

"Yes. How much does it cost?"

The tailor named a figure amounting to nearly twice the price of the suit.

"So much as that?" said Lucy. But in inspecting the cape he could see that it was of the highest quality: double-stitched and lined in silk, with fox fur ringing its hood. In a breezy tone of voice, as though it were half an afterthought, he told the tailor, "We will put that on the bill as well."

The tailor hesitated. "Mr. Olderglough makes no mention of this in the letter."

Lucy waved his hand. "It's nothing to him, I wouldn't think."

"I'm certain that's so. But I should like to ask him first, if you don't mind."

"As a matter of fact I do mind," said Lucy.

"I'd be glad to hold it for you until I receive his reply," the tailor told him.

Lucy shook his head. "You will either hand over the cape now, and make a nice profit in the bargain, or forget it altogether, and content yourself with the few modest coins earned on the suit."

Long moments passed with the tailor staring up at the cape. Lucy knew the only way his attitude would prevail was if the man was a merchant at heart, rather than someone idling in a temporary position. As it happened, the tailor had been raised in the shop. It was his father's before him, and before that, his grandfather's. The world of commerce was all he knew, and all he wanted to know; and while his not confirming the purchase with Mr. Olderglough was a clear breach of protocol, he couldn't pass up the opportunity to unload the cape, and so he took his chance, acknowledging the coup with a curious, twirling twist of his forefinger, followed by a birdlike, trilling whistle. Lucy did not believe these gestures were meant to pinpoint any one specific emotion, but rather were meant to celebrate, in the round, another fruitful day on earth. And so it was.

While the cape was being wrapped by the same invisible assistant, the tailor and Lucy were toasting brandies in the upstairs office, chatting about any little thing, as though they were old friends with shared histories and attitudes. Lucy felt very worldly and pleased with himself. He managed to drink his brandy without gagging, and what a relief this was, for it would have ruined the entire adventure had it happened otherwise.

Klara opened the door to find Lucy standing in the darkness, a package tucked under his arm. After welcoming him in, she moved to the stove to pour out water for tea. Lucy sat at the table, the package on the bench beside him. The state of his nerves was such that he found himself growing overwarm. He removed his coat, and then his cap, laying this on the table to study it. Klara spoke with her back to Lucy.

"I see you got your hat."

"Yes," said Lucy. "Was it very hard to find?"

"It was, actually."

"Well, thank you for it." He laid the package on the table before him. "And for the note, as well."

Klara said nothing to this, but brought the tea to the table. When she saw the package she asked, "What's that, there?"

"What, this?" Lucy said.

"Yes," said Klara. "What is it?"

"This here?"

"Will you tell me what it is or not?" She poked the package with her finger.

Lucy pushed it nearer to her and she said, "What now? Am I to open it?"

"Yes."

"But why?"

"Because it's for you."

This seemed to startle, even upset Klara. When at last she un-did the ribbon, she used only one hand, leaving the other to rest upon her lap. The package bloomed, a crinkling, staggered blos-som, and when she spied its contents, her spine went stiff.

"What is that?"

"It's a cape. Don't you like it?"

"Why did you bring me this?"

"It's just that I noticed your shivering the other day, in the mar-ketplace," he explained. When he said this, a look of shame came over Klara, and here Lucy recognized his mistake.

"You must think me very shabby," she said quietly.

"No, Klara."

"A shabby girl in need of charity, is that it?"

"That's not what it is at all."

But now she was rewrapping the package, and Lucy saw the moment was getting away from him. "Stop," he said. "Wait." When she did not stop, he said it again: "Stop."

She paused to look across at him.

"Why did you bring me my cap?" he asked.

Her eyes hooded when he asked this, as though she thought he wasn't playing fair by bringing it up.

"Why did you?" he persisted.

"You seemed to think we didn't like you," she said. "I wanted to show you we did."

"But that's all this is," he told her, folding back the wrapping.

She drew a hand across the cape's collar. "It's too dear."

"Who's to say, though?" Lucy took up the cape and stood, hold-ing it out before him. "Won't you try it on, at least?"

"I shouldn't," she said.

"Please," said Lucy.

"I can't."

Memel's voice called out from next door: "Cease torturing the boy, already."

"And us," Mewe added.

"Try on the cape," said Memel.

"It's obvious you want to."

At this, Lucy and Klara both went red in the face; but their self-consciousness soon gave way to stifled laughter. Lucy relocated his courage and approached Klara with the cape; when she stood, he rested the garment on her shoulders, and now she wrapped herself up in it, moving to the mirror in the corner of the shanty that she might admire herself. Lucy followed and stood behind her, watching her face, her pleased expression, and then his own. Closing his eyes, he was run through with a streak of pure happiness, for now he knew he truly was in the midst of an intrigue, just as Mr. Olderglough had said. When he opened his eyes, Klara was watching him in the mirror with a look of fondness or perhaps, for all he knew, something more than that.

"Thank you," she said.

"You're welcome," he answered.

"How does it fit?" Memel asked.

L ucy awoke to the sound of the area war. Sitting up in his bed, he trained his telescope over the mountain's face and to the pivot of the battleground. He took an idle pleasure in witnessing the birth of the cloud-puffs, these "rudely bloomed" (the phrase had ambled into Lucy's mind) then thinned by the wind, only to be replaced by yet more puffs when the following volley occurred. He could make out the soldiers' movements but not their faces, and this was preferable to him. From this distance it all seemed something more like an elaborate stage play than actual combat—some ambitious re-creation of a factual happening.

He worked all that morning assisting Agnes in the cleaning of the larder and ovens, then chopping and stacking wood through to lunchtime, but with his afternoon free, he wandered into the village. He had his pipe with him, the pipe he'd yet to master; it smoldered and had to be relit time and again, but no sooner had he done this than the wind would shift and hurry the smoke up his nose or into his eyes. Coughing, and with tears skating down his face, he put the pipe away. The puppy sat in his coat pocket, as before, taking in the sights with interest.

Lucy saw Klara standing in the marketplace, showing off her cape to a half-dozen village women, a meaty group of red-faced peasants turning her about as they studied the garment. Klara was smiling with pride as they handled and rotated her. Lucy stepped nearer, and now he could make out their conversation.

"And what does master Adolphus think of it?"

"Do I know any Adolphus?" Klara asked innocently, looking this way and that. "I see no Adolphus around here."

"And how long has he been gone this time?"

Klara threw her hands up in the air. "Bah!" she said. Lucy entered into the group and Klara, beaming, told the others, "Here, now. This is the gentleman who brought the cape."

The women swarmed Lucy, grinning devilishly, prodding him with stubby digits and speaking of him as though he weren't there at all:

"What are his intentions, do you think?"

"Will he give her a ring next?"

"Adolphus will rip this one in two."

"Clean in two, I should think."

"Will he buy me a cape? You can plainly see the state I'm in."

They slapped at Lucy's back, laughing and congratulating him for his boldness. He smiled weakly but said nothing; he didn't suppose there was one among them he could better in a fair fight. Once they dispersed, Lucy was left alone with Klara, and these two stood awhile, looking at each other. Winter sunlight spilled across her face; Lucy's vision smudged and blurred.

"Would you walk with me, Klara?" he asked.

"Yes, I'd like that," she answered, and they fell into line, stepping through the marketplace, neither of them knowing just what to say. When Klara spied the puppy in Lucy's pocket, she took her up to hold her, asking Lucy what she was called. He explained the name hadn't arrived yet, and now Klara grew thoughtful, peering at Lucy from the corner of her eye. "Perhaps you might name her after your sweetheart, wouldn't you think?"

"I suppose I could," he said. "Only, I don't have a sweetheart."

"Oh no?"

"I did have one, once. Marina, she was called."

"That's a pretty name. And whatever became of her?"

Lucy watched his breath horseshoe in the wind. An unpardonable lie came to him, and he clapped his hands to welcome it into the world. "If I'm to tell you the truth of it," he said, "she died."

"Oh, no," said Klara. "I'm so sorry to hear that."

"Yes, thank you."

"But how did she die?" Klara asked. "That is, if you don't mind talking about it."

Lucy held up his hand. "I don't mind at all."

"You're certain?"

"I don't mind in the least. Which isn't to say I enjoy talking about it."

"Of course not."

He cleared his throat. "Yes. Well. We were happy enough, Marina and I—in our modest fashion. But then she got it in her mind to marry, and when I wouldn't go along with this, she became so distraught about it that she killed herself."

Klara gasped. "Oh, but that's dreadful!"

"It was a sorry occasion," Lucy agreed.

"And why wouldn't you marry her?"

"She was not my own true love," he stated simply.

"But you were hers?" Klara ventured.

"I suppose I was. As a matter of fact, I can state that I surely was, for she told me this many times over. So, when she came to understand I would never be hers alone, then did she hang herself—and from a tree before my own house."

Klara covered her mouth; Lucy nodded sympathetically.

"Perhaps worst of all," he continued, "she had pinned a note to her dress, a note addressed to me, but which all the citizens of the town read before I had a chance to. In this way, all were made to know the finest details of her ruination." Here Lucy paused, as if the memory were too much a burden to recall.

Klara laid a tender hand on his forearm. "Is this why you've come here?" she asked. "To get away from the memory of it?"

"That's partly the reason, yes."

"Only partly? I would think that would be reason enough, all on its own."

"Yes, surely it would be. But then the matter was compounded by another unpleasant element, this in the shape of a local man, named Tor. He had always been after Marina, but he was such a stupid and ugly and sickening individual that she rebuffed him at every pass. This ate at Tor like a rot; then, once she had hung herself, for another man no less, Tor swore an oath to all who would listen that he would avenge her honor."

"By coming after you, do you mean?"

"Just that."

"And did he do this?"

"Yes, he was a man of his word, I won't deny it. In fact, hardly any time passed at all before he broke into my house and came upon me like a storm while I slept."

"While you slept!"

"Yes, yes."

"A madman," Klara said, shaking her head in wonder.

"Not mad," said Lucy. "Just simple. A barn animal, really. I might put his mental age at that of a five-year-old, and not a particularly bright five-year-old, either."

"But whatever did you do?"

"I defended myself, naturally, and forced Tor from my home. Not without a knock or two to remember me by, I might add."

"You? Oh, but you are so slight."

"I am agile, is what."

"Is that so?"

"Very agile and quick and fit."

"I wouldn't have guessed it."

"I could cross a room in the time it takes you to blink your eyes."

"Well."

"Yes. So it was that I sent him packing that first night, thinking that would be the end of it. But he was relentless, and it seemed that each time I left my home, then Tor would come barreling around a corner and make for me."

"Who in the world could live under such circumstances?" asked Klara.

"Not I."

"No one could." Klara became thoughtful, and again she regarded Lucy from a sidelong angle. "Perhaps it is that this misfortune will lead you to something better," she said.

"Perhaps you're right," said Lucy. "As a matter of fact, I'm sure you are."

This made Klara happy, and she hooked her arm in Lucy's. "But, what shall we name the puppy?" she asked.

"I don't know." Lucy was staring at her snaking hand.

Wistfully, she said, "I like the name, Rose."

"Rose?" said Lucy.

"Rose," she repeated.

Her hand came to rest atop Lucy's, and he said, "We'll call her Rose, then."

And they did do this.

She invited him over for tea, which led to supper, with only the two of them in the shanty, as Memel and Mewe had gone away to Listen to work the crowds at a solstice celebration. The hours drew past, and there was nothing like a slack moment, for no sooner did Klara answer a question of Lucy's than she would ask a question herself, and then back again, until the village had gone quiet, and all were in for the night. At one point Lucy screwed up his courage and said,

"Just who is this Adolphus?"

Klara looked away. "He is a soldier I knew."

"Knew or know?"

"Know. I don't know. I haven't seen him in months. And I don't know where he goes, when he does."

"But you wish you did?"

"Sometimes I do." Klara looked back at Lucy. "Perhaps you might find it flattering, that I have an inclination to lie to you about this."

"Perhaps I might," he said.

Rose lay on the table, dozing in between them; they both stroked her but were careful never to touch each other's hands. Lucy could have stayed up all night, but when Klara stifled a yawn, he stood, and said he would take his leave. Klara nodded; her hair was mussed and she smiled at him as he stood at the door. He walked through the village and up the hill to the castle, crossing the still entryway and pausing at the bottom of the stairwell to fish out a squat candlestick from his trouser pocket. Rose began to squirm, and so he let her down onto the ground. She disappeared around the bend of the stair and Lucy, lighting the candle, followed after. The bulbous flame was jouncing up and down as he took the steps; arriving at the mid-point landing, he paused, thinking of how pleasing Klara's face had appeared in the candlelight, and of the way she'd hid her smile in the shadows. He recalled looking over to find she was drawing her cheek back and forth against the fur collar of her cape; and this was a proud moment for him, one that he knew he would revisit any number of times in the coming days and months.

While cataloging these happenings, he'd been peering absently into the darkened recess of the landing; and to look at him was to see a young man without a care or concern, a person for whom life posed no problems whatsoever, only opportunity, and adventure. But gradually this look left his face, and by degrees was replaced with an ever more severe and serious one. A thought had entered his mind, a terrible suspicion, which was that the darkness into which he had been gazing was not empty at all, but that it held, or hid, something; that it held someone. He stared with an increasing intensity, scarcely drawing a breath. There was no movement in the darkness, but with each passing moment he became surer and surer that there was a body hiding in the recess; and, furthermore, that it was aware of his being there—that it was watching him as well.

Now a sound became audible, but this was so slight at the start that Lucy couldn't be sure he was hearing anything at all. Soon it increased in volume, not so very much, but loud enough that Lucy could not deny its existence. He wasn't certain what the sound was, but thought he could identify it; and he hoped with great fervency that he was mistaken. Alas, as it became louder, his suspicion was confirmed, and he lamented this, because of all the noises to hear, at this late hour and in this lonely location, here was the one he least wished to witness, and it filled him with the direst dread. It was the sound of someone hungrily, gutturally eating.

Lucy raised his candle, and this cast a jewel of milky light in the darkened corner, where he could now make out the proportions of a man, and a wretched man at that, crouched on the floor and outfitted in nothing more than ragged tweed trousers. His bare back was all bones, the flesh coated in grime, and the bottoms of his feet, tucked under his legs, were painted in the blackest filth. Lucy could not see what the man's feast consisted of, his face being hidden behind a curtain of long and grease-matted hair, but he ate with something beyond gusto, groaning slavishly, his body shuddering as the consumption of his meal reached its pleasurable capstone. Lucy's hand was trembling, and so the candlelight also was trembling. *Where is Rose?* he thought.

The man ceased eating and turned toward Lucy. His face was covered in blood, and he held in his hands the remains of a small animal, its middle section eaten away save for a ribbon of black fur connecting its halves. A smile crept across his face as he stood; fur and red-purple flecks of meat and entrails clung to his emaciated body. He was panting, and his eyes were so wild that Lucy could not regard them directly. The man was laughing, but stifling this, as though he didn't want to make any sound, as though he might disturb someone; or, bizarrely, as if fearful of offending Lucy. He stood and moved closer, holding the remnants of his feast up to the candlelight. Lucy found he couldn't not look down, and in doing so he was at once encouraged and discouraged to see not the body of Rose, but that of a very large rat. The man too was watching over the carcass, only with something like adoration, or satisfaction. When he lifted the remains to his mouth and lovingly chewed at the stubborn string of fatty fur to halve the thing, Lucy's revulsion was such that his world became liquid, and he lost consciousness, falling away to the ground.

He awoke the next morning in his own bed, Rose licking his face, his head gauze-wrapped, his skull lumped and tender. There came a knock on his door and Agnes entered carrying a breakfast tray. He sat up and she set the tray upon his lap; pouring him a cup of tea, her face was nearer to his than it had ever been before——he noticed she had a downy cheek, and the balled red ear of a newborn. She placed a spoon in his hand and moved to sit in the rocking chair, patiently and wordlessly observing Lucy while he ate. After he had finished, she removed the tray and set it by the door before returning to the chair. Folding her hands, then, and with what seemed to be repressed irritation, she said, "Now, I'd like to know just what it is you think you're doing here, boy."

Lucy said, "Ma'am?"

"Did you not hear what I said?"

"I heard. I suppose I'm not sure I understand the question. A position was offered to me, and I accepted the position."

"But surely there's some other type of work where you come from?"

"Not so very much. Nothing that suited me, anyway."

"And what is it about this appointment that suits you, can I ask?"

"It's far away," he said. "It's different."

She spoke as though they had hit upon something key: "What if it's too far away, Lucy?" she said. "What if it's too different?" Now she fished a single gold coin from her smock pocket and laid this on the bed. "Here is your return fare. And I would like for you to go home, if you please."

Lucy looked at the coin but didn't pick it up. "You're terminating me?"

"It wouldn't be my place to do that."

"Does Mr. Olderglough want me gone, then?"

"I don't suppose he does. But then, Mr. Olderglough is not currently of a mind to make such judgments."

"How do you mean, ma'am?"

She assumed the demeanor of one wondering how much she might prudently say. "Do you not find him a peculiar man?"

"Frankly, ma'am," said Lucy, "most everyone I've met since I've left home is peculiar to me in one way or another." Agnes was visibly dissatisfied by the response, however, and so Lucy added, "But yes, I suppose I do find him so particularly."

She nodded, and asked, "Now, would you be surprised to know that he is *more* than peculiar?"

"I don't know what you mean by that," said Lucy, which was true—he didn't.

Here Agnes began removing hypothetical bits of grit from her smock. "Far be it from me," she said, "to besmirch the man's good name. God knows I looked to him for support and guidance any number of times over the years. But I can't say, Lucy, that I would look to him for guidance at present." A sadness came over her, and she said, "Listen to me, boy. Can't you see that a mistake has been made in bringing you here?"

"But I don't want to go home, ma'am," said Lucy. "I'm not happy there."

"You're happy here, then?"

Lucy didn't answer for a moment. He was thinking about Klara. "Possibly I am."

"You understand that you're in danger?"

"Yes."

Agnes stood. There was an air of finality or defeat to her carriage, so that Lucy felt he had let her down in some way. She said, "What happened to you last night will happen again if you stay here. The situation will not improve. On the contrary." With this, she turned to go. Lucy asked her,

"But why do you stay on, ma'am?"

She lingered in the doorway, considering her reply. Speaking over her shoulder, she said, "Many years ago, I made an agreement with a friend. So long as he remains, then so will I stay as well." Her eyes were kinder now, smoky, and crowded with emotion. "Hold on to that coin. If the impulse to go seizes you, I want you to heed it. Will you do that for me, boy?"

"All right."

"Don't just say it to say it. That's what Mr. Broom did, and look what it got him."

It sent a shiver through Lucy, to hear Broom's name. "What is the matter with him, exactly?" he asked.

"The matter with whom?" Agnes asked.

"With Mr. Broom."

Agnes shook her head, and she regarded Lucy as though he were a pitiful individual indeed. "You really don't understand at all, do you?"

"Understand what?"

"Mr. Broom is long dead, Lucy. The man you met last night is the Baron."

Lucy sat for a long while after Agnes had left, trying to connect the author of the elegantly lovelorn letters he'd been delivering each day with the feral and cretinous apparition he'd seen on the landing. When he found he couldn't link these two, he elected to let it lie awhile. A restlessness came over him and he dressed, descending the stairs and crossing the entryway for the outdoors. Stepping into the cool morning air, he pulled on his cap, careful not to disturb the officious bandaging. He felt an affinity for his head wound; was there not a certain sweetness in its aching pain? He wondered what Klara's reaction to his injury might be, and he imagined her gentle hands searching his skull to pinpoint the epicenter of tenderness. He would tell of how he came to be hurt, and she would swoon and marvel at his trial of fright, afterward comforting him with a cup of tea, and perhaps a slice of poppy-seed cake. And this moment, would it not make the entire ordeal worthwhile for Lucy? Alas, this was not to be, for when he arrived at Klara's door he discovered she was not there, and neither was Memel, and neither was Mewe, which isn't to say the shanty was empty, for it was not; in fact it was filled to capacity, filled with soldiers, the same group Lucy had met when he'd first arrived at the castle. All were standing save for the exceptionally handsome man, who sat in the center, at the table, and he held Klara's cape in his hands. His face was drawn and grim, and he was not in the least pleased with Lucy.

V

—

ENTER ADOLPHUS

The exceptionally handsome man spoke. "I am Adolphus, Lucy from Bury. I apologize for not introducing myself when last we met. But possibly it is that you've heard my name since then."

"Yes," Lucy said.

Adolphus held up the cape. "It has come to my attention that you've brought my Klara a gift. Is that so?"

"It's so."

"And why, may I ask, have you done this?"

"Because she was cold."

"I see." Adolphus turned to the soldier on his right. "Are you cold?"

"Yes, I'm cold," the soldier answered.

Adolphus turned to the soldier on his left. "And you?"

"It's cold. I'm cold."

"And so am I cold," Adolphus said. He turned to Lucy. "We're all cold. But you'll not furnish us with capes, will you?"

Lucy remained silent. A look of violence came over Adolphus, and he said, "Here's how it's going to go, boy. I'm going to give you back this cape. And you may give it to another village lass, or you may wear it yourself, or you may set it afire. You may do with it what you wish, for it is yours. But there is one thing which, I'm here to tell you, you may not do with it, and that is return it to Klara. As a matter of fact, I should think you and she have no further business together, is that understood?"

Lucy didn't answer. The soldiers were standing unnecessarily close to him, he noticed. "May I ask what you men are fighting about?" he asked.

"We fight so that others need not," Adolphus said.

"And who are you fighting, that I need not?"

"They are bastards and will die bastards." Adolphus gestured at the men standing about him. "Now, we've a significant campaign beginning soon, which will see us through to the spring. I've quite enough to do in preparation for this without having to worry about some non-regional cast-off wagging his tiny pink pecker at my bride-to-be. Will you heed me, yes or no?"

He stood and crossed over to Lucy. *If only he weren't so much larger*, Lucy thought. *If only he weren't so bold.* Lucy couldn't look him in the eye, and when Adolphus thrust the cape into his arms and pushed him out the door, there was no option other than to accept its happening, and so he did.

Walking numbly through the village, he caught sight of Klara in the marketplace, shivering in her old, ragged coat. He approached her, and was aware of an anger gathering within him. Standing before her now, he wondered if he didn't hate her.

"Adolphus says you're to be married," he said.

When she faced him, he could see she had been crying. "Anyway, according to him we are."

"I suppose I should offer you my congratulations, then." He bowed. "A long and happy life to you both."

She was wounded by this, and retreated a pace. Staring at the cape in his hands, she said, "Is that all you have to say to me, Lucy?"

He had hoped to communicate an appearance of cold control and indifference, but in looking at Klara's face, and in knowing he had been bettered in love, then did his heart turn against him, and an expansive sorrow welled up in his chest. "Long life!" he said, and spun around, retreating for the castle, his face gone hot with tears. By the time he'd climbed the stairs to his room he had exhausted himself, and felt as though there were nothing inside him at all. Acting automatically, he pulled his valise from under his bed and packed his belongings, including Klara's cape, and Mr. Broom's telescope. He pocketed Agnes's coin before taking up pen and paper to compose a short farewell letter to her and Mr. Olderglough. Leaving this atop his pillow, he scooped up Rose, gripped his valise, and descended the steps. Crossing the entryway, he saw the Baron had left a letter on the side table. Setting down his valise, he stared at it. He opened it up and read it.

Last night I took up a razor, that I might open my own throat with it. How simple this would be: a flick of the wrist and the life would pour from my body, the room would dim, and I would have my rest. I am not afraid to die, and have not been for some time now. And yet I found I couldn't perform the gesture, knowing you are still drawing breath. If you yourself were passed, it would be nothing, but the knowledge that you remain lulled my hand. I will live until you come back to me, then. If you do not come back, then I will die waiting. This is my pledge to you.

Lucy recognized his taking solace in giving up; he was familiar with the comfort which existed in the acceptance of failure. In turning back from his own pain and fear, he had experienced some stripe of validation; for these feelings were justified, after all, and his leaving was necessary, and wise. Despite this, the Baron's letter conjured in him a shame which eclipsed these other emotions, and so he did not strike out for the station as planned, but removed the cape from his valise and walked back down the hill, and to the village. As he knocked on Klara's door, he could feel his heartbeat in his hands. She answered; she was alone. He passed her the cape and told her, "You can't marry Adolphus."

Her face was so pale, and she looked at the cape with such superlative sadness.

"Why," she asked.

"Because of the fact that I love you."

Lucy said these words and he watched as Klara's sadness drifted away, her eyes brightening in pulses, and now she was beguiling again. Stepping closer, she reached up and kissed Lucy on the mouth, lightly, and again, on the neck. She retreated into the shanty and Lucy followed after. He watched as she shed her coat and put the cape on, standing before the mirror, as before, and admiring herself. "Yes, hello," she said, "and who is this young lady?

She looks so happy, doesn't she? I wonder what's got into her. Perhaps she's heard some good news. Perhaps she's heard just what she wanted to hear." She was swiveling back and forth, smiling at herself. "Oh, but she *does* look happy, doesn't she? Well, let's see how long it lasts, shall we?"

The recent turn of events instilled in Lucy an unheralded emotion which he couldn't at the start identify but which he eventually decided was euphoria. And it was in this state that he begot a plan or a strategy, one which he recognized as inspired but also humanely necessary, so that upon returning to his room the next white-lighted morning he threw himself into the task of realizing it, toiling with pen and paper for long hours until his hand was cramped and stiff, that he might get his words to sit just so.

Lucy wrote a letter to the Baroness Von Aux. He introduced himself, describing his position at the castle, and then imparted his opinion in respects to the mental state of the Baron. For, in spite of the dire and unmistakably darkened tone of the Baron's letters, Lucy thought the Baroness was likely unaware of her husband's true condition, and that, if she became conscious of it, and if she possessed any remnant of affection for the man, then she would surely respond in one manner or the other. Well, Lucy was no scholar, and had never before undertaken such a task as this, attempting to transform the fates of others using naked language alone. It was a tedious business, he decided, and he felt no envy of the learned men and women of the world for whom composition was their stock-in-trade. The following morning, upon rereading his work for the hundredth time, he declared the missive sound, and slipped it into the envelope alongside the Baron's daily offering.

All the time he had been writing this letter, and as he set out to deliver it, Lucy was filled with a righteous feverishness; for he knew the deed was correct, and essential. But then something peculiar occurred, which was that the moment the letter was snatched from his hand, the moment his plan was enacted, and had ceased existing in thought alone, now he was visited by a premonition, presented as divine truth, which was that he had just made a significant and imminently consequential mistake. He stood on the platform awhile, wondering about this, becoming fearful of it. Once the train rolled out of sight, then did he push the feeling away, banishing it, for he had other and more pressing, pleasing considerations. Turning his back on the station, he struck out for the village. Smoke was pouring from Klara's chimney. Lucy began to run.

VI

—

LUCY & KLARA IN LOVE

T he days were growing warmer, and Adolphus was away on his campaign. Lucy and Klara took hours-long afternoon walks through the forest, their fingers twining together. They spoke of small things; or of things which seemed small when spoken but which afterward remained fixed in Lucy's mind. One day Klara commented that when the snow melted away, the exposed grasses looked like the fur of a newborn foal or calf.

"But the earth is not an animal," Lucy said.

"Yes it is," Klara told him, and she gripped his fingers ever tighter.

Now Lucy was spending his nights in Klara's bed. He found it in his ability to make her laugh, and this was so pleasing to him that he sometimes overdid it, and the next day she would complain of a tender stomach. Typically he awoke at dawn, while she and Memel still slept, and repaired to the castle. His suit had arrived from Listen, and his flesh was greatly contented as he eased into this dashing ensemble each morning.

Rose sometimes accompanied him on his rounds, but just as often she would loiter at the door of the shanty as he was leaving, and he knew this meant she wished to stay behind, to play with her brothers and sisters and mother. Whenever this happened, Lucy felt a mild betrayal; but Rose was too large to rest in his pocket any longer, and he knew he had to allot her a life apart from his own.

Upon completing his work, Lucy would change back into his old suit and sheepskin cap and return to the village. Some nights he and Klara would socialize with Memel and Mewe; some nights they were alone. Time passed in this way, and life was but one comfort after another. It was all so natural. Later, and Lucy would wonder how many days this phase had been made of.

A week of ceaseless rain, this followed by baking heat, and all at once it was spring, and the chirping insects trilled in the valley. Lucy and Klara lay in the tall grasses above the village. He was leaning back on his elbows, a sleepy expression on his face. Klara was curled at his side, watching the daffodils bowing to the ground when a bee would light upon them. She put her hand on Lucy's bare stomach and he looked down at her.

"Have you ever done that with anyone else?" he asked.

She nodded. "Have you?"

He nodded. Stroking her hair, he asked her what to do about Adolphus.

"What do you mean?" she asked.

"Do you want me to fight him?"

"No."

"Why not?"

She wasn't certain how to put it. "It would be unwise."

"You think he would win, you mean?"

She touched his face. "Yes."

"I suppose he would, after all."

"You mustn't ever try."

"I don't know that I'll have a choice, when he comes back."

She shook her head. "I'll speak with him. He'll be hurt. But he's not a bad man."

Lucy thought of it. "What does he want, exactly?" he said.

"To be a hero," Klara said. "That's actually all."

"And what are you meant to do?"

"I believe I'm meant to coo."

Lucy laughed. He said, "I feel I *could* fight him, though, do you know? I'd only have to think of you two, together, like this."

Klara sat up, startled. "Adolphus and I . . . It never came to that. And I'm not sorry, either."

Lucy experienced a great relief, this followed by a greater curiosity, which he wished to ignore, but could not, and so did not. "Who was it, then, if not Adolphus?"

"It was only once," said Klara. "And it didn't mean anything." She lay back down. "I'll tell you about it, if you really want to know."

"I really want to know."

"All right, then."

The Inveigling of Klara
by the Strange Eastern Stranger,
Godless Corrupter

I t was the way the stranger had looked at Klara, as though she were something to be consumed—something that would be. No one had ever looked at her like that before, and it was troubling in several ways, the foremost being that she liked it, or some part of her did. He entered the village in his tottering cart in the early afternoon; his arrival represented diversion at a slack hour and the villagers assembled to gawk and wonder, asking every question which came into their minds: Where had he come from? Why had he left? Where was he going? What was awaiting him there? They were after the news of the world, and the road-weary vagabond fielded these and other queries patiently but without enthusiasm. A lull revealed itself and he removed his hat, asking if he might stay overnight in the village, to rest and replenish his supplies; when his wish was granted, he returned his hat to his head, grinning a grin that Klara identified as devoutly impure. As if intuiting her recognition, he jerked his head to locate her in the crowd, staring levelly and with something more than boldness; and as he was handsome in that dark and brooding way which certain impressionable young women find irresistible, she discovered she couldn't look away from him, and she became afraid in a manner she couldn't pinpoint or define.

Climbing down from his cart, the stranger moved through the crowd, and to Klara. He wore a dirty jerkin with nothing underneath; his bare arms were wiry and hairless and deeply tanned. He had a gold tooth and was missing the lower half of his left ear, and when he took up her hand she began shivering, tremors rippling up her back and to the shoulder. He kissed her across her knuckles. She looked down at the cool spot where his lips had met her skin, and this was the end for Klara. It was as good as done.

She spent the rest of the afternoon in perpetual movement, running non-pressing errands and paying visits to people she did not much care to see, just so long as she wasn't alone with her thoughts, or with the stranger himself. Fearful he would come to her in bed, she made Mewe sleep beside her. When the stranger didn't come, she couldn't understand why this bothered her so, as though they'd had a plan to meet and he'd broken it. In the morning she awoke early and made her way to the well to wash her face. In passing the stranger's covered cart, she cleared her throat. Laying out her soap and towel on the well wall, she washed, and waited. After a time she heard a rustle of grass behind her, and she smiled, but didn't turn around; when something bristly pressed against her leg she drew back, gasping—but it was only Memel's dog arching against her, and she laughed at herself. When she was finished rinsing the soap from her face, she reached for the towel but it was no longer there.

"Why do you hide away from me?" asked the stranger. He was standing at her back, and very close to her. She gazed at the marble-black sphere of the water's surface at the bottom of the telescoping well. Her heart was thumping so violently she felt it might unravel. "I don't trust you," she said. "You make me feel strangely."

He put his hands on her hips and turned her around to face him. The towel was resting over his shoulder. "Isn't it somewhat pleasant, though?" he asked.

"I don't know if it is or not," she said. "It's something like a fever, actually."

Water was dripping from her hair and nose and chin, and the stranger took up the towel and began drying her. He did this gently and thoroughly, and when he'd finished he wrapped the towel around her throat and breastbone. She was shivering again, and she asked, in a quavering voice,

"When will you go away from here?"

"Soon. But I'm not ready to go yet."

"When will you be ready to go?"

He laid his hand on her face. "I will be ready to go after."

She nearly gasped when he said it. He turned and walked back through the grass and to the village, the dog following in his wake.

In the afternoon she tried another tack, which was to attempt to make friends with the stranger. He was leaving the marketplace and she fell in step with him; in a convivial voice she pointed to his ear and asked, "How did you come to be wounded, sir?"

He looked at her amusedly, as though he was aware of what she was playing at. Tugging at what remained of the ear, he said, "That is a question I can't answer. One morning I woke awash in blood, and it was away."

"It was severed in your sleep?"

"Yes."

"By whom?"

"Some enemy or another. No one came forth to claim responsibility."

How matter-of-fact he was, she thought, as though the incident hadn't been a bother beyond the mess it had made. "What sort of man would do that to you?" she asked.

"Why do you assume it was a man?"

"Oh, but a woman could never do such a thing."

The stranger became remote, his thoughts gone back in time. Soberly, he said, "I've known them to do worse."

Klara blushed at this. It made her inexplicably but unmistakably jealous, and she was frustrated by the feeling. When she gathered herself, she asked politely, "Do you have many enemies?"

"As a matter of fact I do."

"And why is that?"

"I can't think of why. But, they seem to gather wherever I go."

Now that same impure grin as before grew upon his face. Klara gathered her hands together and rested them atop her hip.

"Why do you smile like that?"

"Like what?"

"That way, there." She pointed. "It's a smile that hides something."

"I have nothing to hide from you."

"Don't you?"

"Well, perhaps I do after all. And good luck finding out what it is!"

The stranger laughed at this, laughed at her, and Klara left him alone once more. She busied herself cleaning the shanty and making dinner preparations, but she couldn't free herself from her thoughts of the man. Mewe came to sleep beside her that night but she sent him away. No matter; the stranger did not appear. In the morning, after breakfast, she sought him out. He was sunning himself in a field of lupine between the village and castle. He smiled at her as she came near. "I don't know how you stand it, living here," he said. "It's so terribly dull."

"It is *not* dull."

"It's consummately dull. It's immaculately dull."

"I love it," she said, and she did.

In a humoring tone, he asked, "Tell me, what do you love about it?"

"My father, and my friends. The animals, the rivers. I love the seasons; I think they're just the right length of time, don't you?"

The stranger didn't answer.

Klara said, "I love the fields, there——" She nodded toward the sloping green expanse beyond the castle. The stranger sat up to look.

"What's over the rise?" he asked.

"More of the same."

"Do you ever go there?"

"Sometimes."

He looked at her directly. "Will you take me there?"

"But why?"

"Don't you think it's about time we were alone?"

"We're alone now."

"Alone, but not alone-alone. I want to be alone-alone."

He stood up and looked over her. He was quite a bit taller than she.

"Will you be alone-alone with me," he said.

He led Klara away, over the crest of the hill. His hand was callused and gripped hers tightly. She could smell his body, and the fluttering in her stomach was violent to the edge of nausea. She wore no shoes, and watched her feet moving up and back through the grass and flowers. She wasn't precisely sure what she was walking toward but she wouldn't have turned around for the world. Once they were over the rise she tucked her hair behind her ears, looking about for a piece of level ground. Finding one, she pointed. "There." They walked toward the place.

Lucy was disturbed by the pride with which Klara told this story; she was pleased with herself for having an adventuresome spirit, and this hurt him. He knew he was being small about it, but there was no other way he could feel. He was putting his clothes back on when he noticed a wasp struggling to free itself from a spiderweb, this attached to the low branch of a nearby tree. The webbing bounced and vibrated and Lucy moved closer to watch, with Klara following after. The wasp's manic buzzing filled her with dread, and she said, "Set it loose, Lucy."

"No," he said. "Look." Over top of the branch came the spider, its legs, its head, its plump, bobbing bottom. It was very large, and its weight stilled the web, and the wasp for a moment ceased struggling. But then, as if knowing what was to come, and with the spider stepping ever closer, it redoubled its efforts to free itself, its buzzing jumping an octave.

The spider circled the wasp, searching out the prime point of attack. It had looped the web two full times before it lunged; as the insects met, then did the wasp plunge its stinger into the spider's face, the reaction to which was instantaneous death: the spider dropped, yet remained attached to the web by a single silver thread strung out from its abdomen. It hung in space, lifeless, rotating in the breeze.

Something about this occurrence displeased, even offended Lucy, and he watched the spider with an angry expression. He held his boots one in each hand. He lifted them to either side of the spider.

"What are you doing?" Klara asked.

Lucy didn't answer, but clapped the soles of his boots together, popping the spider like a grape. Klara was disgusted by this.

"Why would you do such a thing?" she asked.

"I don't know," Lucy admitted. He was surprised at himself.

"Well, I think that was terrible, your doing that."

Lucy didn't know what to say. He turned away from the web and sat to put his boots on. Klara stood by, quietly fuming. She felt she deserved an apology, though she didn't quite know why. She walked away, toward the village, and Lucy watched her go but didn't call after her or to try to win her back. Returning to her shanty, she wept on her bed for near an hour. The next day Lucy apologized, and all was as it had been before. Neither one of them understood this argument, and they agreed not to speak of the spider or the strange Eastern stranger again.

A village woman had taken ill and left her infant child with Klara for some days; she and Lucy set up to play house in a manner which was at first light of spirit, but which took on a certain seriousness, then an absolute seriousness. *This is how it would be* was Lucy's thought, and it worried him because he had never been so satisfied before.

The child's name was Anna, and she had purple eyes and was fat as a piglet. Her mood was typically jolly, her laughter quick to come and difficult to arrest, but on the third night something upset her so that she wouldn't cease crying, and if she was enthusiastic in her laughter, then she was doubly so with her weeping. She sat in a quaking crimson heap in the center of Klara's bed, fists trembling, gulping for air. They thought she was ill, or that a sliver had pierced her flesh, but she had no fever and there was nothing on her person like a blemish, and they were at a loss as to what they should do.

Klara was looking at the baby out of the side of her eye. A thought came to her, and she left the room; thus abandoned, Lucy made a sequence of grotesque faces at Anna. When this summoned no reaction, he made his sounds: the knock-on-wood sound, the horse-trotting sound, and finally, the bullfrog-on-a-lily-pad sound. But Anna only raged on, and Lucy gave it up. "I've made all my sounds," he announced.

"Wait," said Klara. She returned shielding a candle, and lay on her stomach before Anna. As Klara drew the candle laterally back and forth, Anna's eye was drawn to the shivering slip of flame, and she followed Klara's movements, and was distracted or charmed by them so that her upset was halved. Klara held the candle still and expelled a steady stream of air, not enough to extinguish the flame, but merely to bend it; it flickered raggedly, recalling the faraway sound of a canvas sail in the wind. Anna had ceased crying now. Klara blew harder, and the flame struggled to cling to the wick; she exhaled sharply and the flame was rent, which produced a *click*. As though it were the punch line to a famous stunt, Anna laughed wildly, as before, her mysterious misery vanishing with the candlelight. Klara smiled at her success, the smoke whorling upward. Lucy had watched all of it. He was astonished.

It was a feeling which stayed in his blood as he slept that night, and then into the morning, so that when he returned to the castle he knew that he was hopelessly mired in love. He brought Mr. Olderglough his breakfast and they shared their comfortable greetings. Peter was scratching in his cage in the corner; crossing over to him, Lucy was struck by a startling truth. He took up Mr. Olderglough's hand mirror from the vanity and held this before the bird.

"What are you doing, boy?" Mr. Olderglough asked.

"Wait," Lucy told him.

Peter was rapt. He tilted his head to better study the stranger before him, and presently issued a hesitant, hoarse croak in the minor key. There followed a dense silence where neither Lucy nor Mr. Olderglough drew a breath, and then, finally, Peter sang his long-lost tune. It came out in purling currents, as though his keeping it in had been an agony. Peter sang to his reflection, sang a love song to himself, for he was no longer alone, and the world was filled with unmapped possibilities. Mr. Olderglough threw his tray through the air, a great clatter and crash, and he leapt from the bed, running about the room in his nightshirt and cap, howling his pleasures.

Still, there were imperfections. There was a sadness about Klara, and Lucy was more than a little intimidated by it. The sadness was buried but existed in her every movement: the way she folded her hands; the way she pulled a lock of hair away from her face and hooked it over her ear; the way her eyes were drawn to the open spaces, as though in search of something familiar, or possibly something new, unknown. It existed in her silences. Lucy was surprised to discover how badly he wished to combat her sadness, to better it, to eliminate it. And if he accomplished this, what would there be to take its place?

Increasingly Klara withdrew, taking walks in the woods for an hour, two hours. Lucy felt an instinctive mistrust of these solitary outings. He asked her,

"Where do you go, when you go into the forest alone?"

"I go into the forest alone."

"Why do you?"

"To be alone in the forest."

"But why?"

"Because I want to be." She looked at Lucy. "You don't."

"I don't want to be any more alone than I already am," Lucy admitted. He was not proud to say this, and neither was she proud for him.

One day he was buying vegetables at the marketplace when he saw Klara stepping through the crowd and away from the village.

She wore a lonesome look on her face, and Lucy followed her. She moved toward the tree line, walking slowly but unhesitatingly; it seemed she had some destination in mind. Lucy might have called to her, but didn't. When she slipped into the forest, he hurried after.

The sunlight was thinned and the wind dropped away. Klara came in and out of view, disappearing behind trees in the distance, then reappearing. Lucy felt ugly to be spying, and he was made anxious by the fact of it, but he couldn't stop, and vowed to see it through. Klara entered a clearing, in the middle of which stood a lone tree, a squat and knotty oak, dead and leafless, its branches filled with ravens. As Klara came nearer, certain of the birds rustled, shaking their heads, unfolding and refolding their wings. She stood before the tree; Lucy thought she said some words to the ravens, but couldn't be sure. When she continued on her way, Lucy resumed trailing her, giving the tree a wide berth, for there was something fearsome about it to him.

Klara walked on and on, and now she was standing before a river, roiling and risen high from snowmelt. When she took up her skirts to sit on the bank, Lucy crept closer, hiding behind a fallen snag, that he might steal a glance at her face and glean just what she was thinking of. The noise of the river was so expansive that it pushed through Lucy, vibrating in his chest. People think of a river as a body of running water, when in truth its physical properties are secondary to its sound.

Klara was watching the sleekly slipping surface of the river, and her face had gone cloudy. Soon she began to weep; she did this openly, frankly, and without shame. In watching this transpire there appeared in Lucy's mind the knowledge that the life she and he were sharing was finite. Its rareness was its leading attribute, after all, and such a thing as this couldn't be expected to carry on forever. A feeling of gratitude was born in him; and it was so powerful as to produce a sensation of lift. In a little while Klara dried her face and stood, walking back in the direction she'd come. Lucy ducked as she passed, and afterward sat alone for long minutes.

Something went mute in his mind as he walked away from the river.

He was moving into the clearing when he stepped on a branch; it snapped crisply in the air and the ravens, as a body, burst skyward. This produced a noise so unexpectedly large, and so violently whole, that it seized his spirit in terror. It was as though some centered part of him had come loose, and it ached, and made him fretful.

There was a heaviness to Klara's movements that night, and she laid with her back to Lucy. His own slumber was troubled and erratic, so that he overslept, awakening late in the morning. Klara was no longer in bed, but in the front room Lucy found she had laid out a pot of tea, a thick slice of bread, a jar of honey, and an apple, peeled and cored. The apple was crisp and tart; the tea had some trace of pine in it. He thought of Klara preparing his breakfast while he slept. A channel of sunlight entered the window, angling sharply to the floor, like a propped beam of milled timber. Dust floated amiably in this, then drew or was drawn into the surrounding darkness, which brought to mind the image of shifting tides. How quiet Lucy's life was just then. He thought he had never been quite so melancholically happy as at that moment.

Clearing the table, he cleaned, dried, and stacked the dishes. The whistle of the morning train sounded down the valley, which meant he had twenty minutes to fetch the Baron's letter and deliver it to the platform. He sat and pulled on his boots, and was lacing them when Klara burst in, short of breath, a bright look on her face.

"Didn't you hear the train?" she asked.

"I heard it."

"Well, get to work, you lazy man!" She pulled him up by the lapels and kissed him. Her smile was easy, and she gripped Lucy's waist, pressing in close to him. Whatever it was that had been bothering her had been set aside; she had made some decision, and this was in Lucy's favor. Pushing him out the door, she told him to return in time for dinner, and he said that he would. As he walked through the village he was so pleased, so relieved, because there was nothing the matter with his Klara, and all was well between them. This feeling of comfort was short-lived, however: as he passed the marketplace, the wily butcher approached him in the road, and said, "Shame about Adolphus, eh?"

"What about him?"

"You haven't heard? He's been taken prisoner."

"How do you know?"

"I met one of his men on the mountain, and he told me all about it. Said Adolphus was shot in the gut, and so the others caught up to him and pulled him away. He was trailing blood, and never had any hope for escape. If he lives they'll only hang him, I imagine. Now what do you make of that?"

"I don't know what."

"I would think you're happy about it, eh?"

"No. I don't know." Lucy didn't like the wily butcher for saying such a thing, even if it was true; and he felt a creeping brood coming on, for surely the news of Adolphus's capture was the reason Klara had been weeping. And even though she appeared to have reconciled herself to its happening, Lucy knew this was not the last he would hear of it. *What a violent thing love is*, he thought. Violent was the word that had come to him.

L ucy stood on the platform with the Baron's daily missive. He was feeling sad-hearted, and his mind wished to wander to its darker corners. As the train approached, the familiar hand emerged, only there was something quite different about the appendage on this morning, which was that it held a letter of its own. The incongruousness of this was such that Lucy failed to lift his letter, but merely stood by gawking at the flapping pink envelope in the engineer's fist. As the train passed, the engineer dropped the letter, and Lucy watched it twirling through the air. When it came to rest down the platform, he cast the Baron's letter to the ground and hurried to scoop up this other, making for the castle at a dead run. As he wended his way up the hill, the engineer sounded his horn, a half-dozen staccato blasts. Of course he had been reading the letters all along, before Lucy was, even.

Lucy found Agnes cutting Mr. Olderglough's hair in the scullery, the latter sitting sheet-wrapped in a low-backed chair, while Agnes stood at his rear, scissors poised. Here was a scenario smacking of the domestic, so that Lucy felt the intruder; and indeed, his superiors wore the look of the intruded-upon, but he offered not so much as a passing apology, as there was no time to linger over faux pas. He pressed the letter into Mr. Olderglough's hand. "She's written, sir," he said.

Mr. Olderglough studied the envelope: front, back, front; he peered up at Agnes, and nodded. He opened and read the letter, sternly, and with the index finger of his right hand pointed upward. When he finished, he stood away from the chair to pace the room, addressing Lucy and Agnes in an earnest monotone. "The Baroness will arrive here in twenty days' time," he said.

Agnes emitted an actual gasp. "She cannot."

"She is coming, Agnes."

"She must not. You will write her at once and explain the impossibility of it."

"She is traveling, and so unreachable. I'm sorry, but it is down to us." He folded the letter into the envelope. "And I'm afraid that's not the worst of it."

Agnes blanched. "Don't you say it."

Mr. Olderglough nodded. "We will be entertaining."

Here Agnes hung her head.

"The guests will arrive two days after the Baroness," said Mr. Olderglough.

"Who?"

"The Duke and Duchess, Count and Countess."

Mr. Olderglough and Agnes shared a look of dire understanding.

"And for how long?" she asked.

"Until the end of the month."

Agnes was quiet as she took this in. "Well," she said at last, "obviously the Baroness doesn't understand the state of things here, otherwise she wouldn't be returning. Certainly not with thoughts of entertaining she wouldn't."

"I believe she does understand," Mr. Olderglough replied, and he read a line from the letter: " 'I ask that the Baron be made to look presentable, so much as is possible in his current state of mind.' "

"She's after ruin, then," Agnes declared. "Or else she's gone mad as well."

"She appears sanguine." Mr. Olderglough glanced at the letter. "Her penmanship is as elegant as ever." This proved a small comfort, though, and Agnes all but fell into the chair, looking as one succumbing to witless panic.

"It's beyond me," she admitted. "Where might we begin, even?"

"I won't deny it seems a task."

"A *task*?" said Agnes wonderingly.

"Task is the word I used."

She looked to Lucy. "We are living in a graveyard!"

Mr. Olderglough moved to stand before her, resting a hand on her shoulder. He spoke firmly, but not without tenderness. "Take hold of yourself, Agnes," he said. "The castle has been dormant; we must bring it back to life. Why do you act like we haven't been through it before?"

"Never so bad as this, though."

"I shan't disagree with you there. And it may well come to pass that we fail. But we have only two choices: to try, or not to try. And I know that you will try, my dear, just as you know that I will."

Agnes sighed the sigh of the damned, then trudged from the room. She had much planning to do, she said, but wanted to spend some time alone before starting out, that she might wallow stoutly, and without intrusion or distraction. After she'd gone, Mr. Olderglough turned to Lucy; all the kindness had left his face. "Now, boy, let us talk about tomorrow," he said.

"Tomorrow, sir?"

"Tomorrow, yes." Mr. Olderglough cleared his throat. "Tomorrow is not going to be a day where we will be visited with thoughts of praising God on His throne."

"No, sir?"

"Tomorrow will not be a day we'll later cherish or clasp particularly close to our bosom."

"Will it not, sir?"

"Tomorrow will be a not-pleasing day for us."

"But why is it so, sir?"

Mr. Olderglough tucked the letter away in his breast pocket. "Tomorrow we must locate, apprehend, and restore to normality the Baron."

VII

THE LOCATION, APPREHENSION, AND RESTORATION TO NORMALITY OF THE BARON

The process of locating the Baron was an unusual experience for Lucy; for whereas before he had thought of this person as one to avoid no matter the cost, now he was actively seeking the man out, albeit fruitlessly, at least at the start.

It was held that the Baron slept in the daytime, and so during the sunlit hours they were hopeful of catching him dozing in this or that nook. But they found no evidence to support any nocturnal habits, however—indeed, they found no evidence he existed at all, save for the occasional discreet puddle or pile. But his chambers remained untouched, and there was not so much as a pinch of salt unaccounted for in the larder. In the night-time, galvanized by Agnes's bitter coffee and an often not-unpleasant sleepless befuddlement, they roamed the halls by candlelight and in stockinged feet, this last at Mr. Olderglough's insistence, for he believed it stealthy. Lucy was disinclined to praise the tactic, as the stone floor was cold, and so his feet were also cold; when he became sullen, Mr. Olderglough loaned him an extra pair of stockings, which Lucy pulled over his own, and which allayed his discomfort so that peace was restored between them. Mr. Olderglough, it should be said, was enjoying this outing to the utmost, and he wondered at his unrealized potential as an adventurer.

Alas, three full days and nights passed them by, and they were no closer to accomplishing their goal than when they'd begun. With only the minimum of sleep shared between them, then did a weariness set in, followed by the chilling shade of doubt, which soon gave way to a sense of outright futility. At last Mr. Olderglough deemed the Baron unlocatable, and was for abandoning the project altogether. Lucy disliked seeing his superior in this state of dejection; pondering the angles, he suggested they were only going about things incorrectly.

"How do you mean?" said Mr. Olderglough.

"Bumbling about in the darkness, sir. In *his* darkness. Would it not make more sense to lure him into the light?"

Mr. Olderglough squinted. "You're suggesting we entrap him?"

"Why not?" said Lucy.

Mr. Olderglough was intrigued, and retired to his chambers to blueprint the stratagem. Lucy was well pleased to have hit upon a possible solution but soon wished he'd never shared his notion, as it steered Mr. Olderglough toward the thought of using Lucy as bait. It was described thus: "You will take to your bed at your usual hour, and all will be as is normal except that your door will be not just unlocked, but fully open."

"Will it, sir?" Lucy asked.

"Indeed it will."

"And where will you be situated?"

"I shall be standing behind the door," said Mr. Olderglough, rather proudly.

"And what will you be doing there?"

"I will be waiting for the Baron to walk into the room."

"And what will commence when this occurs, sir?"

"I will step away from my hiding place and tap my employer atop the skull with a stubby switch of birch wood."

"Is that so?"

"You may count on it, boy."

"And what next, I wonder?"

"After he's been knocked unconscious, then shall we bring him to his chambers and manacle him to his bed. We will force-feed him, and bathe him, and shave him, and cut his hair and strive to resurrect his interest in sophisticated society." Mr. Olderglough rubbed his hands together. "Now, what do you think of it?"

Lucy said, "I think it is somewhat far-fetched, sir."

"Are you not up for it?"

"I'm not, actually, no. And to be frank, sir, I don't believe you are, either."

"What sort of attitude is that? Let us rally, boy."

"Let us come up with another plan."

"Let us look within ourselves and search out the dormant warrior."

"Mine is dormant to the point of non-existence, sir. There is no part of me that wishes to lie nakedly abed and await that man's arrival."

"I tell you you will not be alone."

"And yet I shall surely feel alone, sir."

Mr. Olderglough looked down the length of his nose. "May I admit to being disappointed in you, boy."

"You may write a lengthy treatise on the subject, sir, and I will read it with interest. But I highly doubt there will be anything written within those pages which will alter my dissatisfaction with the scheme."

"Well I'm sorry to have to tell you this, boy, but it must come to pass, and it will."

"I believe it will not, sir."

"Do you want to maintain your position here?"

"You know full well that I do."

"Then what is there to speak of, after all?" With this, Mr. Olderglough stepped to the window to survey the world. "Now, where has that sly old sun gone to, eh?" In searching it out, he leaned too close to the window, and knocked his forehead lightly upon the pane of glass.

All this to say, Lucy did take to bed that night, and the door was left open, and Mr. Olderglough did hide away with a birch club gripped in his hand and a look of dogged resolve stamped upon his face. He had told Lucy they were not to speak, and so they did not. At one point Rose crept across the room to sniff and nip at Mr. Olderglough's foot; Lucy collected her and fetched her back to his bed, rubbing her bare belly, which made her restful, and soon she slept, ignorant to the woes of her master.

Lucy's dread was consistently urgent. Time and again he thought he heard the shuffling approach of the Baron, and yet the doorway remained vacant, and Lucy could only gaze into the bottomless darkness and wonder at what it held. An agonizing hour crept by, and then a half-hour, and now he became aware of an unfortunate fact, which was that Mr. Olderglough was sleeping standing up, this made apparent by the man's gentle, wheezing snore. Lucy had thrown off his blanket that he might cross the room to awaken him when he saw the Baron hunched at the top of the stairwell, completely naked, bathed in grime, panting, and staring at Lucy with a puzzled derangement.

Lucy said, "Mr. Olderglough, sir."

The Baron stepped sideways into the room.

"Mr. Olderglough."

The Baron moved ever closer to Lucy.

"Mr. Olderglough!"

Mr. Olderglough snuffled, and the Baron, hearing this, peered over his shoulder at the door. Stepping nearer, he drew the door back, and there stood Mr. Olderglough, leaning against the wall, arms slack at his sides, mouth agape, dozing babe-like. The Baron studied him for a time, as though in distant recognition; reaching up, he laid a hand on Mr. Olderglough's cheek. At this, Mr. Olderglough awoke, and upon seeing the Baron before him he let out a brief yet sincere shriek, raised the club high, and brought it down over the Baron's skull. The Baron dropped where he stood and lay motionless on the floor.

Mr. Olderglough was studying the birch wood admiringly. "Do you know, I enjoyed that," he conceded, and his face bespoke an exhilaration, for how curious life was, how unfathomably novel, and occasionally, wonderful. Mr. Olderglough moved to lay the Baron prone on his back. Taking up the man's filthy wrists in his hands, he said to Lucy, "Get his feet, boy, will you?"

Shortly after he was tied to his bed the Baron came to, and upon registering the fact of his apprehension, then did he begin to flail and wail, to curse and spit, to roar from his depths, taken up with such manner of rage that he lost control of his functions; or perhaps it was that he intentionally encouraged this action as a non-verbal means of expressing his ire—either way, Lucy found it a grisly spectacle. Mr. Olderglough, conversely, took it in stride, and with something beyond patience; one would have thought he was looking after a temperamental infant rather than a raving, matter-smeared psychotic. Shy of the dawn, however, his years began to show, and he excused himself to rest and regroup. Lucy was ordered to stay and watch over the Baron, and he did this, sitting at a distance and monitoring the Baron's ongoing tantrum, until such a time as the man exhausted himself, dropping into spent sleep; and so too did Lucy succumb to fatigue, sitting upright in his chair. They were the both of them awakened some hours later by the fact of the too-bright afternoon daylight. When the Baron spied Lucy from the corner of his eye he swiveled his head, and a calm came over his face. Perhaps it was his having rested, or possibly his mania had temporarily receded of its own accord, but he was, all at once, human again.

"Who are you?" he asked.

"I am Lucy, sir. Hello."

"What are you doing here?"

"I live here, sir. I've taken over for Mr. Broom."

"Broom." The Baron said this gloweringly, as if the man were antagonistic to his well-being. Suddenly there was a seriousness about his person, as if some pressing thought had come to him. "You will untie me, now," he said.

"I mustn't do that, sir."

"You will untie me or you will be dismissed."

"I'm very sorry to disagree with you, sir, but I have my orders from Mr. Olderglough, and I shall defer to him."

"Mr. Olderglough," said the Baron; and it was clear by his tone that he felt a fondness for the man. "And where is he now?"

"Here I am, I always am," said Mr. Olderglough, entering the room looking greatly refreshed and carrying a steam-trailing soup bowl. "Wherever I find myself, and there I be." He sat at the Baron's bedside and, recognizing his present-ness, rejoiced. "Oh, welcome back, sir. It does me good to lay eyes upon you, and that's the purest truth."

The Baron smiled. "How have you been, Myron?"

"Up and down, sir."

"More of the same?"

"The trials of a life."

"What of the melancholy, may I ask?"

"Stubbornly persistent, I'm sorry to say."

"If only modest joy were so dogged, eh?"

"You said something there, sir."

The Baron gestured with his chin to the bowl in Mr. Olderglough's hands. "What have you got, there? Agnes hasn't been knocking about in the scullery again, I hope."

"I'm afraid that she has, sir."

"And I suppose you'll want me to partake, is that the idea?"

"It is indeed."

"May I ask what's in it?"

"Better you go in blind, is my thought, sir. Just know that it'll revitalize the spirit." Mr. Olderglough brought a spoonful of broth to the Baron's mouth. The Baron reluctantly received this, his face screwing up to a squint.

"Her admiration for pepper has not waned."

"She is devout, sir."

The Baron was peering into the bowl. "What is that floating, there?"

"One way to find out, sir. Let's get on with it, and see what else the day has in store for us, what do you say to that?"

The Baron acquiesced, and the meal resumed. In watching this pair, Lucy wondered at the years that had passed between them. They were so perfectly comfortable with one another as to appear of a piece; it seemed the most natural thing in the world that one should be spoon-feeding the other. After the bowl had been emptied, Mr. Olderglough asked,

"Now, was that so bad?"

"You know perfectly well that it was," the Baron answered, though he did look ever more hale. "Now," he said, "I believe the time has come to address the fact of my being tied to my own bed, in a state of undress, and in need of several concurrent baths."

"Yes, about that, sir," Mr. Olderglough said. "It goes without saying I'm sorry you find yourself in such a condition as this. But at the same time, I can't claim it wasn't a necessity, because it was."

"I have been—misbehaving again?" said the Baron.

"For some months now, sir, yes. Do you not recall it?"

"Somewhat I do." Here he peered through time, and shuddered at what he found there. "It is unpleasant to consider," he said.

"You'll get no argument from me there, sir. Possibly it's best not to dwell."

"Yes."

"Let us look to the future rather than mull over the past."

"It's a nourishing thought, Myron, and thank you for it." The Baron sniffed. "And will you untie me, now?"

"I will not, sir, no."

"Do you have a time in mind when you might?"

"Quite soon, I hope."

"You were always a fair man."

"I like to believe it, sir."

The Baron grimaced. "Why does my head hurt?"

"Well, sir," said Mr. Olderglough, "you were in such a state that I was forced to club you."

"*Club* me, did you say?"

"Indeed."

"I didn't know you had it in you."

"Nor did I. Actually, and if I may be so bold, it was somewhat thrilling."

"Surely it must have been. You'll have to tell me about it one day."

"Yes, sir."

"Has anyone else been injured?"

"You clipped my wing some time back, but I'm one hundred percent at present. And you gave young Lucy here a fright that resulted in a knock on the skull, isn't that right, boy?"

The Baron looked across at Lucy, and a sorrowful mien came over him, as though contemplating Lucy's porcelain countenance in the honest light of day brought his sins back to him, so that a shame took hold of him, and he turned away to bury his face in his pillows and bedding. He was for a time consumed by his sadness, his tone a high, whining wheeze; and Lucy studied the Baron as a pitiable but highly sympathetic individual. But Lucy's empathy was short-lived, as a brief while later the Baron's voice took on a gruff edge, and now did his rage come creeping back, and he began once more to rant and spit and curse, his alter ego having reclaimed stewardship of his spirit. Lucy found this disheartening, not to say frightening; but Mr. Olderglough was not the least surprised. He led Lucy from the Baron's chambers. In the hall he regarded him kindly. It was to be, he assured his protégé, an undertaking.

Some days and nights passed. Lucy and Mr. Olderglough sat with the Baron, together and separately, feeding him and speaking with him and leading him away from his manias the way a child might be led away from a carnival. One morning Lucy entered the Baron's chambers and found the man was no longer manacled, but sitting upright in his bathtub, and his hair had been cut, his scraggly beard shaven, revealing a handsomely angular face. He was reading the letter the Baroness had written with a look of horror.

"Are you not pleased that she's returning, sir?" Lucy asked.

The Baron folded the letter and set it upon the side table. "All I know, boy, is that life is, on occasion, entirely too vast for my tastes." Here he submerged himself, and afterward did a great many bubbles rise up from the depths of the bathtub, this due to the fact of the Baron screaming underwater.

There was a period of frantic activity at the castle. While Lucy and Mr. Olderglough had been tending to the Baron, Agnes had traveled to Listen and back; and in the coming days there followed in her wake deliveries of grain, flour, spices, candles, fowl, fish, kegs of ale, crates of wine and brandy, and all manner of culinary rarities Lucy had not heard of, much less tasted. The tailor arrived, three assistants in tow, and these four worked in earnest to prepare a new suit of clothes for the Baron, and another for Mr. Olderglough, whose outfit had devolved to something beyond shabby. The offending garment was burned, and now Mr. Olderglough moved sleekly through the halls in an ink-black morning coat, the portrait of surefooted elegance. He went about his work with a surplus of energy Lucy had not witnessed in the man; and Agnes, too, was all the more vital in her exercises. It was as though, with the re-awakening of the Baron's senses, so did the health of his longtime subordinates likewise resume focus. Only now did Lucy understand what fond memories Mr. Olderglough and Agnes had been clinging to; only now did he appreciate the satisfaction they received in doing their work. And it was no small surprise that he found himself feeling similarly, but so it came to pass: the castle was sunlit, and all about there was the sense of hopefulness for the future.

Which is not to say Lucy had an easy time of it. Three days before the Baroness was to arrive, Mr. Olderglough ushered him into the ballroom and said, "I would like you to please tidy up the area, now."

"Which area, sir?"

"The location as a whole."

"Meaning this room, sir?"

"All right, yes."

Lucy considered the size of the space. "When you say 'tidy,' sir."

"Wash the windows. Wash the floors. Wash the walls. Wash the ceilings."

"Wash the ceilings," said Lucy.

"Air the room. Clean out the grates. Uncover the furniture. Polish the trim and accoutrements. Once you're through here, then move on to the next room, and the next, and so on."

Lucy said, "It sounds, sir, that you're asking me to clean the castle from bottom to top before the Baroness returns home. Is that correct?"

"Is there a problem with that, boy?"

"In that it's not possible to achieve I would say that there is, yes."

Mr. Olderglough thought this an unfortunate attitude, and furthermore voiced a concern that Lucy was becoming too familiar for one in his position. But in the end he gave way, and Lucy was allotted a small allowance with which to hire help from the village. He enjoined a half-dozen of the meanest-looking women about, the same group who had teased him in regard to Klara's cape, the idea being that they possessed the necessary fortitude to attack such an outsize endeavor. The scheme bore fruit in that the group cleaned with palpable anger, as though the accrual of dirt were an affront to their honor. This hostility was a boon for the task, but proved less advantageous in other ways. Lucy was afraid of the women, and they knew this, and exploited it by pinching and prodding and harassing him; they made crude jokes at his expense for the pleasure of seeing him blush; the stoutest of the bunch at one point pinned Lucy's head to the wall with her behemoth breast, so that he flailed his arms and was panicked to catch a breath.

Indignities aside, Lucy's plan was a success: the work was completed without flaw, and the castle was returned to a state befitting a Baroness. The feeling among the staff was an invigorating concoction of jubilation and acute agitation, both of these held in check, at least so much as was possible.

In the center of this bustle was the Baron, and it was days before Lucy could take his eyes off the man, this due not only to the fact of his remarkable return to civility, but because the person who had emerged from those ghastly shadows was the most alluring sort of gentleman imaginable. To watch him simply enter a room was in itself an entertainment; he was a *danseur noble* crossing a stage, his every movement so unhesitatingly graceful as he reached in one fluid motion for a book, an ashtray, a pitcher of water— effortless performances which led Lucy to wonder at the standards or qualities of noble blood, and whether or not one in his own modest position might will his blood to clarify, to improve itself. He thought not, ruefully.

Beyond the physical, there was ever more to admire in terms of the Baron's temperament and personality. In the days preceding the Baroness's arrival, he oversaw each aspect of the castle's rehabilitation with a firm hand and meticulous eye; and yet he was never anything other than gracious to his underlings, instilling in the same sequence both sympathy and command—here were the attributes, Lucy realized, of the true leader. He was particularly admiring of how the Baron addressed Agnes's scullery shortcomings. Sampling her stew, for example, he might act as though he were partaking of a delicacy, his abhorrence completely hidden away, afterward lavishing her in praise, which she drank up greedily. Agnes thus mollified, the Baron would then say something like, "I do wonder if the pepper isn't dominating the dish, my dear, when your beautiful roux is clearly the leading light of the show?"

Here Agnes's mind would set to turning, and she would ask, "Do you think we might do with less pepper, sir?"

"Excellent idea, Agnes—and just as you say, why not try it?"

So, Agnes would re-create the stew, halve the pepper, the dish would become suddenly edible, the Baron would proclaim her a genius, and she would float about in a cloud of pride and adoration all the rest of the day.

The man was charm personified, in other words, and Lucy was unabashedly in awe of him.

On the evening prior to the Baroness's arrival, Lucy watched from his window as the Baron roamed about in the field separating the castle and village. He walked for long moments with a still face, his hands behind his back, but then began murmuring to himself, then speaking, and with increased animation, gesturing this way and that, a sly smile on his face. Lucy recognized that the Baron was imagining he was with the Baroness, and practicing the things he would say to her. At one point he drew his hand to his mouth, searching for some suitably clever phrase, perhaps; upon locating it, then giving voice to it, his eyes grew bright with pleasure. Lucy found a commiserative affinity for the man growing in his heart, and was made apprehensive by this fact. For if love had so degraded a personage of the Baron's powers, what might it do to him? Folding up his telescope, he pushed the thought from his mind. It was too unsettling to regard directly.

VIII

—

THE BARONESS VON AUX

On the appointed day and at the appointed hour, the Baron stood on the platform awaiting the return of the Baroness Von Aux. His hair was combed severely and his expression was severe, and the flowers he held in his hand were gripped with severity, fixed as he was in fevered expectation. Mr. Olderglough was somber; he stood beside the Baron, and Lucy beside Mr. Olderglough. They were each of them looking straight ahead, beyond the tracks and into the unpeopled, forested lands. It felt as though the train were late, this because it was.

"She herself has held it up," muttered the Baron.

"Oh, sir, come now," said Mr. Olderglough. "Why would she do that? And how would she, even."

"She has found a way—just to niggle the wound. And I'll wager that when she does arrive, she'll have some handsome young valet at her side."

"She would never, sir."

"Wouldn't she? You forget the fiasco with Broom."

"I have forgotten nothing. But I don't see the purpose in making such assumptions before we've set eyes on her. It is a new day, sir."

"It is a day like any other."

"It is a fine and clean and just-born day. There has never been a day quite like today."

"Bah," said the Baron, and he stepped away to privately putter.

Lucy asked Mr. Olderglough, "What were the circumstances of Mr. Broom's departure, did you say, sir?"

"I didn't say."

"Would you say now?"

Mr. Olderglough made a pained face. "A wickedness took hold of him, so that his position became untenable. He tried to shed the wickedness, and I also tried to help him in this. Alas, at day's end there was nothing to be done about it."

"But how did he die, sir?"

"He fell down the Very Large Hole," said Mr. Olderglough, this stated as though it were elementary.

"A very large hole," Lucy said.

"*The* Very Large Hole, yes." Mr. Olderglough turned and pointed to the loping hills beyond the castle. "There's only the one. Though one is enough, I should think. Just ask Mr. Broom, eh?" He shook his head. "It was a poor ending for the boy. I was sorry about it. I had hopes for him. Ah, but his greeds and desires got away from him, as greeds and desires are wont to do." Mr. Olderglough chuckled. "I've just had a recollection, boy. Would you like me to share it?"

"All right."

"I don't want to force it on you."

"No, I'd like to hear, sir."

"Very well. I was but a lad, sitting at the breakfast table with my father. Unbeknownst to him, I'd taken and eaten the last sausage, knowing it was his by rights, for I'd already had my fill. When he saw the empty plate, he looked at me and said, 'Some wear greed as a fine suit of clothes. But you, my son, bear its stamp ever more poorly.' Now, what do you think about that?"

"I don't know what to think, sir."

"Do the words not resonate with you?"

"Not so very much, I don't think."

"They did with me. And after he said it, I remember, he stuck me with a fork."

"With a fork, sir?"

"Jabbed me, really. I don't mean to imply the fork was horizontal to my flesh. It was more a punctuation of the thought than actual physical torture. Father was a performer in that way."

At the far end of the platform, the Baron was speaking plaintively into the air. Lucy watched him awhile, then turned back to Mr. Olderglough. "I can't imagine your having a mother or father either, actually, sir."

"No? Perhaps you think I was hatched from an egg, eh? And perhaps I was—I'll never tell, boy." He bent his ear. "Did you hear a choot?"

"A what, sir?"

"A choot."

"Is that a type of bird?"

"It is the sound the train makes. *Choot, choot.*"

The train was indeed approaching, and the Baron returned to stand beside Lucy and Mr. Olderglough. The flowers were trembling in his hand and he said, "I've gone all shivery, Myron."

"Think of the glad times you've passed with her, sir. She is still that same fresh young woman you courted those many years ago."

"If only that were so, I shouldn't have a care in the world."

As the train pulled into the station, the Baron cast the flowers into its wheels and screeching machinery; the three men watched as the petals were consumed. When the train came to rest, they were drowned in surging clouds of steam, and they each of them closed their eyes.

The Baroness's disembodied voice was deeper and richer than Lucy would have thought it might be. There was nothing masculine about it, but it possessed a weight at its center—it cut the air and carried itself.

"Will no one help me down, I wonder?"

A smart wind reared and drew past, yanking the steam clouds away, and there she was, in the crisp blue air at the top of the stair, in black and shining fur, her hand outstretched, gloved and likewise black. Her face was sublimely beautiful, and yet there was a darkness residing in her eyes, a cold remove, and Lucy knew that the woman in the painting was not she who stood before them. Whereas the woman in the painting was filled with a humble grace, this person had been corrupted clean through. Lucy was afraid of her, and made no move in her direction; and so was the Baron stuck fast. Finally Mr. Olderglough stepped across to receive her, leading her down the steps to stand before the Baron on the platform.

At the start these two stared at each other, saying nothing, and without so much as shaking hands. The Baroness was a portrait of restraint: her thoughts and feelings were mysterious, and she watched her mate with her chin held at a tilt. The Baron managed to mimic her composure for a brief time, but soon his facade began to twitch, and at last he came apart, consumed by naked emotion. Weeping grotesquely, he dropped to his knees, gripping the Baroness about her legs, heaving and sobbing and acting as one oblivious to opinion and utterly without shame. The Baroness did not have an immediate reaction; she merely observed, and with a half-interest. As the scene played out, however, then did her features take on a softer light, and now she removed a glove to stroke the Baron's head. Bending down, she whispered some encouragement into his ear, and he nodded, standing stiffly and re-establishing or attempting to re-establish his dignity.

They stood face-to-face. Returning her glove to her hand, the Baroness drew her thumb across his cheek to dry it. She kissed him. It was a kiss both lengthy and delicate, and at its halfway point, Lucy felt a hand clamp his arm. Mr. Olderglough's eyes were damp; he was transported by this performance. The Baron and Baroness walked side-by-each toward the castle, speaking softly to one another, and behaving as lovers reunited.

Behind them, an overworked porter was stacking the Baroness's numerous steamer trunks on the platform. He was peripherally aware of the spectacle taking place nearby, but he paid the Baron and Baroness no mind, as he had quite enough to worry about without concerning himself with the dramatic affairs of others, thank you very much.

Memel's Lesson to the Children

The Baron and Baroness were hidden away in their quarters for the evening, and so Mr. Olderglough gave Lucy the night off, his first in many days. He made haste for the village, entering Klara's shanty without knocking, anticipating a glad reception, but the fire was dim in the stove, and no one was about that he could see. He heard low voices in the rear of the shanty and followed these to find Memel bed-bound and wrapped in quilts, though it was not at all cold. His flesh was gray and he was obviously very ill. Klara and Mewe stood at the foot of the bed; sitting on the floor beside them were seven or eight village children, all staring up at Memel as if to receive his instruction. There was a goblet of wine in Memel's hand. He spoke evenly, placidly.

"One winter," he said, "when I was a young child like you all, my father and I went to Listen together, to sell our cow. None of you ever laid eyes on my father, but I can tell you he was a man of honor. He had his religion, and he was well liked by all, though he did suffer from one peculiarity: it was said that he had never, in his life, laughed aloud. It was not that he was an unhappy man, but his existence was such that there was not any time left over for idle celebration.

"We couldn't afford the train, and so we walked to Listen, which took three days, through deep snow. We camped beside the tracks each night, throwing a blanket over the cow and sleeping underneath her to keep warm. When the trains passed, the wind whipped up in a great, frigid current that would rustle the blanket and stoke our fire, with sparks and embers tumbling after the caboose. I still don't know why Father asked me along on this trip. I was just another thing to worry about, after all, and my mother could have used my help at home. Well, I like to think he wanted me there for my company. But who can say what goes on in a man's head, eh, children?

"It was dusk when we arrived in Listen, and Father was leading the cow by a rope, while I held on to its tail. Father was anxious about getting his price, because whatever money we made on the sale was meant to see us through the winter. I waited outside the auction hall for him. By the time he emerged night had fallen and I couldn't make out his expression, and so couldn't tell how he'd fared. But then he said to me, 'We'll stay in town tonight, what do you think of that?' And I knew he'd done even better than he'd hoped, for he meant that we would rent a room, at an inn, which was unheard of for us. I told him that I liked the idea very much, and we headed off together, through the crowded square, and we were happy together, my father and I.

"At this point in my life I had never ventured outside the village, and so I was amazed by what I saw in Listen. The street lamps, the shop displays, the bustle of men and women—all perfectly unknown to me. I gripped my father's hand from fear of this strange world, but as the crowd pressed in on us we were separated. I looked all around me but couldn't place him anywhere. I saw only the bodies of strangers, and none of them had any time or concern for me. They knocked me about, pushed me out of the way, and I was so frightened, then, and had begun to cry when I felt a pair of hands heft me up from behind. It was Father, of course. He put me on his shoulders, patting my knee and saying, 'You mustn't cry, my Memel. Don't you know I would never leave you on your own? You're safe with your papa, do you understand?' I said that I did, and my heart swelled up with love for this man, because I knew what he said was the truth.

"We came to the inn, and after stowing our baggage in our room, repaired to the tavern downstairs. Much like the town square, this was full up, so that we had to eat our supper at the bar. Father pulled up a chair for me to sit on, while he stood at my side, and after we ordered our supper we took in the spectacle all about us. Father was as pleased as I had ever seen him. He had had the price of our supper folded into the bill for the room, and so was feeling very worldly and shrewd. He was drinking a beer, and he looked over the patrons as though he found them a satisfactory group. I thought I saw the trace of a smile on his face, but this may have been a trick of the candlelight. Certainly he didn't laugh, though this was the closest I had seen him to laughter.

"We'd just had our suppers placed before us when a man in a ratty coat happened by. As soon as he saw Father he doubled back, pointing his finger, and with a perplexed look on his face. 'Yes?' my father said. 'What is it, sir?' The man slapped his forehead. 'You're going to pretend you don't know me, eh? Come here, you scoundrel!' The man took up my father in the warmest embrace, lifting him clear off the ground and shaking him about. Father naturally was baffled by this, and he broke away from the stranger, who appeared hurt, or insulted. 'But why do you push me away, my brother? Has it really been so many years you don't remember your own flesh and blood?' My father explained he had no brother, that it was a misunderstanding. And at first the man could not believe it, but then Father spoke further, assuring the man he had no family other than his wife and myself, his only son. A moment went by, and the man shook his head. He was terribly embarrassed all at once, and he said, 'Of course, now I can see that you aren't my brother at all. Please will you forgive me, sir? What a fool I am! And here your supper is growing cool.' He was very put out by his mistake, but Father said there was nothing to be ashamed of, it was only a simple misunderstanding, and he wished the man luck in finding his actual brother, and bid him a happy evening. The man bowed to my father, and turned to take his leave of us. But before he departed, he looked at me, and in such a way that Father could not see, he winked.

"My father had begun eating his supper, but for my part I couldn't take my eyes off this man, and I watched him go. It seemed to me that, for one who had only seconds earlier been begging forgiveness, there was a curious lightness to his step. He actually leapt over the threshold at the entrance before vanishing into the crowd outside. 'And what do you make of that?' my father asked me, slurping up his stew. I said that I didn't know what, but that the man had been a strange one. Father agreed, and now we ate our supper, before returning to our room, where we eased into the soft feather bed. The sound of celebration coming up from the streets carried on into the night, and as I drifted off I felt closer to my father than ever before. We were, the pair of us, a portrait of pride and contentment.

"All this went awry in the morning, however. For when it came time to settle our bill, we were greeted with a cruel fact, which was that my father's purse was missing. We searched our room, and retraced our steps from the day before, but this came to nothing, and finally we had to admit the money was gone. It dawned on my father that the man in the tavern who had embraced him had been a charlatan—a pickpocket. When he explained this to me, I recalled the carefree manner in which the man had skipped over the threshold. Likely he knew by the weight of my father's purse that he had happened upon a significant payday, and was eager to begin his spending. And while I was on the one hand sorry for my father, and fearful for us as a family, so too did I feel a curious sympathy or kinship with the thief.

"Now, the question has come up in my mind oftentimes over the years: just where did this sympathy come from? My mother and father never so much as told a lie, and I had been raised to believe that the more you toiled, then the purer you became, and so were well poised to receive God's favor when you passed into His kingdom. I had no reason to doubt my parents, both of them being good, kind people. Be that as it may, from the moment I saw that scallywag making away with Father's money, I was transformed."

Memel took a sip of wine from his goblet, seemingly chewing it before welcoming it into his stomach. He took a second sip, and made a sound like "Ah" or "Hah."

He said, "It was not just the fact of the man's thieving which was attractive to me, it was also the way thieving apparently made him feel. How I longed to cross a threshold in just the same manner as he! I couldn't get him out of my mind, and began to live my life in such a way that my following after him became an inevitability. And so it went, children. I devoted my every energy to play, to shirking, to laughing, to non-working. I ran from every type of responsibility presented to me, be it chores or schoolwork or what have you. My mother and father battled valiantly against my rebellion, but I would not be discouraged, and soon embarked on my own career as a pickpocket—and a deservedly storied career it has been, if you don't mind my saying.

"All through my apprenticeship and my eventual mastery of the art of thieving, you may be interested to learn I never for a moment misplaced my religion. In actuality, I became more devout all the while, though my God was not the God of my elders. For it had always been unattractive to me that He should reward His servants for drudge work—indeed, that He should desire servants in the first place. Being dissatisfied with their God, then, I created a God of my own, and mine was not one to honor labor, but one who repaid the bold.

"The farmer, upon seeing a healthy crop in his fields, kneels and gives his thanks. A shopkeeper will gaze with gratitude at the profits recorded in his ledger. For my part, whenever I came upon a wealthy merchant passed out in his first-class compartment, this was the instant I would pause to reflect, to praise my Savior. It was He who had guided me to these fruitful pastures, to these half-men crying out to be robbed. God wished them taught a lesson, and I, brave Memel, was His instrument."

He looked away from the children, and to a spot high on the wall. "Even now, when I dream, I dream of a compartment filled with the slumbering bodies of wealthy men. I am a younger version of myself, and my energy knows no limits, and I am afraid of nothing in the world. I strip them of their possessions, and their red faces are so peaceful and glad as they sleep, for they themselves are dreaming, of a full table, let's say, a banquet held in their honor, and their hands grasping at this, at that.

"My Klara has spoken over the years of a time of reckoning for me. A day when I would feel my feet in the flames, at which point I would repent, and beg forgiveness. But it would seem that time is approaching, now, and I can say it truthfully: I was right, and my mother and father were wrong. I loved them both, but they were fools. There is nothing noble in suffering, nothing worthwhile in mindless labors. And if you see something you want, children, you should take it. Because the fact of your wanting it renders it yours."

Memel closed his eyes. "That's all I wanted to say to you," he said. "Thank you for listening to me."

The children left the room in a peaceable and orderly fashion.

Memel soon was sleeping, and so Klara and Mewe left him alone, with Lucy following after. Lucy asked what was the matter with Memel; neither Klara nor Mewe answered for a time. Finally Mewe stirred, and said, "We don't know what."

"How long has he been ill?"

"It's been coming and going for months. But not so bad as this."

A pause, and Mewe said he was tired; now Klara led him to the front door, whispering in his ear as he left. Mewe nodded, and they shared a sad look. After Mewe had gone, Klara began chopping an onion for a stew. Lucy approached but didn't touch her, sensing something was wrong beyond the fact of Memel being unwell. He said her name, but she only continued chopping, as though he weren't there at all.

He asked, "Are you angry with me about something?"

"No," she said.

"Will you tell me what's the matter?"

"Nothing is."

Lucy was watching the side of her face. "Has there been some news of Adolphus?"

Klara ceased chopping. She was shocked he had simply asked it. It took a moment for her to answer: she shook her head, no.

"Is it very hard for you, Klara?" said Lucy.

Another pause, when she set her knife aside and turned to Lucy, clutching him, pressing herself against his chest. She was trembling; he thought she was crying, though she made no sound. He asked her again what was the matter but she only said that she was sorry. She wouldn't say why she was sorry.

Later that night they drank some of Memel's wine, after which she became friendly and loving once again. She was simply tired, she explained, and she had missed Lucy, and was worried for her father. They retired to her room, and all was as it had been before. In the morning Lucy fed Memel some broth, along with the castle gossip; the old man was pleased for both, and did seem heartier when Lucy bid him good morning.

Klara kissed him at the door, helping him into his shirt. She framed his face with her hands, peering into his eyes with a determined adoration before saying her fond goodbyes. Lucy's heart was full as he crossed the village, and he told himself he mustn't let so many days pass without visiting, as the time apart was not healthy for his and Klara's courtship. That was surely what the problem had been, he decided; and yet, some small voice doubted his reasoning. And then, too, why did the wily butcher leer at him so knowingly as he passed the stall?

The Baroness sat upright in her bed, reading a book. Lucy entered with her breakfast tray and stood at a distance. She knew he was there but didn't raise her eyes right away; exhaling sharply, she clapped the book shut and said, "I for one find it an annoyance when a story doesn't do what it's meant to do. Don't you, boy?"

"I'm not sure I understand what you mean, ma'am."

"Do you not appreciate an entertainment?"

"I do."

"And would you not find yourself resentful at the promise of entertainment unfulfilled?"

"I believe I would, ma'am."

"There we are, then."

"We are here," Lucy agreed.

The Baroness set the book on her bedside table and looked at Lucy. "So, this is the infamous letter writer."

"Am I infamous, ma'am?"

"In that you've been on my mind, yes. May I ask what prompted you to write it?"

"I felt it justified. Are you displeased with me?"

"Shouldn't I be?"

"I suppose you must."

"It upset me greatly, your letter."

"I'm sorry, ma'am."

"I dislike urgency of any kind."

"Neither am I fond of it. But all was not well here, and as your absence seemed the source of the problem, then I took my small liberty."

"You call it a small liberty."

"I do, ma'am."

"I spilled tea over my dress reading it."

"He was eating rats, ma'am."

"What?"

"The Baron was eating rats. All was not well here."

She gave him a queer look. "Is that meant to be funny, boy?"

"It's not meant to be, no."

"You're a strange one."

"Possibly I am, ma'am, yes. Probably I am." He considered it. "I am," he said.

She drew back her blanket and sat on the edge of the bed, her bare feet hovering above the floor. A shiver ran up her spine, and she yawned, and asked, "What is your aim, here, exactly?"

"I have no one aim, ma'am, other than to perform my duties agreeably. In regard to the present moment, my hope is that you'll forgive me my imposition."

"It seems likely that I will."

"That's my hope." He held up the tray. "Where would you like me to put this?"

The Baroness didn't answer, having drifted into some private mood, gazing dreamily at the wall, or through it. Lucy set the tray on a side table and said, "If you don't mind my saying, ma'am, it's good that you've come."

"Good for whom?" said the Baroness absently.

"For everyone."

"I don't know about that." She came away from her reverie and turned to Lucy with an expression of amusement, as though he had said something humorous.

"What is it, ma'am?"

"I don't know what," she said. "I just felt so happy all at once. Strange." She touched the pads of her fingers to her fine, pale forehead. There was something in this small gesture which startled Lucy; and he suddenly understood how this person could drive a man like the Baron to the depths to which he had recently sunk.

Lucy wished to mark this understanding of her powers, to comment upon it. He said, "You're just as Mr. Olderglough claimed, ma'am."

She slid off the tall bed and moved to sit on the bench before her vanity mirror. "Is that so," she said, her ribboned hair halfway down her back. "And just how did he describe me, I wonder."

"He said that you were a light in a dark place."

She was stealing glances at herself, from this side and that; and now she studied her face directly. What entered into a beautiful woman's mind when she considered her reflection? Judging by her expression, she was not thinking in admiring terms. "Anyway, it *is* dark here," she told him. Taking up her tresses in both hands, and in an uninterrupted corkscrewing motion, she coiled and stacked her hair into a tidy pile atop her head; and pressing the bun down with her left hand, she pinned it in place with her right. Lucy had never before seen such effortless feminine pruning, and was impressed by the seamless brutality of it. The Baroness was watching him in the mirror. "So we're to be friends, you and I, is that right?" she asked.

"Yes, ma'am."

"All right, then, friend. Bring that tray over here and feed me while I get ready."

Lucy thought she had merely been acting playful in saying this; but as she sat by expectantly, now he saw that she was serious, and so he did as she asked, taking a seat beside her and feeding her fruit and porridge and sips of tea while she appraised her face, altering it here and there with creams and powders and coloring, these set out neatly before her in jars and canisters and spray-bulb bottles. Lucy enjoyed his feeding her to the utmost; there was in her eyes a sorrow so profound that it invoked a drop in his stomach. He had no wish to protect her from it, or alleviate it, as he did with Klara; he merely wanted to witness it, and to recall it later when he was alone. He admired her in the way one might admire an avalanche, and his mind meandered, for he was intoxicated by his nearness to so rare a person as she. At a certain point he realized the Baroness was pinching the top of his hand.

"Did you hear what I asked you, Lucy?"

"I didn't, no."

"I asked if you might accompany me on a walk later."

"Yes, ma'am. And where shall we walk to?"

Her eyes became distant. "I will lead the way," she told him, then asked him to leave, that she might dress for the occasion. Afterward Lucy stood in the hall outside her door, staring in wonderment at the smarting red smudge on his hand.

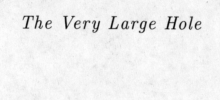

The Very Large Hole

The Very Large Hole was very, very large. From the moment Lucy saw it he was made apprehensive by its existence, for all about them was solid earth, and then this gaping and godless emptiness, and he felt he couldn't credit it. It shouldn't be called a hole at all, he decided, but a chasm, a canyon. He and the Baroness circumnavigated the expanse, walking together but saying nothing, the both of them eyeing the void as if something were meant to occur there. This created a tension of expectation in Lucy, so that when a bird shot free of the hole and into the sky, he flinched. The Baroness gripped his arm to hearten him, but Lucy couldn't rid himself of the thought of Mr. Broom's demise, so that he mistrusted the ground to hold them. "Perhaps we shouldn't walk so near the edge, ma'am," he said.

"And why not?"

"I'm thinking of Mr. Broom's accident."

She looked at him pityingly. "But there was nothing accidental about that."

Lucy felt sickened at the thought of it. "How can you be sure?"

"I knew him well enough," said the Baroness. Cheerily, then, as one making teatime conversation, she asked, "Do you yourself ever think of suicide?"

Lucy pondered this. "No more than what is customary, ma'am."

The Baroness looked on approvingly. "That is a stylish reply."

"Thank you."

They stepped into a bank of sunlight, and she ceased walking to bask in this. She shut her eyes and Lucy could see the miniature cluster of pale blue veins branching across her eyelids.

"And do you ever think of it?" he asked.

"Mmm" was her answer. She opened her eyes. "It's such an odd sensation, being back among you. I was so certain I'd never return."

"But why did you leave here at all, ma'am?"

"Oh," she said, "they were becoming impossible."

"Who was?"

"The Baron. And Mr. Broom."

She pointed at a patch of lush grass some distance back from the hole. "This is where Mr. Broom and I would come," she said, and she sat, pulling Lucy down with her. Looking about, she seemed to be recalling the time she had passed there, and fondly.

"May I ask what the nature of yours and Mr. Broom's relationship was, ma'am?" said Lucy.

"He was my young man, of course," she answered.

"And what was it that drove him to such despair?"

Here she grinned impishly, but said nothing. Reaching down, she plucked a dandelion and blew away its seeds. These traveled on the air and over the Very Large Hole, where they were caught in its drafts. They drew up in staggered ascension, then hurried down, nearly out of sight, before climbing up, up again. This cycle went on for some time, and was a hypnotic thing to witness. When a downdraft yanked the seeds out of sight, the Baroness gasped. She asked, "How long has it been since I've been surprised by anything?"

"I don't know, ma'am."

"Far too long." Pulling up a shock of grass, she said, "The guests will be here soon, Lucy."

"Are you not happy about it, ma'am?" For when she'd spoken, there was in her voice some element of unease.

"I don't know what I am," she told him. The green blades of grass were slipping from her hand, and she and Lucy watched this.

"Why have you returned, ma'am?"

The Baroness shook her head. Leaning in, she kissed Lucy's cheek, then stood and resumed walking, alone now, adrift in her strange and terrible beauty.

IX

—

THE COUNT & COUNTESS, DUKE & DUCHESS

On the morning of the guests' arrival, Mr. Olderglough had taken Lucy aside and told him, "I will look after the Duke and Duchess, and you will mind the Count and Countess. Is that quite all right with you, boy?"

Lucy answered that it was, but it struck him as curious, for Mr. Olderglough had never positioned an instruction in so accommodating a manner before. "May I ask why you prefer the Duke and Duchess to the Count and Countess?" he said.

Here Mr. Olderglough nodded, as if he had been found out. "We have been through a good deal together, you and I, and so I feel I can speak to you in confidence, and as a peer. Are you comfortable with that?"

"Of course, sir."

"Very good. Well, boy, if I'm to address the truth of the matter, none of the coming guests is what might be called desirable company. Actually, I have in the past found them to be distinctly undesirable."

"In what way, sir?"

"In many ways which you will, I fear, discover for yourself. But your question, if I understand correctly, is to wonder which of the two parties is the worse, isn't that right?"

"I suppose so, sir."

"Then I must tell you that the Count and Countess merit that prize, handily. And while I feel on the one hand duty-bound to take the heavier burden unto myself, I must also recognize that I simply haven't the capacities I once did. To look after people such as those who are coming to stay with us is a young man's game, and I am not young any longer, and so I take the simpler path, though you may rest assured that when I say simpler, I do not mean simple. The Duke and Duchess are no stroll in the park, and I can attest to that personally, and at length." Mr. Olderglough stepped closer, his eyes filled with ugly memories. "Be on your guard with these people, boy. They answer to no one. They never have, and they never will."

These words played in Lucy's head as he stood on the platform awaiting the Count and Countess's arrival. As the train came into the station, he could hear a man's wild cackling; when the Count emerged from his compartment he was quite obviously drunken, swaying in place, a cigar planted in the fold of his slick, blubbery mouth. His skull was a softly pink egg, his eyes blood-daubed yolks—he drew back from the sunlight as one scalded. Once recovered, he focused on Lucy, gripping him by the lapel. "Ah, Broom, happy to see you again, boy."

"Yes, sir, nice to see you, as well. Only I'm not Mr. Broom; my name is Lucy."

"What?"

"My name is Lucy, sir."

The Count stared. "You're Broom."

"I'm not he, sir."

"Well, where has Broom run off to?"

"He has died, sir."

The Count leaned back on his heels. Speaking over his shoulder and into the blackened compartment, he said, "Did you know about this?"

"About what?" said the Countess.

"Broom is dead."

"Who?"

"The servant lad? Broom? You were so fond of him last time we visited."

"Oh, yes, him. Nice boy—nice coloring. He's dead, you say?"

"Dead as dinner, apparently."

"How did he die?"

"I don't know how." The Count looked at Lucy. "How?"

Lucy said, "He was possessed by a wickedness and so cast himself into the Very Large Hole, sir."

The Count made an irritable face.

"Did he say a very large *hole*?" the Countess asked.

"Yes," said the Count.

"Large *hole*?"

"Yes."

The Countess paused. "Well, I don't want to hear another word about it." And with this, she emerged: a corpulent, panting woman with frizzed black hair, a crimson neck, and a fierce displeasure in her eye which Lucy took to be travel fatigue but which he would soon discover was simply her root mood. When he held out his hand to help her from the train, she cracked him across his knuckles with her folding fan, a stinging blow that took his breath away. Pushing past him, she stepped up the path and toward the castle, murmuring vague threats or regrets to herself. Once she was clear of earshot, the Count addressed Lucy breathily, and through a shroud of bluish smoke.

"When is the dinner service?" he asked.

"Six-thirty, sir."

"Unacceptable." The Count pressed a coin into Lucy's palm. "If you could scare me up some type of holdover, that would suit me."

Lucy studied the coin. It was a foreign currency, and quite useless to him. "Holdover, sir?" he said.

"Something to chew on."

"Something to eat."

"I like salt. A meat. Don't let the Countess see."

"No, sir."

"You're on your own if she does."

"Yes."

"And I suppose a bath is in order. Can you see to it?"

"Surely, sir."

"Fine. Now you fetch us our baggage and then get started on the rest. You seem a good lad, but how many have let me down in the past? Indeed: too many to name." He trundled up the hill on stumpy legs, and Lucy turned to watch the porter off-load the trunks and cases. It was the same porter Lucy had seen before, when the Baroness arrived. They were much the same age, and Lucy approached to assist him.

"What did he give you?" the porter asked, and Lucy showed him the coin. The porter smiled, and produced an identical valueless coin from his own pocket. They each cast their coin to the ground, and as the train pulled away from the station the porter swung onto the caboose. He bowed at Lucy, and Lucy bowed at him, and the both of them returned to their work.

The Count was listlessly fingering the contents of his steamer trunk. He was naked as the day he was born, and other than his height, looked much as he had at that initial emergence. The Countess, on the opposite side of the room, sat at the vanity, admiring her toiletries, laid out in some obscure codification of her own hostile design. In the corner, unseen behind a folding screen, Lucy was pouring out the final cauldron of water for the Count's bath. He had a sizable salami up his sleeve and was waiting for the moment when the Countess was not about, that he might unsheathe and present it to the Count. He was hopeful this would happen sooner rather than later, as the salami was cold and oily and felt repugnant against his bare flesh.

The Count held a white silken shirt up before himself. He turned to face the Countess, who told him, "You'll want to go darker. You're so ruddy these days."

The Count sighed.

"You take too much tobacco," she said.

"It's more the drink, I fear."

"Well, whatever the culprit, you mustn't wear white if you can avoid it."

He stood before the tilted looking glass, dolefully assessing his countenance. "So many pitfalls in a life," he said.

"Yes."

"The consequences of our appetites confound me. But, you

know what my father said: 'A modesty of appetite represents a paucity of heart.'" He swapped the white for a blue shirt, and appeared pleased, for it truly did mask his hue. "I find myself wondering what's for dinner," he said, to no one.

Lucy stepped out from behind the screen. "Cold dill and yogurt soup, sliced calf tongue in butter, pork knuckle in nettle sauce, and for dessert, a fruit tart."

The Count and Countess stared at Lucy.

"Did you know he was in the room?" the Count asked.

"I did not," said the Countess.

"Nor I."

"I wish I had known."

"As do I."

"I knocked before entering," said Lucy.

The Count said, "I heard nothing like a knock."

"Neither did I," said the Countess.

"You should knock harder," said the Count.

"I'm sorry, sir," Lucy said.

"Or offer a verbal greeting."

"I didn't want to disturb you."

"But you've done just that, haven't you?" said the Countess. She turned to the vanity, and in a spasm of pique began passionately combing her hair. The Count set his blue shirt to the side, for he had located something of consequence in his navel, and now worked fingers like pincers to remove it.

"Is my bath ready?" he asked Lucy.

"It is, sir."

The Count padded around the screen and submerged a thumb in the water. Finding the temperature to his liking, he daintily drew a leg over the lip of the tub and eased into the bath, emitting a puff of air as he did so. "Tell me more about this tart, boy," he said.

"It's a peach tart, sir, soaked in brandy."

The Count raised his eyebrows. "Brandy?"

"Yes, sir."

"Have you yourself ever tried it?"

"Yes, sir."

"And what is your opinion of it?"

"I have a high opinion of Agnes's tart, sir." And this was true—Agnes's tart was her lone certainty. The Count seemed pleased to hear as much; he drew up his lips like a purse's drawstring. In a whisper, he asked,

"Did you bring the meat?"

Lucy nodded, and patted his sleeve. "It's here, sir." Now the Count made a beckoning gesture, that Lucy should come nearer and produce the salami, but before this could be accomplished the Countess, whom neither Lucy nor the Count had heard approaching, was standing beside the screen, watching them with a sour expression.

"He was going to scrub my feet," the Count explained.

"Scrub your own feet. Boy, come with me."

Lucy followed her across the room and soon found himself regarding the clammy folds of the Countess's naked flesh as he untied her corset. Once freed from the garment she sat awhile, expanding. Sniffing at the air, she said, "You smell like a salami, boy."

"Yes, and I'm sorry about that, ma'am."

"It's something you're aware of, then?" she asked.

"Yes."

"Oughtn't you do something about it?"

"I surely will, ma'am."

"It is not insurmountable. One doesn't have to smell like a salami if one doesn't wish it."

"No, you're absolutely right, ma'am."

"Fine," she said. "And now, away with you. I should like a rest before the evening's festivities. Wake me up one hour before dinner service." Bowing, he turned and crossed the room, stalling as he passed the screen, behind which the Count waved frantically from the bath. Lucy moved closer, rotating his wrist to and fro that the salami might come loose; but the cuff was snug, so that the tubular meat became lodged in his sleeve. He was fumbling with his cufflink when the Countess, who had been watching his progress, thwarted his delivery: "I said away, boy—away!" He made a helpless face at the Count and exited the room, very nearly colliding with Mr. Olderglough, who was happening past. They walked together, toward the scullery.

H ow does it go, boy?"

"They are as you said, sir."

"Are they not, though?"

"Indeed, and they are."

"Tell me."

Lucy regaled his superior with details of his experience up to that moment, leaving out his having a salami in his sleeve, for it was an unfortunate, even shameful fact; and beyond that, he had taken it from the larder without asking permission. Mr. Olderglough listened to the rest, his head down as he took it in. At tale's end, he said, "Gluttons of the basest category."

"Yes, sir," said Lucy. "And what of the Duke and Duchess?" He had seen them only in passing, when they entered the castle some hours earlier. They appeared to be of a piece with the Count and Countess in terms of temperament, though were ever more stylish and healthful; the Duchess in particular was something of a pouty beauty, horse-limbed and taller than the Duke by a head.

Mr. Olderglough said, "My experience has been much like yours. I find it something like corralling children, wouldn't you say?"

"It is."

"But you are holding up, my boy?"

"Oh, I'm fine, sir." Actually, Lucy found the task of tending to such people amusing; and this was reflected in his bearing. Now Mr. Olderglough had ceased speaking but was only watching Lucy, and with fondness.

"What is it, sir?"

Mr. Olderglough considered his answer. "Just to say that I'm glad you're here with us, boy. Your very mettle has been tested within these walls, and for what it's worth, you've impressed me, and you have my thanks."

How curious for him to have spoken these heartfelt words, and seemingly out of the blue; and curiouser still, that Lucy should have found himself so touched by the sentiment. But there he was, swallowing a lump in his throat, and when he replied, it was with sincerity. "Thank you very much, sir. And I hope you know that I'm glad to be here with you all, also."

"Good, then." Mr. Olderglough patted Lucy's back. They approached the scullery, and a mischievousness came into the older man's voice: "Now, boy, I hope this doesn't offend, but we've taken a liberty tonight."

"Oh?" said Lucy. "And what do you mean, sir?"

"A liberty has been taken, is all. Blame Agnes. We needed the extra hand, and she believed it would please you." Mr. Olderglough opened the door and bade Lucy enter first. Stepping into the scullery, he found Klara standing in the center of the room, wearing a maid's uniform and a timorous look on her face. Her hair had been cleaned and combed and was pulled away and back; her forearms were bare; her white filigreed smock tied tight about her tiny waist. Here was Klara, only a wholly separate version of her, all the more elegant and feminine, and as Lucy absorbed this unpredicted dream of beauty, then did he feel himself falling in plummeting love a second time.

Agnes, from the larder, called for Mr. Olderglough, and so Lucy was left alone with Klara. He moved to stand before her.

"Who did this?" he asked.

"Don't you like it?"

"I like it."

"Agnes helped me with my hair."

"I like it."

"She has rougher hands than my father."

"I think you look very nice and I like it very, very much."

She was smiling, staring at the floor. "But do you *really* like it?" she said.

"I like it. I love it. I love you."

She looked up now, pleased and relieved by his reaction; for life in the village had never afforded her such finery as this, and she could see how impressed Lucy truly was. Stepping in closer, she reached out for him. Gripping his arm, she paused, and drew her hand away. "What is that?"

"A salami."

"Why do you have a salami in your sleeve?"

"It's not my salami."

"Why—do you have a salami in your sleeve?"

Mr. Olderglough returned from the larder and, upon seeing Lucy and Klara so closely paired, began to loudly clap his hands;

over the sound of this, he called to them: "No time for the cooing of doves! Klara, you will go with Agnes in the larder! Lucy, you will assist me in preparing the dining room! We shall cease living for ourselves but only for the others! Servitude is an art! Now and now!" He continued his clapping and encouragements as he walked from the scullery and into the hallway. "Search within yourselves! Excellence! Magnificence!"

Lucy and Klara were smiling. He kissed her forehead and followed Mr. Olderglough but cast a final look over his shoulder before exiting the room: Klara straightening her dress; the loveliness of her profile as she spun about, girlishly, and stepping to the larder. Lucy hurried after the sound of the clapping, which was ongoing.

The banquet table was buffed and gleaming, the cutlery polished, napkins pressed, the grand room bathed in the golden coloring of the numberless white candles. The three couples were likewise gleaming and pristinely groomed; they sat upright, nodding politely to one another but speaking little, their conversation stilted and faceless, dealing mostly in governmental gossip. The Baron and Baroness chatted lightly to their guests, but the others wouldn't be drawn out, and Lucy, in delivering the soup, could read a justifiable concern on the faces of the hosts, for the mood was restrained to the point of creating unease, and the evening was in danger of foundering. But, as the second course was served, and the wine began to pour, the group relaxed, and the banter became freer. By the conclusion of the third course the party was gay verging on raucous, heads tilted back in mad laughter, the Count's complexion red-going-purple as he spat up some partially chewed morsel of food. The more they drank, then did the traits of the individuals become ever more vague, and now the party took on a single presence, and there was at the edges of this small society an accrual of unkindness, even menace.

Lucy thought he noticed, then was sure he did, that the Count was watching Klara each time she entered the room. At the start he did this only in stolen snatches, but as the evening progressed his attentions became more overt, so that whenever she came near he made it a point to initiate some slight contact—to touch her wrist when she took up his empty plate, or to stroke her back as she passed by. When he touched her, she froze, and her face was empty, plain; but Lucy knew she was oppressed by the Count's attentions, and each time it occurred, his stomach pitched. At one point, when Klara had left for the scullery, the Count asked the Baron, "Where did you find that one?"

"Oh, she's just a village girl."

The Count found this fascinating. "So she's not in your employ?"

"Not typically, no. But we hadn't the time to hire full staff, and so we're just getting by in the meantime. Why do you ask? Are you unhappy with her?"

"Quite the opposite!"

"My husband is smitten, I think," the Countess explained.

"Ah," said the Baron, nodding. "Well, one could hardly blame you. Though I think you may have some competition in young Lucy, here."

The group turned to stare at Lucy, who had been standing at the rear of the room, mutely seething.

"Is that a fact?" said the Count.

"See how he draws up when she comes near," said the Baron, smiling fondly at Lucy. "Take note of the forlorn look in his eye when she departs. Obviously he has given himself over to her, heart and soul." He laid his hand on the Baroness's. "It is something which only one in love could identify."

The Count was watching Lucy. "Well, lad, how about it? Sabers at dawn?"

He was merely making sport, and yet there was an undercurrent of true violence at play as well. You had but to look at the man to see he'd never in his life asked twice for anything he desired. What would it feel like, Lucy wondered, to push a blade into a person? Would it be quick, as when you sliced your hand through a ray of light, or slow, and heavy, like an oar through water? Either way, at that moment he really did want to run this Count through, and so in reply to the query he said, "At dawn, by the light of the moon—just as you wish, sir."

The celebrants thought this very fine, and they laughed a long while about it. The Baron himself stood and saluted Lucy, and the Baroness clapped her white gloves in his direction. Lucy bowed to the group and left the dining room to find Klara standing on the other side of the door, flushed and beaming, for she had been eavesdropping, and had heard Lucy's response to the Count's challenge. Lucy was taken up by an uncommon boldness, and he kissed her there, listening to the swish of her uniform against her skin. A moment of this, and she stepped back, watching him with a look of wonderment. A nameless resolution formed in her eyes, then she led him by the hand, away from the dining room and into the cavernous space of the ballroom, closing the door behind them.

She was not shy, which made him feel shy. She had pressed him against the far wall of the ballroom, and as she undid his trousers Lucy studied her with an idolization so vast it took on physical properties in his heart; the size and weight of it was frightening for him in that he felt he could not contain it. At certain moments in their coupling she became feverish, and it seemed to Lucy she was not herself at all, but possessed by some spirit he hadn't yet known. He gripped her skull and marveled at its diminutive delicacy, puzzling over how it could be that so frail a vessel might possess such a force as Klara possessed. At the apex of his passion his body was flooded in light. Lucy had never been so moved.

Klara stood and corrected herself, straightening the hem of her dress with a sensible tug of the wrists. She was smiling with sly pride, and she told him, "I'll go first." Lucy nodded but didn't answer. After she had gone he remained leaning against the wall, legs atremble, trousers still bunched at his ankles. *What an eventful day I'm having*, he thought.

This sentiment was compounded when the doors swung open and the partygoers entered in a hysterical troupe. Lucy slipped crabwise to stand behind the curtain at his right; he could think of no way to pull up his trousers without bringing attention to himself, and so was forced to leave them be. He stood for a time in the darkness behind the heavy fabric but soon folded back the edge of the curtain, that he might catch a glimpse of the group; and it was from this vantage point that Lucy could and did witness and catalog the strange and terrible ballroom goings-on. All were present save for the Count, who some moments later scampered into the room, the tart wrapped up in his arms like a swaddled infant, his face descriptive of a perceived immortality.

"Look at how merry he is," said the Countess.

"Remarkably so," the Duchess commented.

"Can one be too merry, I wonder?" asked the Baroness.

"One can not," the Count announced, resting the tart atop the table. "For joy carries no consequence, and is desirous of nothing save for more joy." As the group digested the statement, the Count stood by, admiring the dessert, smiling sleepily, the picture of satisfied docility. But then some black violence or another occurred in his mind, and a look of cruelty came over him. He punched his fist dead into the center of the virgin tart.

The Strange and Terrible
Ballroom Goings-On

The Count, in his negligence, as if to intentionally cul-
tivate his negligence, was eating the tart from the cup
of his palm, with all the aplomb of a hog lapping slop.
Clenching his hand to a fist, he watched the remainder push between his fingers, watched the drabs fall to the floor; he wiped his
palm on his trouser leg and regarded the assembled group with
glazed eyes. Said the Baron to the Baroness, "Our guest is happy
with the tart, my love."

"It would seem so," said the Baroness.

"And if he is happy, then we are happy also, isn't that right?"

"We most certainly are."

"For what is the function of the host, after all?"

She spoke as one performing elocution: "The function of the
host is to ensure the comfort and amusement of his guests."

He patted her hand, and they shared a look of wholesome admiration. Now the Baron addressed the others. "I wonder if the rest of
our friends are as well pleased as the Count?"

The Duke said, "I'm feeling very well, myself." He turned to
his wife. "Is there anything you're in need of, dear?"

The Duchess shook her head emphatically.

"Nothing at all?"

She continued shaking her head, and smiling—it seemed she
was too intoxicated to speak. In fact, all in the group were by this
point thoroughly drunken, their cheeks aglow with wine and good

cheer; it was only natural that they should, in spite of their societal positions, abandon formalities. Still, it was troubling to Lucy that the Count, presently grinding the tart droppings into the carpet with his spat-covered boot, should behave in such a way and receive nothing like a reprimand; for surely he had crossed the line which separates the ready celebrant from the boor. And so Lucy was pleased when the Countess spoke up from her perch on the settee, saying, "Oh, but you're making a mess of it. Don't you see that you'll spoil it for the others?"

The Count ceased grinding the tart. He was staring at the Countess. She ran her finger along the lip of her glass, regretful of having spoken up, apparently. "Well, I'm sorry," she said, "but it did seem to me you were ruining the dessert for the rest of us, after all."

His gaze drifted away, and across the room, as though he were taking in the furnishings. An awed expression appeared on his face; one would have thought some profound knowledge had arrived at the forefront of his mind. Regarding the tart, then, he took up yet another handful and crossed over to the Countess, walking with the deliberate steps of a man who was compromised by drink but focusing with all his might on purposeful movement. Standing before his wife, he held his tart-dripping fist out between them. His breathing was erratic.

"And just what do you intend to do with that?" she asked.

The Count reared his hand and slapped her viciously in the face. She reeled backward on the settee and lay still awhile, silent but in a fair amount of pain, it would seem. The Count was pleased with the blow, and returned to his post beside the tart, exhibiting the pride of one having done his duty. The Countess sat up. Though she was bleeding freely from her nose, no one rose to assist her; actually, no one seemed to feel anything at all like concern for her, and it struck Lucy that they were each of them watching the scenario unfold as though it were some type of entertainment or diversion; and indeed, judging by their rapt faces, their reverent silence, that is precisely what it was for them. Lucy had the impression that this spectacle of violence was something which had happened before, and perhaps many times before.

The Countess stood and stepped away from the settee, the smear of tart over her face soaking up the blood, the crumbs crimson and plumped. She did not appear displeased, or in any way offended; quite the contrary, she wore a look of regal defiance, as though she thought herself the most bewitching woman in the room. She began to undress, and the moment she did this, the Duchess and Baroness came to her side to assist her, wordlessly helping her from her gown and untying her corset. Soon she was naked before the assembled ladies and gentlemen, blood dripping from her chin and decorating her bare bosom, pooling in the slit and snaking down her rounded belly. She moved to the tart and took up the entire tray, delivering this to the Duke with a bow of her head. He accepted the tray automatically but his face expressed dubiety. He turned to the Count.

"And what shall I do now, old friend?" he asked.

"A gentleman must do as a lady wishes," said the Count.

"You're certain of it?"

"I've never been more certain in my life."

And so the Duke, too, grabbed a handful of tart and, just as the Count had, jammed it over the Countess's face.

"Harder," she told him.

Yet another handful, and this applied with increased forcefulness, which sent her toppling, her feet in the air like a tumbler. As before, she lay still awhile, translating her pain, during which time the Duchess began undressing, as did the Count, and Duke. Lucy noticed that when the Duchess stepped from her gown it stood independently, stiff, truncated, to ghostly effect.

And what of the Baron and Baroness? Lucy had been so transfixed by the others he hadn't thought to check their reaction; when it occurred to him to look he was surprised to find the pair, whom he had come to regard with something like veneration, were also disrobing, pawing at each other and staring into each other's eyes with an animal craving. The group as a whole were evolving or devolving, becoming increasingly alert and agitated, and there was in the room the most terrible sense of expectation which drew Lucy's stomach taut, a crab-apple knot of abhorrence. He wished to quit the room, but there was no way to achieve this. He wanted to look away but he could not. He watched the proceedings with a dumbstruck sense of horror. A numbness spread in his mind and body as he waited for the filthy pageant to pass.

At a certain point the salami, which had been gradually pushing proud of his cuff, dropped away, hitting the ground with a slap and thud; and while no one noticed this happening, Lucy felt that if an errant salami were spied on the floor, and so nearby his person, it would surely invite investigation. He dared not bend down to retrieve it, but decided to kick it away; alas, he did this over-enthusiastically, and the salami rolled halfway across the room, coming to rest mere inches from the Count's naked foot. The Count caught sight of the salami and stared at it; its appearance was disturbing to him in some way. He looked up and around the room, as if for any further clue. Finding none, he nudged the salami with his toe, then stepped uneasily away to rejoin the others.

The Duke was leading the Countess by the hair to kneel before the Baron.

"Why not have a go yourself, Baron?" he asked, and he handed over a plateful of the tart.

The Baron smiled good-naturedly at the Countess; to the Baroness, he said, "What shall I do, my love?"

She scooped up a piece of tart and deposited it in his palm.

"You're certain?" he asked.

She nodded, and the Baron lightly slapped the Countess's cheek. The Countess wore a deflated expression; she looked to the others, as if for intervention.

"No, no," said the Count.

"We're doing it harder than that, Baron," said the Duke.

"Much harder," said the Count.

"Try it again, but with more force," said the Duke.

"Just as hard as you please," said the Count.

But the Baron hesitated. "You're certain you want me to?" he asked the Countess.

"Hard," came her breathless reply.

Now the prevailing abandon took hold of the Baron, and eschewing the tart, he offered up a grand wallop which found the Countess sprawled on the floor yet again. This was roundly applauded; you would have thought by the group's reaction that the Baron had shared some great witticism or insight. The Countess clambered back upright to kneel once more before the Baron, who instructed her to open her mouth, and when she did this he began pushing in handfuls of tart, one after the other, until she gagged and retched, involuntarily spitting the tart out and onto the ground. She was told to eat this up and she acquiesced with great eagerness, as though there was nothing she had ever wanted to do quite so badly. By this time the group were all completely naked, their circle shrinking to a cluster.

There came a phase of general copulation among the partygoers. Lucy did not know and could not deduce what format or protocol they were guided by, but it did seem there were invisible cues of etiquette being adhered to: the manner in which they came together, the labor itself, the business-like briskness with which they parted. Perhaps the most shocking aspect of all this was the absolute lack of humanity in the room, for there was never so much as a kiss shared, never a caress. At a certain point the Count momentarily broke away from the Duchess to fetch the salami. He returned, re-entering her, this time from behind; wielding the salami like a truncheon, he fell to flogging her all about the back and buttocks and head. The others had completed their transaction and now were gathered around to watch this final spectacle. As the Count's thrusting became more frenzied, so too did the whipping, and when he was through, the salami was mutilated, a mere stub in his greasy grip. He stood away from the Duchess, his body blotchy, clammy, his chest and stomach rising and falling in countertime. The Duchess was perfectly spent; she lay groaning on her stomach, her back coated in welts and bits of meat. The Count threw the stub of salami at her head; it ricocheted off her skull and bounced away, under the settee. In this way the matter was settled.

"Now," said the Baron, "who is ready for a cigar?"

At the mention of this, the Duke and Count expressed enthusiasm which struck Lucy as outsize to the proposition, clapping their hands and hurrahing. The Baroness, too, was acting strangely, her cheek and neck gone red, her face drawn to a tight smile, as one withholding a private pleasure; she approached the table in the center of the room and climbed atop it. The Baron distributed cigars from a cedar box and the men drew closer to her, stepping luxuriously, as if strolling the promenade of a fine spring morning. The Baroness was in position, her face pressed to the table-top, arms splayed out before her, backside pushed high into the air; the Duke and Count appraised her naked behind while the Baron clambered onto the table, reaching up to the chandelier and removing a lit candle, careful as he descended to preserve the flame.

The moment he had put his hand to the candle, then Lucy had an inkling of what was to come, and he hoped with great sincerity that he was incorrect, but he was not, and when the unlit half of the candle disappeared up the Baroness's rear passage, he found himself wondering at the dark state of man, pondering the notions of freedom, and battling with a distant nausea. One by one the men leaned in and lit their cigars, then stood back to smoke and stare reverently at the woozy candleflame. Perhaps a minute passed. The Baron asked the Duke,

"Whatever became of the shipping situation in your township?"

The Duke stuck out his lower lip and shook his head. "Tempest in a teapot."

"You seemed concerned when I saw you last."

"All for nothing. The union organizers were run out of town, and peace has been restored."

"I'm happy to hear it. And how have your profits been this year?"

"Better all the while."

"And the weather?"

"We've had a mild winter, thanks to God. And you, what of your interests?"

"As before."

"Money always came to you."

"It always has, actually."

"Money comes to money, they say," the Count offered.

"They say it and it's true," the Baron said appreciatively.

The Duchess and Countess, meanwhile, were warming themselves by the fireplace. There was a copious bouquet of yellow roses on the mantel; they began to take up the flowers, one by one, and toss them into the flames. The Baroness had lain still for some minutes but now removed the candle and walked to stand beside her friends. Reaching for a rose, she likewise cast this over the flames, and then again. And so: three naked and unspeaking women threw roses into a fireplace, one after the other, until the bouquet was gone. The men had returned to the settee; they watched their wives perform this mystifying endeavor with somber expressions on their faces. When the roses had gone to ash, and the cigars were snuffed out, the group dressed, bade one another goodnight, and retired in twos, first the Duke and Duchess, then the Count and Countess, and finally the Baron and Baroness.

Once alone, Lucy pulled up his trousers and stepped from behind the curtain. Agnes entered as he approached the door.

"Where in the world have you been?" she asked.

"Here, ma'am. The others have gone to bed."

"Yes, that Count mentioned they were done. Did it seem that they enjoyed themselves?"

"Yes."

"And did they enjoy their dinner?"

"Yes."

"Did they enjoy the tart?"

"Yes."

"They found it tasty?"

"Yes."

"Did they actually say as much?"

"No."

"But you got the impression they liked it, is that it?"

"Yes," said Lucy. An unpleasant thought came to him. "When did you speak with the Count, ma'am?"

"He came into the scullery just now. Looking for a nibble, he said."

"Where is Klara?"

"She's also in the scullery, washing up."

"Who else was with them?"

"No one."

Lucy quit the room. Clear of the doorway, he started running. Agnes stayed behind, pouring herself a brandy, and sitting with a sigh on the settee. She sipped her drink, looking about with a wary expression. There was something about the ballroom that had always bothered her.

When Lucy entered the scullery the Count had Klara pinned in the corner. He was pulling up her dress, rubbing her underside, and licking her face; when she struggled to free herself he began to thrash her, shaking her about, that her head might roll from her shoulders. Lucy crossed the room in broad strides, as though he were floating, almost, or sliding across ice; snatching up Agnes's marble pestle from the butcher's block, he swung this at the back of the Count's head, thinking to knock the man out, but at the last moment the Count turned, and so caught the pestle in the mouth. His skull was ricocheted off the stone wall and he dropped to his knees in a halted stupor. His top row of teeth was gone and rich, red-black blood drew down his face and into his shirtfront. It was moving faster than Lucy thought blood could move. He gestured to Klara, and she came and stood behind him. He was holding the pestle so tightly that his finger-nails were sinking into the meat of his palm; when the resulting pain of this occurred to him he loosened his grip, and the pestle fell to the ground, breaking in two. He hadn't struck anyone in his life before this.

The Count stood, leaning against the wall and watching Lucy and Klara with a divine confusion, as though he'd never seen them before—as though he'd never seen anyone before. He drew a finger across his chin and looked at it. Staggering to the basin, he inhaled, then spit out the shards. Straightening his lapels, he spun on his heels and addressed Lucy, his words made spheroid by the thick blood and dearth of teeth.

"How do I look, boy?"

"You have blood all down your face, sir."

The Count pulled his kerchief from his breast pocket and dabbed at his cheek. "And now?"

"There is still a good deal of blood."

He wiped the kerchief all around his face, smearing the blood and disimproving his state considerably. He offered Lucy a questioning glance.

"Much better, sir."

The Count bowed to Lucy, and then to Klara. "Well," he said, "the Sandman is calling me, and so I shall retire. Thank you both for a pleasant evening."

"You're welcome, sir," said Lucy.

"You're welcome," said Klara.

The Count left the scullery, and Lucy and Klara watched the empty doorway. The Count reappeared, and Klara gripped Lucy's hand.

"Which is my room? I can't recall."

Lucy pointed. "Up the stairs, sir, and second on your right."

The Count left again. Lucy felt faint; he found himself blushing, and so was shy to face Klara. He closed his eyes as she wrapped her arms about his waist and pulled him closer. They held each other, and kissed, and were so very much in love.

In the morning, the Countess opened her eyes to find her husband's face a butcher's display of dried blood and flesh so raw and swollen as to produce a shine. She began to scream, and she continued screaming for a good long while.

The Count had no recollection of the incident with the pestle. Lucy had cleaned away the blood and tooth fragments in the scullery, as well as the button-like droplets which ran down the hallway and to the base of the stair. When this was deduced to be the blood's point of origin, it was assumed the Count had tripped. The guests and their hosts re-enacted this happening the next morning, and they were very excited to be doing so, all except the Count, who stood back from the others, purple and ghastly. The Baron knelt to touch the blunt edge of a stone step, perhaps the very same one the Count had collided with, and a collective shiver ran through the assembled. The Count attempted to speak but his words were unintelligible. He repeated them, but only the Countess could understand, and she translated:

"He wonders where his teeth went."

The Duke leaned forward. "Likely you ate them, my good man!"

The Count winced at the thought, then winced from the wincing.

"I suppose you'll find out soon enough!" said the Duke.

The Duchess, who was suffering from a headache, said, "He's not gone deaf, dear. Please keep your voice down."

They moved to the breakfast table, where it was decided a medical presence was necessary. The Count agreed but would not consider seeing any doctor other than his court physician. The Baron said he would have a letter sent at once to fetch the man;

but no, the Count preferred to recuperate in the comfort of his own estate. This point was argued but the Count was immovable, and now a pall settled over the table, for the premature departure of he and the Countess signaled the collapse of the group. And what of the Duke and Duchess? Yes, it would seem that they, too, were formulating plans to leave; already they were speaking of future meetings, and the unfortunateness of the Count's taking a fall— the pity of it all. The Baron looked on, aggrieved, and a glint of desperation flashed in his eye. He pleaded with the others to stay, speaking of grand dinners and as yet untapped kegs of the finest wines; but none could be persuaded, and now all was silent save for the clattering of cutlery.

Something had gone wrong the night before, something which wouldn't be mended. Who could say whether this was a shared sense of loathsome shame stemming from the ballroom happenings, or some lingering hostility which had taken hold of the group permanently—Lucy wasn't sure the performance of the evening prior was not ongoing. But whatever the reason, the joy vanished from the guests, and also the Baron, and most acutely, the Baroness, who, upon recognizing that the happy times had once more ended, left the table without saying goodbye to her old friends, disappearing into her private chambers and locking herself in.

Lucy and Mr. Olderglough were kept busy all that day and into the late afternoon, assisting the guests with their packing, and transporting their baggage to the station. The Count was acting the infant, but was clearly relishing being the center of sympathetic attentions. Lucy was made uncomfortable by the man, fearful he would suddenly recall how he had come to be injured; but he only looked to Lucy as another body to lean upon and moan at. Lucy and Mr. Olderglough escorted the Count onto his train; when this pulled away, Mr. Olderglough said, "It looks like we'll have a quieter time, boy, and I daresay we've earned it." Lucy noticed he was smiling but trying to hide it.

"What is it, sir?"

Mr. Olderglough cleared his throat. "Well, I find myself wondering what exactly *happened* to the Count last night. You wouldn't have any idea, would you?"

"Ah, it seems he fell, sir."

"That is the theory, yes. Must have been a nasty fall, eh?"

"It must have been."

"If it was indeed a fall, that is."

"Yes."

Mr. Olderglough paused to ponder. "And I wonder, too," he continued, "just what happened to Agnes's pestle?"

"Her pestle, sir?"

"Her pestle, yes. Didn't you know that she found it this morning, split in two?"

"Is that right?"

Mr. Olderglough nodded.

Lucy shook his head. "That's a shame."

Mr. Olderglough nodded. "Lastly," he said, "I am curious as to what happened with young Klara's uniform."

"Her uniform, sir?"

"Agnes tells me it was ripped at the neck and sleeve. I hope she hasn't come to any harm?"

"No, sir, she hasn't."

"She got home safe, then?"

"Safe and sound."

"Thank goodness for that. She seems a very nice girl."

"She is, sir. And thank you for saying so."

They walked for a time in silence. They were both smiling, now. Mr. Olderglough said, "Would you agree that the most appealing thing about a mystery is the fact of its mysteriousness?"

Lucy considered this. "Perhaps I would, sir."

"But also the most frustrating, wouldn't you say?"

"Perhaps it is. But as is not unrarely the case, sir, I must admit to not knowing quite what you're talking about."

"No?"

"No."

"Well, no matter." He looked away. "You may take the night off, if you wish."

"I would like that very much, sir, and thank you."

"Yes, boy. Off you go, now."

Lucy walked toward the village then, listening to the chirring of crickets in the dusky air. He found himself drawn once again to the sight of the smoke spilling from Klara's chimney. He wished he might live forever in that wonderful hovel.

As he came nearer the village he noticed a crowd had assembled outside the shanty. Stepping to the front of the pack, now he saw the focus of their attentions: Adolphus stood before Klara's door, famished and decrepit, in filth and bloodied rags, held up on either side by two of his comrades. One of these men knocked, and Klara answered, standing in silence and stillness, regarding Adolphus as though he were a specter. When she took him in her arms, a burst of jubilation came up among the villagers. She led him inside, and the crowd dispersed, all except for Lucy. When he recognized it was not possible for him to enter the shanty, he turned and walked away.

X

—

A BLUE BOY

There followed a desolate era where Lucy didn't know quite where he stood with Klara. It was only days before and they had been connected as if by blood; now he heard nothing from her, and neither did he hear from Memel or Mewe. It was said among the villagers that Adolphus had been tortured and starved and was still very much in danger of dying, but time passed with no news of his demise, and as the smoke continued to spill from Klara's chimney, Lucy knew she had to be nursing and feeding him and tending to his wounds. Meanwhile, and as if in concert with this unnerving scenario, the mood among the castle inhabitants grew ever more removed, with the Baroness forever breaking away from the Baron to be alone in her chambers, and the Baron chasing after her, his voice gone high and pleading. Finally they retired to their respective rooms, and a cruel silence existed in every hall and doorway. From the scullery, Agnes and Mr. Olderglough spoke only in whispers, and their words were unsure, for they were the both of them fearful of what was likely to come. It was an in-between time, and Lucy shirked his duties to spy on the village with his telescope, as when he had first arrived.

One morning he watched Klara walking through the village and to the shanty, a bundle of kindling in her arms. He studied her face, but she wore no expression whatsoever; seven days had passed since Adolphus's return, and a hard kernel of contempt had formed in Lucy's heart. Why had she not come to him? Surely she knew he was aware of Adolphus staying with her; surely she knew he was in pain about it. What did it mean that she hadn't bothered to address this? Well, what else could it mean? He told himself it was a matter of pride to wait for her, when in fact he was simply too frightened to go himself. When he thought of the way she might phrase her goodbye, he was sickened.

Klara dropped her kindling and stared with an awestruck expression into the distance. Adolphus had emerged from the shanty and was standing under his own power in the doorway. The sun glanced off his face, and while it was plain he was not yet healthy, he was far healthier than before, and he smiled easily, beckoning with his hands for Klara to come nearer, and she did this. They stood before one another awhile, speaking unknown tender words. When Klara reached up her hand and stroked Adolphus's cheek, then did Lucy know he had lost her. This is how it happened that his heart was so superbly broken.

Lucy was disinclined to leave the castle, and took to maundering in the halls, carrying his burden here and there, eating little, sleeping less, and saying nothing, for he found speaking to be actually painful for him. At last he retreated to his room, blacked out his window with ash, folded and stowed his telescope, and took to bed. At the start he had no specific thoughts or notions but was merely inhabiting a deep, even ache; then came the visions of merciful death, and he pondered the variants with a swooning reverence. On the third day of this, Mr. Olderglough came to visit, and Rose was at his side. As they entered the room, Lucy drew the pillow over his face. "Please don't," he said.

"Don't what, boy?"

"Don't say it."

"Don't say what?"

"Don't say anything."

Mr. Olderglough sat on the bed. "Are you not well, Lucy?"

"I'm not, no."

"What's the matter?"

"I'm not well."

"I suppose it's something to do with Klara, is that it?"

Lucy didn't answer. Mr. Olderglough bowed his head, and his forelock came uncoiled. "What may I do to help you?"

"Nothing."

"And when will you be better, I wonder?"

"I don't want to be better."

"That's no kind of attitude."

"I can't help it."

"Must you speak with the pillow over your face?"

"I must, yes."

Mr. Olderglough set his forelock in place, looking sterner. "Lucy," he said, "I'm here primarily because of my being worried about you. But there is also the fact of your being paid to perform services in the castle, and it has been some days where you haven't done so. Now, we all come down with a trace of gloom from time to time, but—"

"You've never once paid me," said Lucy.

Mr. Olderglough scowled. "Oh, come now, boy. That can't be true." He thought a moment. "*Is* that true?"

"Never once."

"Well, that's just terrible." Mr. Olderglough paused, then brightened. "What if I *did* pay you? Then would you work?"

"No."

"This is all very discouraging. May I ask after your plans?"

"I have none."

"But surely you must. What of the future?"

"There isn't one."

Mr. Olderglough sighed. "I cannot claim to be enjoying this conversation, if I'm to be honest. As a matter of fact, I'm going to go away, now. I'll leave Rose here with you, if you don't mind. I found her wandering the halls this morning."

"Fine. Goodbye, sir."

"Yes, goodbye." Mr. Olderglough left. Rose climbed onto the bed to lie next to Lucy, who presently returned to the swamp of his own self-pity, which was a relief, for as a habitat it was magnificent in its direness; and since it had been created from his own fabric, he felt some stamp of gratification as he wallowed there. There had always been something comforting in melancholy for him, as though it were a purposeful tradition he was taking part in.

The next afternoon, Memel called on Lucy. Lucy did not cover his face for the visit, but stared away at the ceiling. Memel said, "Mewe is down with the grippe. Will you and Rose come for a walk with me?"

"No."

"Why not?"

"I'm too sad to."

Memel puckered his face. "You shouldn't talk like that."

"Why."

"It's sort of disgusting, don't you think?" He sniffed the air. "Why don't you empty your pot?"

"I don't care about it."

"Clearly you don't."

There was a discordant note to Memel's voice; Lucy looked at him, and was shocked to see how unwell the man appeared. He'd lost weight, and his color was gone, and he was trembling. "You're still feeling poorly, Memel?"

Memel said, "There's something gone sour in me. I can't seem to get rid of it, whatever it is." He regarded his stomach, then turned back to Lucy. "Won't you come along? I don't feel like being alone today. And besides that, there's something I want to show you."

Lucy did not in the least want to go, but Memel seemed so nakedly vulnerable that he felt duty-bound to come along, and so he rose from the bed and dressed, and they struck out, with Rose leading the way. Memel made some weather-related comments in hopes of conjuring a conversation, but Lucy would not be lured into speaking more than a word or two. Finally Memel asked him what was the matter. When Lucy told him nothing was, Memel pointed out that this was a lie.

"Isn't it true that you're having troubles with Klara?"

"I suppose that I am."

"Because of that soldier?"

"Yes." Lucy felt strange discussing Klara with Memel. "I wonder what she wants," he said pallidly.

"I couldn't answer that, boy. And I doubt she could, either." Memel laid a hand on Lucy's shoulder. "I don't know what she sees in that other one, to tell you the truth."

"Don't you care for him?"

"I have no regard for a man so willing to give his life for an *idea*," said Memel, and he spat on the ground to emphasize his indignation. Lucy, for whom the war was still a mystery, said, "Yes, and what is the idea?"

"Precisely," Memel answered, pausing to catch his breath, though they'd not been walking at all briskly. Lucy offered him an arm; Memel accepted this, and they continued, heading for the tree line. They were passing a section of forest he'd never seen before, and presently they came to a clearing in the wood, a grassy knoll, uneven rows of homely tombstones: the villagers' cemetery. Lucy followed Memel through the rows. They arrived at a grave and Memel pointed. "Klara's mother," he said. "Alida, was her name." Kneeling, he said, "I suppose I'll be joining her soon enough."

"Don't say that."

"Why not? It's true. I've already written my epitaph. Would you like to hear it?" Lucy said that he would and Memel cleared his throat, speaking skyward, as one reciting a poem:

> *"He wandered here and there over rolling hills.*
> *He never saw the ocean but*
> *dreamed of it often enough."*

He turned to Lucy with an inquisitive expression.

"It's very nice," said Lucy.

Memel bowed his head modestly. "Have you ever visited the ocean?"

"No."

"A man once told me it was wide as the sky and twice as blue. Do you believe it?"

"I suppose I do."

Memel shook his head at the wonder of this. "What do you think your stone will say?" he asked.

Lucy had never thought of it. What was an epitaph meant to be, exactly? A summation of accomplishments? A representation of one's general outlook? Fine, only he had as yet accomplished nothing, and he had no overarching opinion regarding his life or anyone else's. Lucy was stymied; he shrugged the question off.

"It will come to you in time, likely," said Memel.

Lucy wasn't so sure. "Why did you bring me here, Memel?" he asked.

Memel nodded, gesturing to Alida's grave. "I was wondering if you were aware that she did the very same thing to me that Klara is doing to you now? And with my dearest friend Tomas, no less?"

It was curious to think of Memel with any other friend besides Mewe. "I haven't met a Tomas," said Lucy.

"You wouldn't have. He's been dead a good long while. A gambler, Tomas was. He and I were as close as could be, since we were boys, even."

"And when did he die?"

"Just after the impropriety was revealed. He was murdered, you see."

"He was?"

"Yes."

"Who murdered him?"

"I did."

Lucy said, "You murdered your closest friend?"

"Yes."

Lucy thought about this. "How did it come to pass?"

"You want me to tell you?"

"I want you to tell me."

"Well then, I will."

How It Came to Pass
That Memel Murdered
His Bosom Confidant, Tomas

emel went to pay Tomas a visit one morning and found him in bed, clinging spiderishly to his wife, and with neither one of them wearing a stitch of clothing. They didn't notice his being in the room, and Memel considered their labors in a stupor. Here was an utterly alien visual, for he hadn't the slightest inkling of anything untoward going on between these two. When Alida spied him in the doorway, she shrieked, and Memel left the shanty to stand in the sunshine, clutching his shirtfront and gasping.

Tomas emerged, half-dressed, and in a dead panic. He took Memel in his arms, but Memel could smell his wife on Tomas, and he turned away, stalking from the village and toward the hills. Tomas followed, calling after him; it was a dry, hot day, and when Tomas's voice became raspy he ceased speaking, but he never stopped trailing Memel. They walked one in front of the other, above the village and through the forest until they arrived at the edge of the Very Large Hole, where Memel's legs gave out. Tomas sat some feet away; after he'd caught his breath he said, "We used to come here as boys, and try to throw stones across to the other side, do you remember?"

"I remember."

"But we never could do it, could we?"

"No, we never could."

"And now I suppose we're too old for it."

"Yes, that's the truth."

In actuality they were neither of them old men; their arms were still wiry with muscle, their backs straight and strong, and yet they had surpassed the mean, the center mark of their lives, and were both aware of an overall dimming.

"Every day, and a little closer to death," said Tomas.

"That's how it is from the beginning, though," Memel pointed out.

"Yes, but did you think of it as a younger man?"

Memel admitted he hadn't. Tomas stood, picked up a stone, and threw it into the hole. Memel did the same. Neither stone went very far.

"I should be able to do better than that," Memel said.

"Yes," said Tomas. "Let's try again, and give it our best."

They picked up stones and threw them as hard as they could. Both went a good deal farther than their first attempts, but Memel edged out Tomas for the greater distance.

"Very nice," said Tomas.

He was standing near the lip of the Very Large Hole. His hands were on his hips; he stared into the abyss, and Memel took up a position behind him.

"And so, what are we to do about this, Tomas?"

"I don't know what. I wish I did know."

"Well, what does Alida want?"

"Who knows what that woman wants." Tomas laughed to himself.

Memel took a step closer to Tomas. It occurred to him to walk softly. "Shall we leave it up to her, then?"

Tomas made a strange sound with his throat, for he was crying now. "I suppose we must do that," he said.

Memel took another step. "And what will become of us?"

"That's for you to say."

"Is it?"

"Yes. For my part, I pray that our friendship will remain."

Yet another step. "You want my wife and my friendship, eh?"

"I know it's impossible. But that's my wish." He took a shivering, sobbing breath. "Oh, Memel," he said. "I love you so much."

Memel lunged, and Tomas was borne aloft and into the void. Memel had pushed with such force that he nearly tumbled into the hole himself; when he regained his footing, he stood wondering at the absoluteness of his friend's absence. It was as if the darkness had eaten not just Tomas's present, but his past also—his history in its entirety. Memel hastened back to the village. He was curious to see Alida's face when he told her.

There was a tactility to this story which startled Lucy. He was unsettled by the image and deed, and by Memel's undemonstrative manner of reportage; and yet he was moved by the tale as well. Was there not a measure of justice in the act, after all? Perhaps it was only natural, then, that Lucy was already reimagining the story so that it was Adolphus at the lip of the Very Large Hole, and he himself stood at Adolphus's back, creeping ever closer. He wondered if he could actually go through with it. His heart was doubtful. "That must have been difficult to do," he said to Memel.

Memel shook his head. "I pushed him. That was all. He didn't make a sound. You'd think he would have screamed."

"He was too surprised, maybe."

"It would be surprising, wouldn't it? Slipping through the air like that, all at once?" Memel paused a moment to consider it. "Well, I can't say I regret it, Lucy. Woe betide those who trifle with Eros, eh?"

"I suppose."

"Cupid is well armed, and so must we be, isn't that so?"

"It is so."

Memel's face grew long. "I do miss Tomas, though. Him and Alida both. I've never got over either of them being gone, if I'm to be honest."

With a degree of trepidation, Lucy asked, "And how did Alida die?"

"In childbirth, nine months after the death of Tomas." He regarded Lucy with a mischievous expression, as if daring him to
inquire further.

"Nine months," Lucy said.

Memel nodded.

"You're saying Klara is Tomas's daughter?"

"I'm saying that Mewe is Tomas's son."

"Does Mewe know this?"

"No."

"He's never asked after his history?"

"He's never asked me."

"When will you tell him?"

"I have no plans to tell him at all."

"But why not?"

"Why should I, is the superior query."

Lucy considered it, and could think of no further argument. He
asked, "Why did you tell me this story about Tomas?"

Memel held up his palms, but he didn't answer the question,
and would say no more about it. At the conclusion of their outing,
he bade Lucy and Rose a good evening, and his footing was shaky
and uncertain as he stepped toward the village.

That night Lucy lay in bed, hopeful for sleep, but sleep wouldn't
come no matter how he approached it in his mind. At last he sat up
and declared, "Well, I'm just going to have to kill him, and that's
all there is to it." He lay back down and made plans to that effect.

Adolphus stood beside the Very Large Hole, looking into it, and whistling shrilly. Lucy sat in a crouch a half-dozen paces away from the lip. He hadn't slept even momentarily all through the night and there was an insistent, throbbing discomfort in his skull. Kneading his temples with the tips of his fingers, he asked Adolphus to stop whistling, and Adolphus did stop. *But now he'll spit,* thought Lucy, and this proved to be true. The soldier marked his spittle's transit with interest.

"Well, boy, where's Klara?" he asked.

"She's coming." There was something in Lucy's voice, some inkling of worry or strife, that caught Adolphus's ear; now he peered at Lucy in a sidelong manner. Lucy's eyes were ringed with gray and blue, and his breathing was hurried and shallow.

Adolphus said, "I know what went on between you two, while I was away."

Lucy said nothing. He had removed his pipe from his pocket and was tapping it against a rock.

"I want you to know that I don't bear you any ill will because of it. Our desires get away from us, and there's nothing to be done about that. I can't say that I blame you, anyway. Her behavior is all the more baffling to me, but then Klara was never one to do the expected thing." He spat a second time, then asked, "What's the matter with you? You sick?"

"Nothing."

"What?"

"I'm not sick."

Adolphus shifted. "But why did she send you to fetch me? And why did she wish to meet here, of all places? It doesn't make sense."

"I'm sorry."

"What for?"

Lucy only stared. Adolphus made a scornful sound at him, and resumed gazing into the hole. "I don't like it here," he admitted.

If he spits once more, then, thought Lucy. Adolphus spat; Lucy set his pipe on the ground and stood.

"I'm sorry," he said again. He drew a breath and lunged at Adolphus, his hands outstretched, arms locked straight at the elbows. But Adolphus had been put on his guard by the eerie light in Lucy's eyes, and so was ready for an untoward occurrence. He spun away and to the side, and Lucy rushed past him, disappearing into the Very Large Hole, headfirst, and quite neatly.

Adolphus looked at the hole awhile, then shook his head and went away. It was odd that Lucy had made no sound when he fell. He was happy, at any rate, that the boy was gone, and so the foolishness with Klara could rest. Only the night before, and she had admitted to loving that runt more than she loved him, if such a thing could be believed. Perhaps she was only cultivating an argument; her father was the same way. Well, now she would once again be contented, which meant that Adolphus could focus his attentions on the area war, which was his pre-eminent concern, his primary source of happiness.

L ucy made no sound as he fell.

Only a moment before and his heart had been beating with such violence as to burst; now it seemed not to be beating at all. He was somersaulting through the air, and so with every rotation saw the light of the sky above him, followed by the absolute darkness below. As he fell farther, the light became softer, and the air ever cooler. When he arrived at the bottom of the Very Large Hole there was a surprise awaiting him there, namely a body of running water, which he plunged into with such violence that he blacked out. A long moment, and his body bobbed to the surface, then eased lazily downriver.

"Have you got him?" asked a breathless voice in darkness.

"I've got him," said a second voice. A pair of hands clamped down on Lucy.

Lucy could not at the start grasp just what was happening all around him, for his senses were stunned, his eyes unused to the darkness; but as he became acclimated, now he deduced that he'd been collected from the water and was lying supine upon the incline of a sandy bank. Two men were attending to him, one young and one old, and both of whom, judging by their looks, had not seen civilization in some time—their clothing was tattered, their hair stringy and wild, and they wore unruly beards not in keeping with the fashion of the day. In spite of their appearance, they were in possession of their faculties and health and, it would seem, their good cheer, and so Lucy did not offer any opposition to their assistance.

The young man was holding Lucy's head in his hands and tilting it this way and that. "I can't tell where it's coming from," he said. "Can you tell?"

The old man's face came into view. Squinting, he answered, "I can't, no. Shall I fill up the boot to wash him?"

"Yes, please."

The old man hurried off, while the younger continued his inspection of Lucy's head. When their eyes met, Lucy said, "Hello."

"Well, hello there. How are you feeling?"

Lucy shrugged. Licking his lips, he tasted blood, and scowled.

"You've been injured," said the young man, nodding. "Though for the life of me I can't locate the source of the bleeding. This is troubling, I won't deny it; but it is also, we must admit, preferable to the wound being highly visible, would you agree?"

"Yes."

"May I ask who you are?"

"Lucy is my name."

"Well, Lucy, you've made a misstep, in case you hadn't noticed. But not to worry; we'll get you cleaned up in no time, and then afterward we'll have a nice piece of fish. What would you say to that?" When Lucy didn't answer at once, the young man asked, "You do *like* fish, I hope?" Judging by his tone, it was a question of some importance.

"I like it," said Lucy.

The young man was soothed by the answer. "Fine," he said. "That's just fine."

The old man returned holding a woman's boot, this filled with river water. Kneeling, he emptied it over Lucy's face, cleaning the blood away, and now the two men regarded his countenance with unabashed curiosity.

"He's just a boy," said the old man. The young man, meanwhile, had located a diamond-shaped wound just below Lucy's hairline and asked Lucy to press his finger over top of this to staunch the bleeding. Lucy did as he was told, and made no complaint as they propped him upright. He took in his surroundings from a seated position.

It was a cavernous space, similar in scope and shape to the interior of a grand church. A moderately sized river emanated from a tall cave on the north-facing wall, then looped the patch of sand upon which the three men sat before disappearing into the wall facing the south. There was a pillar of sunlight shining down from above; this spotlit a circular section of river before the island. In staring absently at this, Lucy saw a fish rise at its center, and as the resulting reverberation rippled outward across the surface of the water, a thought came to him. To the old man, he said, "You're Tomas, the gambler. And you're not dead at all." Next he addressed the young man: "You're Mr. Broom. I hope you don't mind it, but I've been using your telescope."

The pair were for a time struck dumb by Lucy's words, and their expressions read of perturbed amazement. At last the young man spoke, asking his aged partner, "Now what do you make of this, I wonder? A mystery come down from the skies?"

"I find myself curious," the old man said.

"That's only natural, and of course I feel just the same. But shall we bombard him with questions all at once, or shall we hold off, and first put him at ease?"

The old man gnawed awhile on his knuckle. "Lord knows I wish to bombard him," he said. "But no, let us resist the impulse."

"Yes."

"He is our guest and so will be comforted."

"Yes, bravo." The young man rested a hand on Lucy's shoulder. "He likes fish, is my understanding."

At this, the two men laughed, a violent laughter which multiplied hugely in the gaping cavern, and was reminiscent of thunder in that it was at once vivid and vague. This laughter went on for what seemed to Lucy to be an inappropriate length of time, and he was not at all certain how he should feel. After consideration he decided he should feel afraid, and so he was.

XI

—

MR. BROOM & TOMAS THE GAMBLER

S upper was served—fish, as promised, though it was not a piece as Mr. Broom had said but rather a fish entire, one per man, unscaled and uncooked, for there was neither flame nor blade to be found in the Very Large Hole. The fish were retrieved live from the river; the two men had built up a network of stone-walled corrals diverting from the current proper, and into which fish would innocently amble. Upon finding their transit blocked they would backtrack, only to discover that the point of entry was now likewise impassable, as either Mr. Broom or Tomas had built up a fourth wall to hem them in. Thus confined, the fish would languish in what Tomas described as arrant boredom until such a time as it was removed from its cell, rapped upon the head, and consumed. Lucy thought the method of capture ingenious, but this ingenuity did little to allay the fact of the meal being repellent to him. He stared at the fish, hanging limply in his hands, and his posture denoted a level of disappointment.

"Well, let's begin, then," said Tomas, and he and Mr. Broom bit into the clammy bellies of their fishes, rending away the flesh in animalistic swaths. Soon blood and scales were shimmering in their beards, a sight which stole away Lucy's appetite completely. Setting his fish to the side, he decided he would not partake, at least not yet, for he knew that if he were to remain he would at some point be forced to follow the others, an eventuality he considered with repugnance. The woman's boot sat in the center of their circle, refilled with water, a communal vessel; Lucy drank from this to wash away the very thought of the taste.

The meal reached its conclusion, and now came the interrogation. After establishing how it was that Lucy had identified them, Tomas and Mr. Broom, so pleased for the company and break in routine, wished to know most every detail of Lucy's life, from the occasion of his birth and up until the present moment. Lucy had no objection to fielding the queries, and his answers were for the most part truthful. He spoke of the melancholy circumstances of his childhood, for example, with a frankness which surprised even himself. Regarding his decision to leave Bury, to say farewell to all he had known in his life, there was not so much as a fact misplaced. And yet, when he arrived at the question of how it was he'd fallen into the Very Large Hole, now he discovered the truth to be insufficient. For would it not have undone the balmy social atmosphere to admit he had attempted to murder a man in a style both cold-blooded and cowardly? Lucy affected the attitude of one in possession of overwhelming sorrows, and when he spoke, his voice was halting, cautious: "I'm not proud to admit it," he said.

"Take your time," Mr. Broom told him.

"By all means, you must," agreed Tomas.

Lucy nodded his thanks. "Yes. Hmm. As it happens, and if you really want to know, I threw myself into this pit bodily."

"On purpose, you mean?" Tomas asked.

"That's right," said Lucy.

"But why would you do such a thing?" Mr. Broom wondered.

"I was despondent."

"Clearly you were," Tomas said. "But what were you despondent about?"

"A great number of things."

"Such as what?"

"The overall circumstances of my life on earth."

"Life in general, you say?" Mr. Broom asked.

"Yes."

"Top to bottom, is that what you mean?" said Tomas.

"That's it."

"No solace to be found?" asked Mr. Broom.

"Anyway I could find none, search as I might."

"As bad as all that, eh?" Tomas said.

"I'm afraid so, yes."

Mr. Broom and Tomas shook their heads sympathetically. A thought came to the latter, and he brightened. "Possibly things will take a turn for you now, have you considered it?"

"I hadn't, actually," Lucy answered.

"This might be your starting-over point."

"It's a thought."

"The moment at which you begin afresh." Tomas nudged Mr. Broom. "From here on out, a new beginning."

"Yes," Mr. Broom said. "It pleases me."

"After all, is that not how it has been for us, my friend?"

"It has indeed, and indeed it has."

The bearded duo sat awhile, digesting. Tomas was cleaning his teeth with a fish bone, while Mr. Broom pinched at the tip of his tongue once, twice, thrice; he plucked away some bit of matter, which he fell to studying. Lucy, in regarding these two, was visited with the chilling knowledge that he would soon be assimilated into their society. Naturally this did not sit well with him, so that he felt impelled to ask after the possibilities of escape. The pair of them nodded, as though anticipating the question; Tomas, holding up a corrective finger, said, "There is no possibility whatsoever."

"Surely there must be," Lucy answered, looking about the cavern, as if to locate some solution.

"The walls cannot be scaled," said Mr. Broom.

"The river, then."

Tomas shook his head. "The downriver route is, you can plainly see, impassable, disappearing as it does into sheer rock. The upriver route presents the only option for escape, and I say without reservation or shame that it cannot be bettered."

"So you've tried, then?"

"Of course we have. In my years alone here I attempted it more times than I care to recall before abandoning the thought entirely. Then, when Mr. Broom arrived, I was swayed by his youth and enthusiasm, and I made several more attempts by his side, each outing a thoroughgoing failure. I suppose it is that you'll want to take a look for yourself, and you're welcome to do this, but I for one will opt out, as will Mr. Broom, I imagine. Isn't that right?"

Mr. Broom nodded, with emphasis.

Tomas pointed upriver. "You enter into the cave," he said, "and walk a hundred yards, at which point you'll come to a fork. You may elect to take the route to your left, or the one to your right; it makes no difference, for whichever you choose will lead to yet another fork, and then another, and another, and on like this, endlessly or seemingly endlessly, and in total darkness. It's slow going against the current, the footing is slick and treacherous, and of course, as you know, the water temperature is not what you'd call inviting." Tomas paused here, remembering. "Our last excursion was catastrophic. We had been away some days when I wrenched my ankle, and Mr. Broom was forced to carry me on his back. We were delirious with hunger and frozen to our bones and I make no exaggeration when I say we had abandoned all thoughts of survival. At last we simply gave ourselves to the current, bobbing along in the darkness and hoping against hope not to be dashed against unseen boulders. Halfway back, and Mr. Broom broke an arm." Here he turned to look at Mr. Broom, who drew back his sleeve, revealing a wrist bent to a grotesquely unnatural angle. "Think of it, boy," Tomas continued. "Floating downriver in pitch black, expecting at any moment to have my skull stove in, and the only sound to be heard other than the rush of the frigid waters was Mr. Broom's screaming, echoing off the roof of the cavern." He made a sour face and shook his head. "It's the devil's own playground in there, and if you don't believe me, then you be my guest."

Lucy stared at the river, puzzling at the fates which had landed him in his present location. What could the future possibly hold for him here? And what of his life beyond the confines of the cavern? He wondered what Adolphus had told Klara of his disappearance. Presumably he'd told her the truth, and so she was mourning his passing. It pained him to think of her being pained, to say nothing of the idea of Adolphus offering his comforts. "We must try again," said Lucy.

"Must we?" Tomas asked.

"Of course we must. Otherwise we'll die here."

Here Tomas spoke gently, and with tranquil understanding. "That's not how we see it, Lucy."

"How do you see it?"

"We'll live here."

They passed a night huddled close for warmth, and in the morning awoke to face another meal, this identical to that of the evening prior. Lucy was very hungry by this point, and yet he still could not deliver the fish to his mouth. Neither Mr. Broom nor Tomas commented, for they had each been through just the same ordeal, and knew Lucy would eat when he was ready. During breakfast, and afterward, Lucy noticed that Mr. Broom was watching him with a woebegone look on his face. This continued for such a time that Lucy asked if something was the matter. Mr. Broom said, "It's just that, I find myself wondering if you're aware you and I arrived here under similar circumstances."

"I'm aware of it," said Lucy.

"And how are you aware of this, may I ask?"

"Mr. Olderglough referenced it, as did the Baroness."

Upon hearing that the Baroness had returned, Mr. Broom's eyes darted away. He was silent for a long while before asking, "When did she come back?"

"Some weeks ago."

"And how does she seem to you?"

"I had the impression she was relieved to have come home. At least at the beginning, this was the sense I had."

"Do you mean to say that something has changed since then?"

"There has been a change."

"And what is the change?"

Lucy was unsure how to describe it. "It seems to me that she is weakening."

"She is ill?"

"Not physically ill, no."

"How is she ill?"

Lucy said, "There is an increasing dearth of sensibility in regard to her actions."

"I don't understand."

"She keeps unsavory acquaintances and engages in unnatural social acts."

"Speak plainly."

"I dare not."

"Tell me all you know."

"I shall not. All that I'll say is that I believe there is an unwellness rampant in the castle."

"What manner of unwellness?"

"A pervasive unpleasantness."

"What is unpleasant?"

"It's something which I can't put into words other than to say I suspect all who live there are affected in time. Did you not feel imperiled at any point during your stay?"

"No."

"Fixed in the clutches of something larger than yourself?"

"No."

"And yet you chased death into the Very Large Hole, where you now find yourself living in rags and eating away at the belly of a raw fish and calling it supper, or breakfast, for that matter."

Mr. Broom could not deny that he had suffered a degeneration. "But," he said, "that might have happened regardless of my location. For love is the culprit, and love grows wherever it wishes." He pointed. "Look at our friend Tomas, here. He finds himself in the same position as I, and yet he's never so much as set foot in the castle."

True enough, and yet Lucy couldn't shake the notion that there was some malicious anathema afoot in the castle. He was visited by the image of the Baron, his bare body smeared with rodent's blood, a memory which invoked a shudder. As though reading Lucy's mind, Mr. Broom asked,

"And what of the Baron? Is he faring so poorly as his wife?"

Lucy said, "Much like she, there is evidence of decline, and it is my opinion that this decline will become dire."

"And what is the nature of their partnership at present?"

"How do you mean?"

"Are they functionally married?"

"How do you mean?"

"Possibly you already know what I mean."

"Possibly I do."

"And are they?"

"Yes."

"How do you know?"

"I've witnessed it."

"I see. You'll excuse me, please." Mr. Broom stood and walked into the water, swimming away and vanishing in the darkness of the far cavern. Tomas gave Lucy a look of mild reproach.

"But what else could I have done?" Lucy asked.

"Lied," said Tomas simply. And here Lucy slapped his knee, as in this one instance the thought to do so hadn't occurred to him.

These two fell silent, and the passage of time grew leaden for Lucy. If only there were a fire, he might gaze wistfully into its heart and ponder the sinister mysteries of life; or if he were tired, he could drift into slumber and dream of Klara stepping through boundless fields of undulating grasses. But there was nothing to do other than speak, and there was no one to speak with other than Tomas, and Lucy felt they had exhausted all topics of conversation save for one. In the interest of creating an event, then, he decided to broach it: "Memel says you were quite close, the two of you."

Had Tomas been expecting this? He didn't seem surprised by it, and his tone was not unfriendly. "We were, at that," he said. "Is it safe to assume he told you how it was that I came to be here?"

"It's safe."

"And he believes me dead?"

"Yes."

"Has he forgiven me, I wonder?"

"He didn't say if he had or hadn't. I believe he felt his actions were justified. Anyway, he expressed no regrets. And yet, he remembers you fondly."

Tomas shrugged, as though he didn't quite believe Lucy. In a self-consciously casual tone, he asked, "And how is Alida?"

Somehow Lucy hadn't anticipated the question, and now he

regretted having brought up Memel at all. Sensing his regret, Tomas spoke:

"Something hasn't happened to her, I hope?"

Lucy said, "In fact, she's died, Tomas."

Tomas's face hardened, a rictus of disbelief. "Died."

"Yes, and I'm sorry to say it."

"Died," Tomas repeated. "But how?"

"In childbirth."

Tomas was staring at Lucy. "When?" he said.

"Some months after your disappearance."

"How many months?"

"Nine."

Here Tomas performed an anomalous gesture, casting his hand sharply across his face, as though drawing a veil over his features, or catching some unspeakable word. Lucy knew that he was watching a man's heart break before him.

"Did the child also die?" asked Tomas.

"The child is alive," said Lucy. "Mewe, is his name. He lives just next to Memel and Klara."

There was nothing but the sound of the river for a time; and to Lucy it seemed the volume of it was increasing. Tomas began digging a small hole in the sand. "Will you tell me about him?" he said. "What does he do? Possibly he's a gambler too, eh?"

"No, he works with Memel on the trains."

"He is a thief?"

"Yes."

"Does he have any talent for it?"

"He has a great talent for it."

Tomas filled in the hole and smoothed it over. "So many days with nothing whatever passing," he said. "And now this."

"He is a happy boy, Tomas. He is happy and well liked."

Tomas nodded. "How is Klara?" he asked. "She would be a young lady by now, I should think."

"She is a young lady," Lucy agreed. There must have been some familiar tone of injury in the way he said it, because now Tomas was watching him with an expression of recognition.

"She wouldn't have anything to do with your being here, would she?"

Lucy said, "Roundaboutly, and yes, she does."

Tomas laughed scornfully. "Well, we're quite the group, aren't we? You and I and Mr. Broom?"

"I would say we are."

"Been led down the garden path, eh?"

"Perhaps we have been."

"Cupid is well armed, it would seem."

"And so must we be," Lucy said, and now the two smiled at each other, sharing a contented moment which did not last long, interrupted as it was by Mr. Broom's return. Trudging up the bank, he said, "We are, the three of us, going to wake up tomorrow, and we're going to strike out, and either we'll escape this place and reclaim our lives aboveground, or else perish in our attempt to do so." As though exhausted by the words, he dropped to his knees, whispering, "We may well perish, in fact." He was studying his hands, now, in wonder at their abilities, perhaps.

Lucy and Tomas looked at each other and raised their eyebrows. "Our friend has been invigorated by his swim," said Tomas.

D ue to the danger inherent in attempting escape, and because of his age and general decrepitude, Tomas was not enthusiastic about this idea at first glance. He became sullen in the afternoon, and it seemed that a rift was afoot, but by the time evening rolled around he had found some deeper reserve of spirit and proclaimed, more loudly than was necessary, that he would join the expedition.

Surely there was a connection between his change of heart and news of Mewe, just as Mr. Broom's decision to leave was informed by the knowledge that the Baroness had returned to the castle. Lucy, for his part, had made up his mind to leave before Mr. Broom had brought it up, even; and he would have gone on his own if need be, for his thoughts were of Klara alone, and his desire to win her back superseded all other concerns. Regarding preparations, there were none to speak of, other than for the men to come to an agreement about the specifics of the method of departure and escape. This was discussed at length, and resulted in disagreement but thankfully not division.

Mr. Broom was for action. He wished to lead the three, for he was, he said, the strongest of the group, a truth which neither Tomas nor Lucy could dispute, though they were the both of them left wondering just what Mr. Broom's strength would avail anyone other than Broom himself. Beyond his physical capabilities Mr. Broom claimed, with an amount of humility or reluctance, to be in possession of second sight. He often felt its influence, he said, and believed that if he were to focus intently and utilize this gift to its utmost, then he would guide the group to freedom.

Tomas sat awhile, blinking. "This is news to me, my friend."

"It's not something one goes about boasting of."

"And why not? Here we've been discussing topics such as our favorite numerals." Tomas closed his eyes. "Tell me, please: what am I thinking about now?"

Mr. Broom shook his head. "It doesn't work like that."

Tomas stuck a hand behind his back. "How many fingers am I holding up?"

"It doesn't work like *that.*"

"How does it work?"

"I believe I can find the way out of here," Mr. Broom said.

"And yet you didn't on any of our prior expeditions. And why not? Sheer modesty, I wouldn't wonder."

Mr. Broom had gone red in the face. "Perhaps you have a plan of your own."

"Perhaps I do."

"Do you or don't you?"

Tomas drew himself up. "If anyone is to lead the expedition," he said, "I believe that should be me."

"Oh?" said Mr. Broom. "And why is that, can you tell me?"

"Because I am the eldest, and so I have the wisdom of time on my side."

"The wisdom of time?" said Mr. Broom. Apparently he found the phrase humorous.

"That's what I said," Tomas answered sternly.

"Does one always accompany the other?"

"In my case I believe it does. Beyond that, and this is inarguable, I have journeyed upriver far more often than you have, and so am more familiar with the terrain."

"That's one way to put it. Another way might be to say that you are more familiar with failing to surpass the terrain."

Tomas leveled a finger at Broom. "I saw the sun set thousands of times before you drew your first breath."

"And so?"

"I was entering women when you were still soiling your short pants."

"And so?"

"I slit a man's throat before you could milk a cow."

"I still can't milk a cow. But I think your plan is pure foolishness."

"It's no more foolish than yours."

"Yes, but my plan is mine, and so I prefer it."

"And just as naturally, I do mine."

Arriving thus at stalemate, the pair lured Lucy into the fray, asking which plan he himself thought best. Believing each one to be equally poor, Lucy admitted to having no preference at all, a statement which effectively offended both men, who together began to chastise him, for here they were busily concocting schemes while he sat by, marking time, contributing nothing whatsoever.

All this to say there was strife among them, and confidence was ebbing with each passing minute. In the end, Lucy did come up with a plan of his own, and as it happened, this was the idea they could all three of them agree on.

The Specifics of the Method of Departure
and Escape from the Very Large Hole

Lucy hadn't eaten in nearly three days by this point. Tomas and Mr. Broom found this alarming in that it had potential to upset their escape, and so they brought him another fish and sat before him; and whereas earlier they were disinterested in whether or not he chose to eat, now they were all the more keen, so that Lucy felt a pressure to please them. His hunger was startlingly vivid; it stabbed and pinwheeled in his stomach and seemed at times to possess the attributes of color. And yet he felt he simply could not perform the action of severing the metallic scales with his teeth, and he told his comrades he wouldn't do it.

"It will give you pluck, and so you must," said Tomas.

"If we're leaving in the morning, as Mr. Broom says, then I can do without."

Mr. Broom shook his head. "We'll be days in the darkness, and it will take our every bit of strength to see this through, if it's even possible to see it through. I'm sorry, Lucy, but we really must insist that you eat."

Lucy glared at the fish, knowing that he would consume the thing but hating it, and unsure just how to start. Tomas touched the tip of his finger to the fish's belly. "Here," he said. "Just shred it away." At last Lucy drew the fish to his face and bit into its flesh; and at the same moment he did this, the fish fairly exploded, shooting out a clammy glut of roe, for it was a female, and had been on its way to the spawning ground when captured in the stone corral.

Lucy was incredulous, and he sat very still, roe clinging to his cheek and chin. When Mr. Broom and Tomas ceased laughing, they took the fish away and fetched him another, a male. Lucy did not dawdle with this, but consumed it with a certain violence or anger. Soon the fish was but a head, tail, and skeleton; and as Lucy felt his body accepting the much-needed nourishment, then did his mood lighten. He lay back on the sand, watching the distant purple circle which was the shading sky framed by the mouth of the Very Large Hole. His stomach squirmed loudly, relentlessly; he was listening to this with dispassionate amusement when a consequential thought, like a bird flown through an open window, came into his mind and perched there. He sat up alertly, looking across at Tomas and Mr. Broom, both of whom had also eaten and were ruminating upon their own concerns.

"The fish head upriver when they spawn, do they not?" said Lucy.

"They do," said Tomas.

"How far upriver do they travel?"

"I don't rightly know. Do you, Mr. Broom?"

"A good long while, anyway," Mr. Broom answered. "Why do you want to know?"

"Well," said Lucy, "if we were to follow one, mightn't she lead us to freedom?"

When he said this, Mr. Broom, too, sat up. Tomas wore a skeptical expression; and yet there was a stiffness or seriousness to him as well. He asked, "And how might one do such a thing, even if we weren't making the journey in total darkness?"

Lucy was staring at the woman's boot, situated once again in the center of their circle. He believed he knew the answer to Tomas's question but he didn't respond right away, forcing himself to act with calm. He took the boot up and poured out the water. Removing the lace, he laid this in a straight line before him, watching it awhile before unlacing his own boots, and tying each of these to the first, tripling its length. Mr. Broom drew his fingers to his mouth in a gesture of surprise and recognition; now he also began unlacing his boots. Tomas didn't understand what was happening, and had to be enlightened; once this was done, he still didn't want to give up his laces. But Lucy and Mr. Broom entreated him, and though Tomas thought it far-fetched, neither did he want to spoil their fun, and so he handed over his laces as well, and these were tied to the rest, so that there was now a single lace of goodly length laid out between them. They studied this for a long while, and with reverence, representative as it was of their last chance for escape. Later, and the men slept, dreaming their dreams of vainglory, the tongues of their boots lolling in the sand as if exhausted.

The idea, of course, was to tie the string of laces to the tail of a fish on its way to the spawning ground and, as one walking a dog on a lead, follow the fish to the river's wellspring. It was, Lucy thought, not just a good idea, but the only idea—the only logical method other than blind luck or brute force which might see them home again. He was prouder, perhaps, than he'd ever been in his life, and it was difficult not to discuss and rediscuss the idea's inception and canny brilliance with the others, neither of whom was, Lucy felt, appropriately enthusiastic or complimentary about it. Mr. Broom seemed to think it almost a shared notion, or one which was so obvious that he would have come to it himself in the blue-skied by and by.

They selected the fish from the corrals, a moderately sized female who had been caught only the morning prior, and so, they hoped, had not had time to become idle. Tomas held her still while Lucy attached the bootlace to her tail. While this was happening she was full of fight, but once transferred to the river she merely floated in place, and the three men stood and stared, waiting. Lucy gave a tug on the bootlace but nothing happened. He gave a second tug, less gentle this time—still nothing. He hadn't considered the possibility of failure, somehow; and in the face of it, he felt a gross despair gathering about his heart. But now, and with no small amount of relief, he saw the bootlace was growing taut, and that the fish was pulling toward the mouth of the cave. She had been temporarily demoralized by her capture and imprisonment, or else was flummoxed by the fact of her tail being fettered and had needed a moment to gather her wits, but the spawning instinct had returned, and she would see the impulse through to its natural conclusion.

Lucy, Mr. Broom, and Tomas, led by the increasingly impatient fish, stepped headlong into the roar of the cavern.

There is darkness and there is darkness, thought Lucy. *This is darkness.*

At the start of the journey they had called to one another, called out their best wishes, laughing at the oddity of their lives, elated by their adventure. But then Tomas's chatter fell away, and after that Lucy's, and lastly Mr. Broom's, and now did the trial of their escape truly begin, and they set to work with wholehearted diligence.

The water was never any more than waist-deep, and the current was not particularly strong, but the fact of their constantly battling against it was enough to wear them down, and they soon found themselves humbled, woefully fatigued, each of them sheltering in his heart a fear of death which was acute, and acutely real. Later their flesh went numb, which on the one hand dimmed their pain, but also made them clumsy, so that they tripped over unseen rocks and boulders and were dunked frequently; each would lurch up from the water with a great, heaving inhalation of sheer discomfort.

Time and again they arrived at a fork in the river, identified by the bisection of sound before them, and time and again the fish performed without hesitation, yanking agitatedly on the lace, which Lucy had tied to his finger. There was no telling if it were day or night but the men walked on just as far as they could, until on the verge of collapse, when they located by touch an outcropping of sand and rock; they crawled onto this and laid their weary bodies down. The fish had no desire for relaxation, and the lace quivered with a relentless pressure Lucy found maddening. Lest he not sleep at all, he tied it to a rock. When they awoke they couldn't guess at how long they had rested, only that they hadn't rested enough. In spite of this they stood, and stretched their aching muscles, resuming the trek upriver, for they knew their time was limited. They could be injured; they could starve; their will might give out; they might freeze—it was paramount to move while they still had their strength, and the unspoken fact was that the chances of survival were shrinking away with each moment gone by. The darkness was so complete that when Lucy blinked his eyes there was no discernible visual difference, which struck him as fantastical or impossible, as one clapping his hands together and finding that this action produced no sound.

Save for sleeping, they paused only to eat; they had two fish apiece on their persons, one in each trouser pocket. After these were consumed, then did their mood grow all the more peculiar. As is typical of long journeys, they lost their desire to communicate with one another, and lapsed into silence; they were as good as alone now, and each found his thoughts more inclined to wander abstractly. This brought about periods of peaceful calm in Lucy, moments where he forgot his hunger and miserable cold, moments when the fish, as though likewise dazed, did not yank on the lace but moved more slowly, so that Lucy could forget the fact of its existence and purpose, as well as his own. These transient instances were merciful but fleeting; soon enough, Lucy's woes would return, announcing themselves cruelly, loudly, inarguably.

Days came and went when finally Lucy crossed some nameless threshold, and began to find everything about his situation very funny indeed. He supposed this was the signal that the end was near, a notion which was of no great concern. When it occurred to him he hadn't felt any tension in the lace for a while, he drew his hand back, and now he discovered it was no longer attached to his finger. This sobered him temporarily, and he called out to Mr. Broom and Tomas, but heard no answer. He ceased walking and waited, thinking they would soon catch up with him, but they never did. The swirling sound of the river encircled him, and confused his equilibrium. He had the sensation he was standing on a steep incline, though he knew this wasn't so; when he closed his eyes it felt as though he were sleeping standing up. What if he were to simply fall away, into the water, to be led back to the safety of the sandy island? But if he were to do this, mightn't he die, his skull dashed on some jagged rock? *No matter*, he thought, and his body was tilting backward when he realized that when he'd closed his eyes, it had become ever so slightly darker. He opened and shut his eyes several times to make sure this was an actuality; and finding it so, he located a hoard of resolve from the innermost region of himself. He took a moment to regroup, and continued apace. The light was increasing.

XII

—

LUCY, LIBERATED

It was a sunbright, late-spring morning, and before Lucy was a level field of tall grasses, and in the center of this, an apple tree. He walked toward it, collapsing at its base. The sun spilled through the branches, and the earth itself was warm; he allowed this warmth into his blood, then his bones, and there were apples on the ground all around him which he ate one after the other, and his life felt a fantasy of luxury. Soon, he slept; waking around noon-time, he returned to the mouth of the cavern and called to Mr. Broom and Tomas, waiting there for an hour and more before walking away, to the east, in the direction of the castle. Possibly it would have been best to re-enter the cave and attempt to locate his friends, but this didn't occur to Lucy until later, and then only dimly. He liked to think the men had been deposited unscathed back upon the sandy bank, and were chattering away yet in their voluble fashion, but in his deeper heart he knew they were corpses, now.

There was a peculiar foreignness to all the world around him which made Lucy feel wary. Some hours later the village came into view, and he thought of Klara, which summoned an anguish in him. Everything he had been through of late, what difference did it make? What was it for that he had survived, even? When he saw her shanty in the distance he knew he had to go there at once, and he located and hefted a heavy stone in his hand, this to nullify Adolphus's skull. Lucy had no plan beyond this, but there was the sense in him that once this was accomplished, then other avenues and possibilities would present themselves.

Mewe was sitting out front of his shanty, staring at nothing, a drawn look on his face. When he saw Lucy, he startled and sat upright. "You're not dead?" he said wonderingly.

"No, I'm not dead. Hello."

"But where in the world have you been?"

"Away."

"Where are your shoes?"

"I lost them."

"Why is your suit in rags?"

"I have suffered through an era of unluckiness."

"Yes, as have we," Mewe said, leaning back. He pointed at the stool beside him and Lucy sat.

"Why do you have that stone in your hand?"

"I'm going to kill Adolphus with it."

"That would be quite a trick."

"You don't believe I'll do it?" asked Lucy.

"I don't believe you will, no. Because Adolphus has already died."

Lucy said, "What?"

"He's died. They've exploded him."

"Who has?"

"They have."

"What does that mean, exploded him?"

"It means that he is no longer of a piece."

"Where is he?"

"Here and there—that's what I'm telling you."

"Where is the main part of him, Mewe?"

Mewe pointed to Klara's shanty. Lucy stood and entered. Adolphus lay on the table in the front room, naked to the waist, and his head was not on his shoulders. It had been taken off cleanly, to the base of the neck. There was a charring at the edges of the wound but his body was otherwise unmarked, and Lucy stood by, considering the incongruousness of this specimen: healthful yet headless. He had no feeling in him as he stared at the corpse, no relief, no sense of triumph. In a little while he laid the stone on the table where the head should have been. Mewe came into the shanty and stood next to Lucy. "It was a cannonball, do you know? A cannonball took his head off."

"Oh," said Lucy.

"They say his body stood awhile without the head, and that when it collapsed, it folded, as though he were lying down to go to sleep. After, they brought him back here, to Klara. Only she'd already gone."

"Gone?" said Lucy.

"Yes, the Baroness has taken her away."

Lucy shook his head. "What does that mean?"

"Klara went to the castle to see if there was any news of you. She and the Baroness met there and came to some agreement. Klara told me she would work for the Baroness as her lady-in-waiting. Anyway, they've left."

"Where did they go?"

"West, is all Klara said. They took Rose with them, too."

"Where is Memel?" Lucy asked.

Mewe pointed to Memel's door and Lucy entered to find Memel lying atop his mattress in suit and vest and boots, hair combed and parted, hands folded across his heart, and his flesh was gray, for he too was deceased. There were candles burning about the room, and long-stemmed flowers had been cast over his body and onto the ground around him. Lucy stood at the foot of the bed, breathing in the scent of the blossoms. Mewe was in the doorway, looking at his old friend with a mournful expression.

"Let me understand it," Lucy said. "Memel has died, and Klara and Rose are gone, and the Baroness has also gone, and Adolphus has lost his head."

"All true," said Mewe.

"Will you explain to me just what happened while I was away, please?"

Mewe cleared his throat. He said, "Adolphus came here claiming you'd tried to kill him. We couldn't picture it, but then you'd disappeared, and when Klara and I went up to the Very Large Hole to look for ourselves, we found your pipe there." Mewe pulled the pipe from his pocket and tossed it to Lucy. Lucy caught it and held it in his palm.

"And so Klara thought I'd died," he said.

"Yes, when we saw the pipe, we knew that you had, and were very sorry for it. Actually Klara was more than sorry for it. Adding to her upset was Memel's decline; after he passed away, Adolphus was always hovering nearby. He got it into his mind that he and Klara should marry at once, and he wouldn't let this alone, so that finally she had to explain it was impossible."

"Impossible," said Lucy.

"Yes."

"And why was it?"

Mewe said, "But of course she didn't love him in that way, Lucy. Not since she met you."

Lucy watched Mewe carefully after he'd said this. He wanted so badly to believe that it was so.

"Adolphus took the rejection poorly," Mewe continued, "so that when there came news of an attack against his troops up the mountain, he hurried off to do his part. The soldiers who brought his body down said he was fighting with something more than bravery.

At last he simply ran toward their cannons, and that was the end of him."

Lucy returned to the front room and stood again before what remained of Adolphus. Flies were socializing at the thickly clotted neckhole and he experienced an obscure pity for his antagonist. "I wonder what they were fighting about," said Lucy.

"Some men just like to kill each other, I expect," said Mewe. He had remained in Memel's doorway, and was looking over his shoulder at Lucy. "And what now?" he asked. "Will you stay on at the castle, do you think?"

"I don't think I will, no."

"Will you return to your home?"

"No."

"When will you leave?"

"Just now, I suppose."

Mewe had turned away from Lucy; he was hiding his face, and Lucy asked,

"Are you all right?"

When Mewe looked back, Lucy saw that he was silently crying. "Everything is ending," he said. He hurried out of the shanty and Lucy watched him leave, afterward standing in the quiet, cool stillness. Thinking of the time he had passed in the space, there entered into his mind an accumulating hum, and now Lucy was struck with a bolt of the most splendid sadness. It overcame his spirit, his breath ran thin, and his legs went stringy from it.

Revisiting Memel's room, he folded back the dead man's lapel, tucking the pipe into his coat pocket. He had never enjoyed using the pipe, and it felt correct for Memel to have it in his permanent possession.

Lucy left the shanty and struck out for the castle.

All was quiet as Lucy climbed the stairs to his room. The state of his suit was past repair and so he shed this, putting on the clothes he'd arrived in. The trousers were blowsy at the knee, the stockings had gone thin, and the buttons on his coat were missing save for one. He pulled on his sheepskin cap and was, for better or worse, himself again. After packing his valise, he set out in search of the others, finding Agnes at the table in the servants' quarters, a cup of tea in one hand, her chin rested in the other. Lucy greeted her and she swiveled to face him.

"I'm leaving the castle, ma'am," he told her. "I thought you should know."

"Leaving?" she said. "But I thought you'd left already."

"I was gone, but I've returned."

"Only to leave again?"

"That's right." Lucy sat opposite Agnes. "Where is everyone else?"

"The Baroness has run off once more, and so the Baron is hiding away in a sulk somewhere. I don't know what's the matter with Mr. Olderglough, but he's gone sulky also." There was a stiffness to Agnes's movements, as though she were in pain; when Lucy asked her if she was feeling all right, she said, "I don't believe I am all right, Lucy, no."

"And will you tell me what's the matter?"

In a tone of confidentiality, she told him, "It would seem to me, boy, that we are all of us getting smaller, here."

"Smaller?"

"Less full, yes."

"I'm not sure quite what you mean, ma'am."

"We are—emptying. Becoming empty." Brightening, she said, "We are *draining*. That's it. We are all draining away, and soon we will be gone." She took a sip of her tea, then studied her cup with a look of mistrust. "Cold."

"Would you like me to boil you more water, ma'am?"

"Why bother? Indeed, it will only grow cold again." She began muttering to herself, and now Lucy noticed the state of the larder: stacks of unwashed crockery teetered here and there; the table linen was blotched with stains; trampled ash decorated the floor.

"Well, ma'am," he said, "I just wanted to say thank you for all your help."

"Did I help you, though?" she asked absently.

"You did."

"And how did I?"

"You were generous with me, and so I felt less alone here."

She looked at him as though she thought he were being foxy. "Do you still have the coin I gave you?"

Lucy patted his pocket. "It is here, ma'am."

"And now, will you use it?"

"I will."

"Well, that's something, isn't it?" She took another sip of the tea, and scowled.

"Goodbye, ma'am," he said.

Lucy left the servants' quarters; Agnes resumed her muttering.

M r. Olderglough sat before his vanity in his rumpled sleeping attire, his cap askew, his face unshaven. He was speaking to Peter through the bars of the bird's cage, this resting upon his lap. When Lucy greeted him he peered up in the vanity mirror. "Oh, hello, boy," he said. "Where have you been keeping yourself?"

"Hello, sir. I apologize for my disappearance, but I fell down the Very Large Hole, and was forced to fight tooth and nail to reclaim my freedom."

"Is that a fact?"

"Yes, sir."

"You fell all that way but lived to tell the tale?"

"I have lived, sir."

"And you stand before me now as one who has cheated death?"

"I suppose so, sir."

"One who has rerouted the fates?"

"Perhaps, sir."

"And was this a very difficult exercise for you?"

"It was, sir, yes."

"Was it tedious?"

"I don't know if I would use the word tedious specifically, sir."

"Well, it certainly *sounds* tedious. But, what do I know, eh? With my head full of stuffing? Happy to have you back, at any rate."

"Thank you, sir. But I've not come back."

"Haven't you?"

"No, sir. In point of fact I'm here to tell you I'm leaving."

"Leaving?" Mr. Olderglough said, as if the very thought were an eccentric notion.

"Leaving, sir, yes, and just now."

"But why would you do that?"

Lucy said, "It seems to me there is no longer any reason for us to stay, sir."

"Oh, but that's not true at all, boy."

"Is it not correct that the Baroness has left again?"

"It is correct."

"Then is it not likely the Baron will once again devolve, as before?"

"It is more than likely. But I don't see what that has to do with the abandonment of my position, and so no, I shan't so much as entertain the thought." Mr. Olderglough shivered and sniffed, and he returned his attentions to Peter, who had, Lucy noticed, gone quiet once more.

"Has he misplaced his tune again, sir?"

"Hmm," Mr. Olderglough replied. He shivered and sniffed a second time, and in looking at him, Lucy could see that all sense had left the man. He was making a kissing noise at Peter now; and as if speaking to the bird, he said, "I will perform my functions. I will do right by my master."

"But if your master cannot do right by you, sir?" said Lucy.

"That is none of my affair."

"It is every bit of it yours."

Mr. Olderglough shook his head and lapsed into silence. Lucy could think of nothing more to say, for there was nothing more, after all, and he was turning to go when Mr. Olderglough called after him, and in a tender tone of voice, "Do you know, Lucy, I've come to think of you as the son I never quite knew." Now he set the birdcage onto the vanity, and folded his hands on his lap. Looking out at the village, and the green-forested hills running away and to the horizon, he said, "I believe I could spend the rest of my days simply peering out a window, boy."

"Any window, sir?"

"Any one, yes. This one, for example."

Mr. Olderglough stared. Lucy left the room.

Lastly, there was the Baron. Lucy found him in the ball-room, standing before one of the portraits of his forebears, hands cinched at his back, rocking to and fro, and humming to himself. He was barefoot, and when he turned to face Lucy it was evident the madness had once more taken root in him. He wasn't possessed by it yet, but was existing in some middle plane, straddling either reality. Lucy wondered just what had occurred over the preceding days; for it was as if some ill-wishing cloud had passed through the valley and rendered everyone simple.

A crooked smile hung on the Baron's face, and at the start he couldn't quite place the person who stood before him. "Lucy!" he said finally. "And how are you, boy? Someone told me you'd vanished into thin air."

"Hello, sir. Yes, no, I've not vanished. How are you?"

The Baron nodded gladly, then resumed his portrait-gazing. Lucy took up a spot beside him and the Baron explained, "This is my great-great-grandfather, Victor Von Aux. He was responsible for the construction of the castle. What do you know of him, may I ask?"

"Nothing, sir."

"You've heard no stories?"

"No, sir."

"That he was a hot-air balloonist who dabbled in the black arts?"

"I didn't know that, sir."

"That he was an expert marksman with a penchant for opium?"

"No."

"That he bred Arabian horses? That he was known to entertain his guests with executions?"

"No, sir."

"Well. I'm surprised you haven't heard any of this."

"Yes, and so am I," said Lucy. "He was a complicated man, by the sound of it."

"A demon," said the Baron flatly. He sidestepped, and was now standing before the portrait of the Baroness. He said, "She's gone away again, boy."

"Yes, sir, and I'm sorry to hear it." Lucy also sidestepped. "Do you know where she's gone to?"

"To the ocean, she says. She tells me she won't be coming back this time."

"Who can say, sir."

"She can, and did. I'm inclined to take her at her word." He looked at Lucy. "She claims to have no affection for me any longer. What do you think about that?"

"I don't know, sir. Just that it seemed to me she did."

The Baron nodded. "Yes, and to me also, boy. Well, possibly she did once. But apparently this has passed." He swallowed, and cleared his throat. "Love leaves us like luck leaves us," he said, and he turned and walked clear of the ballroom. Lucy stood by, looking up at the Baroness and considering these words. He took up his valise and left the Castle Von Aux forever.

The conductor inquired after Lucy's destination and Lucy asked if his coin would take him to the ocean. "It will, just," the man replied, and Lucy settled into an empty compartment. An hour passed, and it grew darker. The strain of his recent adventures had worn him down; he felt so weak, and that he might sleep for days. He gave in to fatigue, his dreams little more than static black curtains and certain colder temperatures. Sleeping through the night, he awoke to a surprising fact, which was that his old friend Father Raymond was sitting across from him, an eager look on his face. The moment Lucy opened his eyes, then did the priest rejoice, reaching over and clasping Lucy's hands in his own. "I didn't want to disturb your slumber, boy," he said, "but it was sheer torture not to, I can assure you."

"Hello, Father. What are you doing here?"

"I've just come from Listen. I've a sister there, perhaps I've mentioned it before."

"You never have, no. Was it a pleasant visit?"

"It was not. In truth I couldn't get away from her fast enough. What was I thinking in traveling all that way to see the likes of her? She of the dying dogs and loamy aromas?"

"I don't know what."

"She doesn't cook, boy—she scalds."

"I'm sorry to hear it."

"At any rate, I'm heading back to Bury, now, and that suits me well enough. But what of you, I wonder? Will you tell me your news? How are things at the castle? You must be living very fine these days, I would think."

"No, I'm not. Actually, I've just come away from there."

"Come away? Not permanently, I hope?"

"I'm afraid so."

"And why is that?"

"Any number of reasons."

"Possibly you'll tell me one of the reasons, or two?"

Lucy didn't know where to begin. He said, "I found it to be an unhealthy environment."

"Unhealthy?"

"Unhealthy and somewhat dangerous, yes."

Father Raymond shook his head. "That'll never do, boy," he said. "But don't you worry, we'll get you some other, better position back home."

"No, I'll not be returning to Bury."

"What? And why not?"

"As it happens, I'm chasing after a girl, Father. For it has come to pass that I've fallen in love."

Father Raymond leaned in. "In love, you say?"

"Just so."

"And what is that like? I've often wondered about it."

Lucy said, "It is a glory and a torment."

"Really? Would you not recommend it, then?"

"I would recommend it highly. Just to say it's not for the faint of heart."

Father Raymond thought awhile. A troubled look came over him and Lucy asked if something was the matter. Said the priest, "Not to besmear your quest, boy, but I find myself curious as to why you're forced to chase after the lass. That is, why is she not stationary? In other words: does this young lady not love you also?"

"Oh, yes, she does. She's only run off because she believes me dead."

"Dead!" said Father Raymond, and he slapped his knee. "That's a good one."

"Yes."

"I suppose it is you'll show her otherwise, eh?"

"I hope to, Father. If I can locate her, that is."

"Surely you will."

They spoke through the morning, and both were happy to be reunited. Father Raymond deduced Lucy was penniless and so slipped him some coins, that he might not go hungry. When the train pulled into the station at Bury, Lucy looked out at the town. All was as it had been, but he was not comforted by the familiar sights, and there was no part of him that wished to detrain.

He noticed a beggar kneeling on the platform. The man's head was bowed, his hands held out before him. A body passed and dropped a coin into the man's palms; when he peered up to judge the coin's value, Lucy saw that this person was the man in burlap, a realization which prompted him to gasp.

"What is it?" asked Father Raymond, working to free his satchel from the overhead.

"The beggar on the platform. He's the same man who came to me when I was so ill. Do you recall it?"

"What, the marauder you told me about?" Father Raymond studied the beggar, then shook his head. "You're mistaken, boy. That's only Frederick."

"You know him?"

"So much as one can know a simpleton. Frederick sweeps out the refectory once in a while for a scrap of bread or sip of wine. He was knocked on his head when he was a child, they say, and he's been that way ever since. You may take my word for it, he possesses no powers, supernatural or otherwise."

Lucy stared. "I'm certain it's the same man," he said.

"More than likely you half-noticed him about before you took ill, then simply imagined his visit. You were delirious from fever, after all. I saw it myself, remember."

The conductor was calling for all Bury passengers to disembark. Father Raymond told Lucy, "I do wish you'd stay awhile. You're certain I can't persuade you?"

"I'm sorry, Father, but no."

"Love is so urgent as all that, eh?"

"It is."

"Perhaps I'm better off without it, then. I never did like to rush. Well, I'm pleased to have seen you, Lucy. Take care of yourself, won't you?"

"I'll do that," Lucy said.

Father Raymond left, and Lucy resumed his study of the man in burlap, who now was sitting back, stacking and counting all that he'd gathered. This was the person indirectly responsible for Lucy's departure from Bury, and all that had happened to him since. When a string of drool slipped from the man's lip, he hurriedly sucked it back up into his mouth, as though it were precious to him, and he didn't dare lose it. The train lurched, and eased free of the station, and Lucy was again in motion.

He had never been west of Bury, and he watched the flatland scenery unfold with an active interest. Here there were no trees, no mountains, only pastures of level green, and it was so very quiet and peaceful for Lucy in the padded, red-velvet compartment. He imagined how it would be when he located Klara, and composed scenarios of surprising her on the seashore, and now in the lobby of a grand coastal hotel. These exercises pleased and excited him profoundly, but in time he grew tired and set them aside. He closed his window shade and sat awhile in the partial darkness. The conductor passed in the corridor and Lucy called after him, asking to borrow paper and pencil. Using his valise as a drafting board, then, he drew an upside-down U shape. Under the dome of this line he wrote some words for the future, the faraway future he hoped. But whether they were needed sooner or later, he knew it was good to get them down:

LUCIEN MINOR
His heart was a church of his own choosing,
and the lights came through
the colorful windows.

Acknowledgments

Philippe, Emma, and Nina Aronson, D. Contumely Berman, Leslie Butler, Rachel Lee Corry (herself a beguiler), Eric Issacson, Azazel Jacobs, Megan Lynch & Dan Halpern & Allison Saltzman and everyone at Ecco, Lee Boudreaux, Peter McGuigan and everyone at Foundry, Sarah MacLachlan & Janie Yoon and everyone at House of Anansi, Leslie Napoles (all grace), Rene Navarette, Brian Mumford, Danny Palmerlee, Max Porter & Aidan O'Neill and everyone at Granta, Steve Schiller, Scoop Short, Dan Stiles, Libby Werbel, my mother, father, and brothers.

In writing this book I considered the works of Thomas Bernhard, Ivy Compton Burnett, Italo Calvino, Dennis Cooper, Robert Coover, Roald Dahl, J.P. Donleavy, C.F., Knut Hamsun, Sammy Harkham, Werner Herzog, Bohumil Hrabal, Shirley Jackson, Par Lagerkvist, Harry Mathews, Stephen Millhauser, Jean Rhys, Robert Walser, and Eudora Welty. My thanks to them.

The Looking-Ahead Artist

U pon our arrival here we were made to fabricate effigies of ourselves. This was difficult work and took a long while, as the effigy was to be of a high quality—much more realistic than a scarecrow, for example. Having nearly been dashed across the rocks and drowned fifteen hours prior (the natives had attended to our scrapes and allowed us to eat and sleep before herding us into this thatch hut working area and putting us to labor with a gentle but never-decreasing insistence), I found the industry pleasing in its nondangerousness. At one point I laughed, a lone guffaw that startled and annoyed Lieutenant Commander Tyler, the only survivor of the shipwreck other than myself. He told me to be quiet and I obeyed the instruction for all of five minutes, after which time I asked in a whisper what he thought we should do, what our chances for escape were. Might we hide ourselves in the jungle? Or steal away in one of the canoes I had seen lining the shore of the beach? But Mr. Tyler had no plan, and no wish to discuss the formation of one. When I volunteered we might speak of it later he said vexedly, "Oh shut up, shut up!"

And so we worked in silence.

The materials for the effigies were brought in as we needed them, and the natives were generous with these, and not the least displeased if we called for more: folded piles of finely woven, multicolored cloth (for the re-creation of flesh and clothing), sticks and branches (for the skeleton), lengths of gut for thread, sewing needles in the form of slim black thorns (these were remarkably hard and without the slightest give, as if petrified), and dried grasses for stuffing. They set one bushel of grass beside my workplace and two beside the much heavier Mr. Tyler, who when he noticed this did not try to hide his humiliation and insult. He demanded to know the meaning of the exercise and the village Chieftan was summoned, entering the hut wearing nothing save for a pair of long pants made entirely of colorful feathers and addressing us in English, which he had learned in his youth working as a trader in the Dutch East Indies: "Whenever you men fall ashore on my island, it is as though you cannot see what you're doing. So I will force you to look upon yourselves; when I believe you can iden- tify your own actions and their consequences, then you may walk freely and without reminder. But until that time, you will wear the effigy." Mr. Tyler gripped a fistful of grass. "What do you mean, wear?" The Chieftan explained we would carry the effigies with us everywhere we went, their arms crossed around our necks in the piggyback fashion. Mr. Tyler asked the Chieftan if he was aware of his, Mr. Tyler's, rank in the King's Navy; the Chieftan chuckled not unkindly, as one finding amusement in an overconfident child, and said, "But of course your rank means nothing here." Now the regal man (his posture was perfectly straight and his eyes suggested an exceptional intelligence and depth of feeling) made a long study of my person. Pointing to Mr. Tyler, he asked me, "You are this man's inferior?"

"Yes sir," I said.

"Not any longer you aren't." Returning his attentions to Mr. Tyler, he spoke once more in the chiding but curiously fond tone of voice. "If I hear you are treating him as a subordinate in any way whatsoever, I will put you out in the rainstorm."

"And what does that mean?" Mr. Tyler wondered, for besides being a fairly tame threat, it was the dry season. The Chieftan took up a squat whistle and blew it. (The sound was similar to a duck call, perhaps an octave lower.) "To be put out in the rainstorm," he said, "you would not like this." He bid us a good morning and exited the hut. Mr. Tyler told me, "When we are alone you will adhere to the rules of rank, is that understood?" I didn't answer. I had not been sympathetic with him on the ship, and there are many reasons why, but here are two. *Reason #1*: He discovered several of the second-class seamen, myself among them, gambling our meager wages belowdecks one evening, and he confiscated the entire pool of money. It is expressly forbidden for second-class seamen to gamble, so it is not so much that he took the pool which offended me, but that he didn't report the incident to his superiors, by which I mean to say that he simply stole our money away from us. He knew we would not report him, for none of us wished to let the captain know of our wrongdoing. Mr. Tyler's wage was fully three times the wage of an average second-class seaman. *Reason #2*: Having found two second-class seamen engaged in the sexual practice in the ship's hold, he reported the pair to the captain, who gave the men twelve lashes apiece. Mr. Tyler had been a second-class seaman in his younger days and doubtless knew with what frequency the sexual practice took place in the hold, and let me say that I myself have engaged in the sexual practice in the hold, and so has every second-class seaman I have ever known engaged in the sexual practice with another second-class seaman in the hold! So, with these two incidents coloring my opinion of Mr. Tyler, and furthermore finding him boorish and small in the main, I was disinclined to show him the proper respect now that we were but two men washed onto this strip of land in the center of an uncharted ocean.

Let me be frank: I did not have faith in him as a man of God.

Franker still: I felt he was a man beneath me.

My effigy took three days to complete and I was genuinely proud of it when I had finished. It was just the same size as me to the centimeter, and the face, drawn over sun-bleached cloth in charcoal, was quite like my own despite my having no mirror to work with, and having had no previous artistic training of any kind. The Chieftan congratulated me heartily, and after hefting the effigy onto my back, he allowed me to leave the working area for the first instance since I had begun the undertaking. (In all that time, in fact, neither Mr. Tyler nor myself were able to leave; whenever we were to get overclose to the exit, a friendly but abnormally muscular native holding a scythelike tool would wave us back with the blade.) Mr. Tyler stood to leave also but the Chieftan, gesturing to his not-nearly-finished effigy (it lay on the ground in shocks and pieces), would not permit this. Mr. Tyler slunk back, casting a brooding glance over his shoulder as he did so.

The Chieftan and me and my effigy stepped into the sunshine. It took some moments to acclimate my eyes to the brightness of the day; when I could finally look about without discomfort, I took in a paradise of sugary sand, bowed palms, and blue-green ocean. The tide was high and the bloated breakers approached the steep shoreline haltingly and with much rippling turmoil before finally leaping forwards and clapping onto the wet sand. Natives dove and swam in the water, children and men and women wearing only the scantiest covering. The women were well bred and shapely and I smiled at them, and they in turn smiled and called to me in a singsong that made my heart whiffle. The Chieftan pointed up and down the beach and said, "In the days after your wreck, many of your shipmates' bodies floated ashore. We have set them aside, in case you wished to visit with them."

"No thank you, sir," I said.

"I thought some of them might have been friends of yours."

"Indeed some of them were. Which is why I don't want to see them."

He nodded his head respectfully. "Perhaps Mr. Tyler would want to see them," he said.

"Perhaps he would. Though, I don't know why."

"Oh?" said the Chieftan.

I paused. "Mr. Tyler had no friends on the ship," I said.

Now he asked my personal opinion of Mr. Tyler. But my reply was indistinct and the Chieftan, recognizing the evasion, encouraged me to speak my mind. "I can tell you don't like the man, why not talk with me about it?"

"That would be regarded as treason."

"Not here it wouldn't."

"In my country, treason is punishable by death," I explained.

The Chieftan lay a hand on my shoulder. "My good man, you don't think you'll ever actually *see* your home again, do you?"

Many miles in the distance I could make out the edges of the black and ash-colored storm that had landed me on the island wheeling away over the horizon.

Mr. Tyler stuck himself one too many times with the sewing thorn and gave up working on his effigy altogether. When he lay the thing at my feet, I bitterly acquiesced to finish it; for no matter what the Chieftan told me I could not believe (and at this point still did not want to believe) I would never see my birthplace again—in my heart, Mr. Tyler still held sway over me. When it came time to draw his face, I spent long minutes looking over his every fold and mole and ingrown hair. He had the swollen appearance of a man cinched tightly at the waist, and one of his eyes wandered independent of the other. I drew the mismatched eyes faithfully but he growled at the sight of it, casting coconut water over the visage and ordering me to start anew. I redrew his face with the eyes in a line and this satisfied him, but not the Chieftan, who when he saw the effigy pointed with the tip of his feathered umbrella and said to Mr. Tyler, "You did not draw the eye honestly."

"It seems a good likeness to me," Mr. Tyler answered.

"No, your one eye follows the sun, and the other the moon. Why are you pretending otherwise? As if we didn't know? Redraw the eyes, and then you will be finished."

The Chieftan exited the hut and I sat beside my effigy (indoors, it was accepted that we should remove them from our backs), watching Mr. Tyler. I fell to thinking of the plight of the ugly man, and wondered if his personality had also been fixed at birth as his face was, or if this had become repellent over time. I suspected the latter—that he had been pure at the start, but as the years passed, his gruesome exterior had poisoned him inwardly. Realizing I was studying him, he threw the effigy at me. "You heard what the savage said. Go on and do your worst."

I stood. "I will not do it," I said.

His face turned puce with disbelief. "You will do it at once!" he hissed.

I held my ground and told him, "You no longer have any power to wield over me. We are equals now, and you must do it yourself."

I picked up my effigy and left Mr. Tyler to assess and dislike himself.

The Chieftan came to understand I couldn't swim, and though I didn't want to in the least, for I was frightened of the ocean (all the more so after the shipwreck), he insisted on teaching me how, as the natives' relationship with the water was profound, and the idea of one living so near it without taking advantage struck him as lamentable, and rightly so. He was a patient and thorough instructor (he had me practice my strokes in the sand), never making me feel embarrassed when I became scared, which was often. Once a tall breaker crept up and crested over the top of my head, tumbling me so that I couldn't tell up from down. I'd taken in a stomachful of water and all was growing dim when I felt the Chieftan's hand grip me by the hair. He pulled me up to face him and the fear I witnessed in his eyes—the fear that I had been hurt while under his supervision—made a bond of true friendship and loyalty between us. He escorted me to the shore (we were both laughing weakly now), and a thought came to me.

"How many white men have landed here, sir?"

"Oh, many, many."

"Where are they now?"

"Sooner or later, they were all of them put out in the rainstorm."

"What happens when one is put out in the rainstorm?"

"Knock-knock-knock," he said, tapping his knuckles on my skull. "Knock-knock-knock-knock."

"Will Mr. Tyler be put out in the rainstorm?"

"If he doesn't hurry up with his effigy he will be. Probably he will be anyway."

"Will I be?"

"I sincerely hope not," he said.

My effigy was propped against the base of a palm up from the shoreline, and as we approached, all at once I had a feeling of fondness for the thing, as though it were my pet—I was glad to see it, and wished to speak to it. I mentioned this to the Chieftan, and he smiled. "You like yourself," he said. "That is good, and understandable."

"But that isn't what I meant," I said softly.

"We like you also," he answered.

The Chieftan consulted with the council of tribal elders, and they decided I was to be assigned a working position within the village—an unheralded event for an outsider. The Chieftan could not directly translate the title of the long-vacant post; the closest he could come up with was to name it "the looking-ahead artist." I was given long swaths of fabric; rudimentary brushes fashioned from bamboo and human hair; supplies of charcoal; the ash of pitch pine (which when combined with water created something like ink); and for coloring, cinnebar, indigo extracted from woad, and the dusted powder of flower petals, similar in texture to pounce or pumice. After these were delivered to my and Mr. Tyler's hut the Chieftan paid a visit, encouraging me to begin the fulfillment of my duties. When I admitted I did not understand just what it was he hoped I would accomplish, he said, "You draw what happens later."

"What do you mean, later?" I said. "Later when?"

"Tomorrow, the day after—many days after."

"You want me to look into the future?"

"I want you to make a picture of the future."

"But I can't see into the future."

"You have tried before?"

"No."

"Try now."

I was at a loss, however, and all that night I lay awake wondering what images I might put to the fabric. Mr. Tyler also lay awake; he could keen my anxiety and encouraged this by telling me I would acutely offend the natives when it was discovered I had no psychic abilities, that I would be slaughtered by them, and furthermore that by engaging even halfheartedly in their future-gazing witchcraft I would be denied entry into heaven. When he finally drifted away to sleep he had all but convinced me of my own ruin, so that by the time the sun came up I was in a state of desperation. At last I drew a simple sketch, not of what I believed might happen, but what I hoped might, for this seemed preferable to drawing nothing at all. The Chieftan arrived to inspect my work; he studied it with no expression whatsoever and I held my breath, certain I had failed the man. But a moment later he called out a series of instructions in the native language, and beyond the hut I heard much hurrying and shouting—and soon came the felling of a palm. This activity stirred Mr. Tyler from his slumber, and he crossed the hut in his dire underthings to squint at my artwork. Pointing at the fabric he asked, "What are you doing, there?"

"Resting in my own private hut," I explained. And by sundown of that day the natives had constructed this just as I had foreseen it, and many among the village came to visit and wonder at my powers. Congratulations and gifts were impressed upon me: gourds of palm wine, fragrant bouquets of violently colorful flowers, a table

and set of chairs, and also a hammock to sleep in—this last a gift
from the Chieftan himself, his face lowered as he handed it over.
"It's only a trifle," he said bashfully.

I took care to set up a reverent area for my many supplies, for I
suddenly felt I could see the future just as clear as the present, and
was eager to begin my transcription.

I drew a naked native beauty visiting my hut by the moonlight,
and this came to pass; I drew a cook and servant both, and these
soon appeared to do my bidding; I drew a feast and celebration in
my honor, and it was re-created faithfully. Any pleasing thing I
could want, all I had to do for it to become fact was sketch it out.
However, there was so little lacking from my life on the island that
after a time I began to feel something of the glutton. Deciding I
had done quite enough for myself I turned my brushes and charcoal
charitably outward. One of the native boys, I had noticed, was often
taunted and teased by his peers. I painted him as a favored son of
the village, and the artwork had hardly dried on the fabric before
his popularity quadrupled, and it was all the chubby, club-footed
chap could do to keep up with his numberless social commitments.

I don't know if the natives were aware I was not transcribing visions, only drawing things I wanted to take place, but it is interesting to note that after involving myself with the above-mentioned
native child, the Chieftan came to my hut and wordlessly removed
my effigy, and I was never to lay eyes upon it again.

It was during this time I began to dream of my home, a place I
did not think of in my waking hours, a place I no longer hoped
to revisit. I had not had a happy life there, truth be told: I had
been orphaned as an infant, my childhood had been a violent one,
and as an adult I had struggled to establish close friendships with
any man or woman. So, these visions of my birthplace came to me

quite against my will—literal recollections or re-creations wherein nothing fanciful or unique ever took place: I would be sitting in a café eating a solitary dinner, or perusing the shelves in a muted, musty booksellers, or stepping through a dense fog beside the canal and nearly walking into a passing lamplighter (neither of us saying a word to each other, no greeting or apology). But the scenarios were so vividly steeped in every sensory detail (the inscrutable gloominess of a bowlful of steam-wrinkled peas; the unpleasant coating of residual grime resting on the palms and fingertips after handling secondhand books; the way a walk beside the canal summoned the need to make water) that upon waking, the feeling of having returned to the place was so strong as to fill me with an overwhelming heartsickness and sense of placelessness. Rising from my hammock, I would find myself comforted by the reality of the village, of the breakers combing the shore, the voices of the children playing in the palm trees, and the coolness of the sand in my hut. And yet my sorrow would linger all through the day, and I was much relieved when the dreams ebbed away, replaced by images of island life, or else a blank space (which was preferable to me), a benign nothingness which unhappiness and regret could never, for unknown reasons, penetrate.

Mr. Tyler eventually finished his effigy (half a month had passed with all but the errant eye filled in), and upon showing it to the scythe-wielding guard, was admitted into native society, looking hopeful for some congratulations, as I had had. But he was to be disappointed in this, as far too much time had passed for there to be any observances, and besides, I had at last spoken to the Chieftan about what type of man Mr. Tyler was, and the Chieftan in turn shared this information with his council, who then informed the rest of the village, and so the prevailing attitude towards him, which was already one of suspicion, had further cooled. Recognizing what had happened, Mr. Tyler gave up on mingling entirely and spent his days pacing the shores of the island, gazing winsomely out to sea, his clothing gone to rags but refusing to wear the native attire, as I had begun to. (At first sight I had been intrigued by the Chieftan's feather pants, and as my outfit grew shabby I requested something similar. The Chieftan presented me with a pair soon after, identical to his own, though with the hem cut just below the knee, whereas his ran to the ankle. At the start I felt conspicuous in these, for here I was a twenty-year-old man in pink-and-blue-feathered short pants, but the gasps of pleasure these elicited in the native women erased my shame, and while it did not occur to me right away, looking back now I can see that my wearing these, when only the Chieftan had worn them before, increased my standing considerably amongst the natives, who took to greeting me as "the Chieftan's boy"; and the Chieftan himself began calling me his "unknown son." I was happy to hear him address me thus, but also vaguely intimidated by the mysterious phrase. I asked him what its significance was, and he told me, "I look upon your flesh and eyes and know you did not come from my body. And yet the feeling is so strong in me that our hearts are twinned." To illustrate this he held his fists together, each mimicking our hearts pumping in concert.) Mr. Tyler's complexion was fair, and as he paced the shores his skin went from burnt to blistered to what can only be called charred. After a week of this I approached him, offering the shade of the Chieftan's feather umbrella. His effigy peered over his shoulder at me and I noticed Tyler had drawn angry eyebrows on its face, and so were his own eyebrows arched drastically downwards. He spoke in a tone of perfect abhorrence: "I will take nothing in the way of assistance from you," he said. "A traitor to your race and country both."

"At the very least you should step back from the water," I told him. "Can't you see it reflecting the rays of light? The sun will burn you alive, Tyler."

"You will call me Mr. Tyler!" he said. "Or Lieutenant Commander Tyler! But you will not simply call me Tyler!" It was obvious to me his hold on reality was slackening dangerously, such was the weight of his solitude. Gently, and with not a little sympathy, I asked him, "What do you think is going to happen, that one of the King's ships will suddenly appear on the shore and welcome you aboard?"

"That is precisely what I think will happen. And when it does I trust you will say your prayers, for after your perfidy against the crown is made public I expect you to be hung without trial, in your feathery knickers, from the stern of the boat. And after your spirit has left your body, this entire heathen population will be eaten alive by the flames of my torch!" He broke away and his pacing began once again, hurrying to and fro with a caninelike exuberance. Over the sound of the breakers, I told him, "If and when a ship appears, it will take a full day before it weighs anchor. Do you truly believe these people will let you stay here and greet your countrymen when they land?"

He, and his effigy, turned to face me. "And just what does that mean?"

"Of course they will hide me away to protect me, Tyler. And you—well, you will not be around to speak ill of us, let me say that much."

His eyes for an instant flashed in surprise, then his face shriveled with righteous scorn. "You are threatening to have the savages kill me, is that it?"

"I make no threats. If I wanted you dead I would only have to paint you so. What I am trying to do is help you. For I suspect you could live a pleasant enough life here if you would only show these people the bare minimum of respect."

"I'd just as soon commune with the animals in the jungle," he said. "And now you have my final word on the matter."

I took the umbrella and walked away from him. The Chieftan had been watching the exchange from up the beach; he sat cross-legged, awaiting my return. I told him, "He shuns all friendship and assistance. He does not wish to have a position in the village. He refused the umbrella and made a mockery of my pants."

The Chieftan's eyes narrowed. He blew his duck whistle and a young villager appeared at his side to receive instructions in the native tongue. I could not grasp the words individually but by the way he knocked upon the boy's head, I understood well enough that he was calling for the preparation of the rainstorm, an evidently laborious process which took many hours to complete. After the villager left, there was an ungainly and discomfiting distance between the Chieftan and myself; hoping to put this to rest I began to speak, but he quieted me, saying, "I prefer the privacy of silence just now."

Mr. Tyler, unaware of his fate, was watching his feet as they were washed over in the mallowy froth of the breakers.

Remarkably, a ship did appear on the horizon, the very next morning as a matter of fact, with the sun painting the sky red, and the village still in purple slumber. Mr. Tyler, having slept on the shore, arose to see this, and after letting out a shriek of tearful relief, he cast his effigy into the surf and ran into the jungle to hide. Soon every native stood as part of a vacillating pack at the waterline, squinting and musing at the vessel. The sight of the ship filled me with apprehension, but the prevailing mood amongst the others was lighter, and in actuality they appeared pleased by the coming of the outsiders—the Chieftan wore a tight smile, I noticed, as though suppressing laughter. Now he clapped his hands to quiet us, and divided us into two groups: those that might locate and capture Mr. Tyler, and those that might complete the preparation of the rainstorm. I was enjoined to go with the first; walking alongside the Chieftan we set out, following the splay-toed prints of my former superior.

The Chieftan's attitude was carefree and breezy, calling out to his subjects and encouraging them to tell their most amusing "singing stories." I asked him if he was not concerned by the approaching ship (I could see now it was a Spanish caravel); he asked me sincerely, "And why should I be?"

"But mightn't they take up their arms against us?"

"I suspect they will not."

"And why do you suspect this?"

"Surely they will be distracted."

"What will they be distracted by?"

"That which is lacking in their lives."

Did he mean to fill the Spaniards with the many native dishes I had come to so adore? The slow-roasted boar, with its crackling, salted flesh? The sweet-pulp coconut beverage with which I greeted each sun-filled day? I asked him to discuss his plan in greater detail, but he would not say just what it was. "It has succeeded in the past, is all you need to know," he told me slyly.

Mr. Tyler was discovered huddled in the pit of a grotto on the far side of the island. He had covered himself in moss and grime to camouflage his flesh, but with his prints leading us to the mouth of the cavern this proved an impotent diversion. He was yanked into the clear by the ankles, mewling and screeching, clawing at the air and generally making an ignobility of himself; presently he lay before us, painted in muck and blood, weeping and panting and cursing a God I suspect he had never fully believed in. When at last he fell silent, the Chieftan told him, "I have given you many chances and opportunities to remain peacefully among us, but you have shown me only your back, and every step I have taken towards you, you have moved away from me two steps. Because of this, I can think of no option other than to put you out in the rainstorm."

Tyler still did not understand just what the words meant, but he knew by the gravity with which it was discussed that the rainstorm had to be something distinctly unpleasant. And so with nowhere else to turn he faced me, making his appeal as a countryman and Christian, promising he would live humbly and respectfully, as I had advised, if only he would be given another chance. His voice took on a tone I did not recognize for its chasteness, and his rogue eye jounced passionately in its socket. I found I

could not look at the man, and my face flushed in shame for him; but after all he did appear to be sincere, and the Chieftan was affected by this.

"What is the opinion of my unknown son?" he asked me.

I searched inside myself for the answer; when I located and recognized it as the truth, I spoke: "Even if he is spared, he will never regard us as peers, and no matter the amount of charity shown to him, in his heart he will only think of revenge and treachery."

"And so you believe my judgment is just?" he asked.

"I do," I said.

With this, they dragged Tyler in the direction of the village, and his mewling and screeching resumed and redoubled.

By dusk the caravel had dropped anchor and two long boats weighed down with musket-wielding Spaniards landed on the shore. The village was quiet and still, and as they made their way up the sand the look of apprehension was very clear in their faces. When a single native appeared in the distance, every musket was leveled in his direction, and their leader called out a threat or command, his voice deep and booming. But now the Spaniards saw the native was not a he but a she, and an attractive one at that—and without any covering over her body whatsoever. She took timorous steps in the direction of the sailors, who were all of them struck dumb by the sight of the naked beauty; their muskets dropped away and the fierceness vanished from their faces, replaced by a pitiful longing. Now another female native made her approach, and another, and so on, until the two groups were of an equal number, standing all together on the beach. The women began to caress the Spaniards, diffidently at the start, but this became more direct and ardent, and soon they were all of them kissing the sailors on the mouth, who after a decidedly brief struggle with propriety returned these affections in kind. Their sense of relief at being received in such a way was palpable: they laughed and called out to one another, and

when the women pulled them up the shore towards a silo-shaped hut in the center of the village, the Spaniards followed happily after, and there was nothing about the men denoting caution or concern.

Inside the hut the native women removed the Spaniards' armor and clothing and lay the men down upon the sand to further caress and make love to them. Strong palm wine was distributed and imbibed; the Spaniards, distracted by their lust, and it being very dark inside the hut besides, did not notice the nimble children of the village stealing away with their muskets and sabers. When there sounded the Chieftan's quacking whistle, all at once the women were up and away, running clear of the structure, ahead of the grasping, cackling sailors. Now a barricade of heavy timber and frond rope dropped shut over the lone exit and the men were trapped—nude, drunken, unarmed, and utterly vulnerable. There came a chorus of laughter on the air and the Spaniards followed the unsettling noise, gazing upwards, where they saw every able male of the village, myself included, sitting far above them on a bamboo overhang which ran all the way around the structure. Beside each of us was a pile of heavy stones.

In the center of the hut lay a mass beneath a covering of orchids. One of the Spaniards tripped over this and in doing so brushed away some of the flowers, thus exposing the bloodied corpse of Mr. Tyler. Presently the men, understanding what was going to happen, started weeping and cursing and praying. Then began the rainstorm, and the prayers ceased, replaced for a time with the cacophonous sounds of unalloyed agony, which gave way to a singularly rich and complete silence.

That evening there was a banquet. The dead were cooked on spits and served with a mango sauce over a bed of aromatic roughage. I had no desire to eat the flesh of man and decided I would not do it when a heavy platter of steaming gray meat was set ceremoniously

before me, and the room all at once fell quiet. I knew at a glance I was looking at what remained of Mr. Tyler; the Chieftan, beaming, motioned for me to eat. I said I did not think I could do it and he leaned in, explaining I was not meant to eat the entire pile, but that a small sampling would satisfy the council. I pushed on, telling him I was repulsed by the very notion of it. Now he looked at me with a sternness I had not seen in him, and he said that if I did not have but a single bite I would lose the goodwill of the villagers, and that it would likely never return. I found myself pushing a sliver of Mr. Tyler into my mouth, then. This rested warmly atop my tongue. Closing my eyes, I made to swallow the morsel, but the taste was so foul my body would not accept it and I coughed it involuntarily back onto the table. This was the source of much hushed, head-shaking discussion; I had caused the most perilous offense, it was plain. The Chieftan called for silence and cautiously took up a piece of Mr. Tyler for himself. Pushing the meat this way and that in his mouth, his face slowly morphed to a scowl—now he, too, coughed Mr. Tyler out with a gag. He turned to me, and a look of amusement fixed itself to his face. "So you see," he said, "the man proved to be of no use to the world whatsoever, not even in the guise of food." He translated the sentence for the natives, who after a pause erupted in laughter. I found myself swept up in this gaiety. Soon we were roaring. It really was quite funny, if you think of it.

Time passed, a month, six months. When it was ascertained that one among the village—the unpopular boy I had assisted with my drawing, coincidentally—was a true and gifted psychic, my position as looking-ahead artist was bequeathed to him, and now, with no purposeful way to spend my days, I fell into a bittersweet melancholy. There came into my life a most distracting and unsettling unmooring, where there was nothing in the space of my mind which I could connect to another one thing in my known world,

and now the dreams of my home returned to me. In one of these: *I was back home after a long voyage. It was winter, and I bought myself a fitted tweed overcoat and a pair of black leather gloves. These had taken up a quarter of my pay, but I was unconcerned by this, and felt very elegant and worthy as I moved through the front room of a drinking establishment in the direction of the exit, the silk interior of the coat sleeve tickling across my bare wrists between the glove and cuff, my spine loose from the strong ale. It was late at night, and I boarded a bus. From the top level I could not see the streets, so dense was the fog. There were no passengers other than myself and I realized at some point that I didn't know quite where I was; the driver had ceased naming the stops but I had been lost in thought and hadn't noticed this. A woman approached and sat beside me. "Do you know what the next stop is?" "No I don't. The driver hasn't been calling them." "I know he hasn't. That's why I'm asking." Her face was pretty, but cold, set—grim, almost. Hers had not been an easy life, and she was in that pivotal juncture where her beauty was perceptibly receding; and there seemed to be a knowledge of this in her carriage, a bitter resignation. She was sitting closer to me than she needed to. "Well," I said. "Hmm, yes." "Goodnight," she told me, and stood and stepped away. I heard her shoes as they skipped off the bus, into the gauzy night. Her heel made a harsh grinding on the concrete, and she laughed, and the very moment I heard this, I patted my breast: my purse was gone, with the remaining three-quarters of my pay.*

I would awaken in my hut feeling wretched, rootless. All was well in regards to my existence in the village but I felt an aimlessness which the Chieftan recognized, and in his sympathy he proposed I teach the youngest natives my own language, and he had a bright, airy hut constructed for this very purpose. I had imagined a handful of villagers would take an interest, for in truth there was no real reason for them to learn my language other than to speak with me, but on the first day of class there were forty-five sets of paper-white teeth sitting on the floor of the hut, and I was sincerely moved by this. An auspicious start, and a misleading one, for it soon

became apparent to me and surely to the natives that I was a hopelessly poor instructor: forgetful, short-tempered, nonthorough, and ultimately disinterested insofar as I had nothing actually invested in my work. By the end of the first week I had taught them nothing, and with so many hours lost among us, my melancholy, and the unsettling dreams of my home, returned.

Again I appealed to my dear friend, the Chieftan. When I mentioned I was learning more of the native language than the natives were of mine, he said the solution was plain to see. I was no longer to be the instructor, but the sole pupil; and contrariwise, the natives were no longer to be the pupils, but the collective instructor. "It should have been so from the start," he said. "Why muddy these children's minds with your language, when they already have a superior one at their fingertips? I have found myself more and more frustrated by your tongue. Why do you make it so hard to say what you mean? It is almost as though none of you want to actually know what the other is feeling."

It was decided, then, that not only would I not teach the natives my language, but that the Chieftan and I would no longer speak English to each other, that we would in fact strike it from our lives—that we would intentionally forget it, speaking only in the native dialect from that time forwards.

It is difficult to unlearn the language of my birthplace, but I find it to be fading further from my grasp every day. And the dreams, though they persist, are also growing ever dimmer, the details of sight and smell waning in realism, and as such are far less painful to endure. Eventually all thoughts of home will be banished from my body and mind, and I will think and converse only in the island language, and this day—the day I reach for some basic word or phrase in English and find it not there—this will be an extraordinary day for me. Indeed it will.

© DANNY PALMERLEE

PATRICK DeWITT is the author of the critically acclaimed *Ablutions: Notes for a Novel*, as well as *The Sisters Brothers*, which was short-listed for the Booker Prize. Born in British Columbia, he has also lived in California and Washington, and now resides in Portland, Oregon.